belle and the pirate

VIVENNE SAVAGE

Also By Vivienne Savage

DAWN OF THE DRAGONS
Loved by the Dragon

Smitten

Crush

THE WILD OPERATIVES
The Right to Bear Arms

Let Us Prey

The Purr-fect Soldier

Old Dog, New Tricks

THE WOLVES OF SAN ANTONIO
Training the Alpha

IMPRACTICAL MAGIC
Impractical Magic: A Halloween Prequel

Better Than Hex (Coming Soon)

MYTHOLOGICAL LOVERS
Making Waves

ADULT FAIRY TALES
Beauty and the Beast

Red and the Wolf

Goldilocks and the Bear

Prologue
12 YEARS AGO

JAMES CLASPED HIS fingers together behind his back and stood tall before his superior officer. Commodore Edward Teach of the Eisland Navy reclined behind his desk, feet propped on the edge and crossed at the ankle. As a child, James had read stories of the man's heroic deeds on the high seas, and more than anything, he'd wanted to be like him.

For over a decade, James had served the navy in any capacity he could, first as a cabin boy and then as a sailor when he reached adulthood. Years later, after climbing through the ranks on his own merit, he'd finally achieved his dream of becoming Captain Hook. Due to his string of recent personal successes and the wealth of his parents' winter vineyards, he'd even gained the favorable attention of the king's eldest daughter.

And soon, they were to be married. To think, if he hadn't delivered her favorite vintage in person to the castle, declaring such an honor could be given to no one else, Princess Rapunzel could have slipped through his fingers.

"I have a special favor to ask of you, James," Teach said smoothly. "Pull up a chair and have a seat with me."

"Of course, Commodore."

The senior officer stroked his black beard and studied James through dark eyes. "Edward. There's no reason why we shouldn't be on a first-name basis, my boy. Call me Edward."

When James pulled up a chair to the desk, his idol removed a sterling silver cigar case and snapped it open. Almost dizzy with enthusiasm, the young captain accepted a cigar, and they both puffed at the expensive, fragrant tobacco, inhaling the aroma of cloves, vanilla, and spice. Maintaining a stoic expression took every ounce of his self-control, preferable to clapping like a giddy child in the presence of his lifelong hero.

"You've come a long way, James."

"I've had good men to model myself after."

"King Harold and I see great things in your future, especially now that you're soon to become his son in marriage. As I'm soon to become admiral of the fleet, we've given some thought to who should take my place."

James straightened in the seat and stared at his mentor. He couldn't possibly mean him, could he?

"My promotion provides the ideal opportunity to elevate a young man with great ambition, intelligence, and loyalty to both the navy and the crown. You are that young man."

Anticipation churned his insides, but James remained still despite the urgent desire to leap to his feet and crow in victory. "I am humbled by your continued faith in me," he said, maintaining decorum. Inside, he celebrated.

"I have a special cargo I'd like you to oversee. A merchant ship from the Ridaeron Dynasty will be transferring it to you."

"Ridaeron? I had no idea we were trading with them."

"Talks about greater cooperation between our kingdoms have been ongoing for some time."

"I see. What's the cargo you'd like me to take on? Weapons?"

"People," Edward replied. "We've purchased labor for the

vineyards."

"Migrant help?"

"No," the commodore said, confirming the younger man's suspicions.

The joy conceived by a possible promotion crumbled like dry pastry, happiness replaced by a sour taste in James's mouth. "What you're asking me to do is immoral, Commodore," he said. "And not merely that. Slavery is outlawed in Eisland."

A thin smile came to the commodore's face as he stroked his black beard. "Not for long. It's a profitable venture and has the potential to bring greater income into Eisland's coffers than these blasted bundles of frozen vines. Think of it, James. Hundreds of workers able to produce results even in the frigid cold of night."

For centuries, the sweet ice wines fermented from Eisland's winter vineyards had provided prestige and money. Their wines were highly sought after across the kingdoms, from their closest neighbor, Creag Morden, to the west and all the way to Samahara in the south.

James opened and shut his mouth, positive the man had given him a test. Was he supposed to oppose it? Agree blindly? No words came to him.

"Have I chosen my man poorly?"

The thick lump in his throat didn't budge when he swallowed. Wary of speaking his mind, he crafted an excuse for his hesitation instead. "No, of course not, Commodore—Edward. I'm merely concerned about our native Eislanders who will be put out of work."

"Ah. There's that brilliant mind. Your concern for our people isn't misplaced, but I assure you, they'll be trained to perform other valuable duties. Have you ever been to the vineyards during a harvest?"

James clutched one fist against his thigh. "I have. My parents both worked my grandfather's land during their youth, and now they own the same vineyard." Thanks to his commission, he had been able to help his parents invest further in the property by purchasing the surrounding land. Their operation had doubled in size.

"So, you know firsthand the dangers faced during the cold season. People lose fingers."

"Without the proper protections, yes."

Edward spread his hands out. "And how much do those magical protections cost? A single pair of drakeskin gloves is more than the worth of five laborers from Ridaeron. Ten if they're young."

"You want to use children?"

"Naturally. If trained at a young age, they'll be more useful in the long run. Children heal faster, too. All in all, we gain more money than we spend."

"I see." He forced down the bile threatening to rise in his throat.

"Good. I need you to be ready to set out two days from now. I'll be sure the Jolly Roger is supplied."

James studied the naval officer who had, until that moment, been his greatest hero. The cigar tasted bitter, no longer pleasant and satisfying. "Does... does the king know of this?"

"My boy, it was the king's idea. As for his board of advisors, that's another matter. But let's not worry too much over the details. You've been chosen to perform a task of great importance for Eisland, and once these bodies have been delivered to the vineyards, we'll prove their necessity to the council."

A week into their sea voyage, the Jolly Roger encountered a ship flying Ridaeron's colors. James had hesitated to share the true purpose of their mission to most of the crew beneath his command, still holding on to his hope that it was a sick joke told by an aging war hero with an addled mind.

Until that moment, James had even tenaciously dared to hope Commodore Teach had been testing his loyalty to Eisland.

Once the Golden Goose moved into place beside them and dropped anchor, her crew slid planks across for transporting their living cargo. Captain Hendrik el'Vartellan's wind-weathered features crinkled with unconcealed delight, wrinkled brows drooping into his solemn eyes.

"Let us get this done, and quick. We'll bring them to you," he called from the main deck. "A storm approaches from the south, and trust me when I say neither of us wants to be caught in that nightmare." One whistle from Hendrik sent his crew scrambling across the deck.

James wiped his damp palms against his pants and gave a salute to the foreign captain. "Is the cargo hold ready, Nigel?" he asked his second-in-command in a hushed voice.

"For supplies, yes. But I'm not so sure now," the lieutenant replied. They'd both been assigned to the Jolly Roger at the same time, eager to prove their worth and value to the navy.

While James had advanced a couple years ago, Nigel had remained one rank below him and happily transferred to serve under his command. "This isn't right."

"We'll have to make do," James replied, voice low.

Four dozen slaves or more—he lost count as each row of shackled men, women, and even children—boarded his vessel. Those small, bruised faces wrenched James's heart the most, and there seemed to be no end of them. The captives cringed whenever a member of either crew moved toward them.

"Can you take it from here, Captain Hook?"

"Aye." James mastered his voice and took command of his emotions, forced to hold a stoic expression in the presence of his equal. "We'll handle it from here. Lieutenant Gaumond, take the… captives below deck to the brig."

Nigel's eyes widened. It lasted a split second, too brief for anyone but James to notice his friend's hesitation. "Aye, Captain," he muttered before he gave commands to the other crewmembers.

Once Captain el'Vartellan returned to his ship, his crewmen removed the planks, lifted anchor, and sailed away. James had barely moved an inch, still staring into the distance until the Golden Goose was little more than a dark silhouette against the gray horizon.

"This can't be real," Nigel said as he returned to the deck.

James found all eyes upon them, eyes filled with skepticism, disgust, and even bewilderment. He couldn't blame a single member of the crew if they doubted him for what they'd just witnessed.

"Captain, are we dealing in the slave trade now?" a sailor asked.

"It appears Eisland has decided there is some value in it, yes."

"Then why are they aboard *our* vessel?"

James swept his gaze over their curious faces. "We've been ordered to smuggle them into Eisland to provide labor to the winter vineyards by Commodore Teach himself. Our instructions are to bring them to Port Progress and unload them in the dead of night."

The ship's only doctor shoved her way to the front of a growing crowd as men abandoned their posts to surround him. Eliza wore the blue and silver robes of a naval physician upon a lean, broad-shouldered frame. He hadn't warned her, and the white-hot fury in her hazel eyes told him excluding her had been the wrong choice. "What's the meaning of this, Captain?"

"It's by no choice of mine. Commodore Teach does this at the behest of the king. This is their experiment, a test to prove the value of the flesh trade to our monarch's advisers," James said.

Mutters went up from the crew and his unease grew. The whole thing went against everything he stood for.

"Many of them are in no condition to sail," she spit out between her teeth.

"Make them as comfortable as possible, Eliza. Please examine them and treat any wounds and ailments you find. Someone instruct Cook to provide water, bread, and stew."

Unable to face them a moment longer, James retired to his cabin and sank into the desk chair.

How could he possibly turn over so many innocent lives? Of course, it occurred to him that some may be criminals, as that was what he'd learned about the Ridaeron Dynasty during his school years. They enslaved their criminals and murderers first, their debtors second. But there had been children among those sad faces, with matted hair and dirt-smudged skin.

"What am I to do?" James wondered out loud to the empty cabin. The wealth of a pampered Eisland office surrounded him, the bed sumptuous and draped in velvet over the frost silk sheets, the wood lacquered and polished to a glossy, mirrored shine.

If he delivered the commodore's chattel then resigned, he'd be surrendering everything he'd worked his entire life to achieve.

And he'd never be able to forgive himself, not for abandoning his dream, but for condemning the innocent to a long life of pain and misery.

"I can't do this. I can't take them to Eisland," he muttered before leaning forward to take the bottle of rum from the desk. As he took his first swig, an idea sprang into his thoughts, nebulous and without form. By the third glass, it had taken shape, overpowering all reason and smothering what remained of his sanity.

The perfect plan. Just as he began to write his letter of resignation, Eliza gave her characteristic three-tap knock and entered. Before he could greet her, she tossed a folded packet on his desk. Her ivory face shone red. He'd never seen her more furious than when he'd thrown fish guts in her hair as a boy.

"What's this?"

"My letter of resignation."

"Eliza—"

"Don't you 'Eliza' me. If this is what our navy is sinking to,

I want no part of it. Mum's letter is in there as well. We refuse to engage in this, and you should be ashamed for agreeing to it."

"You're right."

"I—what?" She blinked.

"I said you're right. I can't turn a blind eye to this any longer," James murmured under his breath. "I'd decided that moments before you arrived."

"What else are we to do? We've received our orders."

"We'll free them." He turned his grim expression to Eliza and poured a shot of rum for her, too. "I plan to sail until we're a day's travel from the coast, then we'll force anyone who wants no part of this scheme to disembark. We've got enough space in the longboats for almost all of the crew."

"Everyone won't go, James."

"I know. I'm counting on it."

"They'll hunt us down. You can't just run off with one of their prized ships, let alone the cargo they paid for." She grimaced at the term.

"Splendid. You always claimed to enjoy a good fight, didn't you?"

"You're serious about this?"

"You should know me by now. As you said, if this is what our nation is turning to, I won't participate. We'll run, and after that, I have no idea what the tides will bring us."

"Mum is already lighting bloody candles and praying to Triton for you to see sense."

"Let her know I have. Then I want you to unshackle the slaves. You're fluent in Ridaeron, right?"

"I am."

"Find out if anyone knows how to sail." James tossed back the remainder of his rum and stood, fueled by liquid courage as he approached the cabin door to make his announcement.

Chapter 1

WITHIN THE HUMBLE wolf den of Mount Braeloch, Tink had found a loving home, surrounded by big people who cared about her, but as time passed, she missed her fellow sprites and often tried to persuade them to befriend the werewolves.

Despite her fervent efforts, the meek creatures didn't dare to travel closer than necessary to spread nature's bounty upon the once-barren ground and replenish the leaves with green and beauty. Such was the power of the sprites who lived in the leafy boughs, the grassy mounds on the ground, and the colorful flowers they tended.

And according to them, Tink was strange and unnatural for their sort. Her closest friends had died of old age over the years since the defeat of Maeval, leaving only new and young sprites in the area who had no love for adult shifters or humans.

"What if the big people eat you?" Splish asked.

"The big smelly one doesn't even call you by your name," Splash, the twin sister of the other fairy, agreed. She shook out her wild silver hair and frowned while studying the mouth of the nearby den. They wouldn't come inside, no matter how hard Tink tried to convince them of the wolf pack's benevolence.

"That isn't Conall's fault, and he isn't smelly anymore," Tink protested, although her friend was right. Bell had been the name given to her since creation, as her laughter sounded like many of them chiming. Each of her friends had similar names, given for their talents and the funny sounds they made. "I introduced myself as Tinker Bell."

Splish snorted. "And like a human, he lacked the wit to understand a proper introduction. None of the big folk ever get it."

Splish and Splash meant well, but they were notoriously hard on the humans. They tended the water flora in Lake Arweg, and their giggles mimicked the relaxing sound of gentle rainfall. And while they were sweet to the other fae folk, they had no patience for mortals.

Tink's shoulders drooped. Arguing with them would be a lost cause and a waste of her time. "All right. Fine. Then don't come."

All she'd wanted was to find six other fairies to accompany her to bless Kendric's birth. He'd turned three months old and, according to tradition, leaders from all the surrounding packs would arrive to pay their respects and gift the family presents.

Sorcha's baby boy was one of the most beautiful things Tink had ever seen, and also the most irritating. No matter what they were doing, or how much fun she was having while playing with Conall, the moment the baby cried, his parents abandoned her to see to his needs.

And he cried a lot.

And he often smelled bad until one of the big people swept him away to change his nappy and freshen him.

And Tink *still* found him precious and absolutely irresistible to snuggle beside once Sorcha washed and swaddled him. Unfortunately, sprites had no children of their own. Instead of relying upon procreation, they were born from a child's first laugh and simply came into existence upon motes of magic soon after, already young adults.

So why did she want one of the stinky little buggers?

Disappointed by her kin, Tink returned to the cavern as the first trickle of visitors arrived. Shifters of all shapes and sizes reached the mouth of the cavern where two werewolves waited like enormous furry sentries.

Finlay became human to greet her, experienced enough to shapeshift with his clothing intact. "Hello, Tink." He made a rugged, attractive man while human, clothed in the clan's scarlet and silver tartan.

"Hello, Fin!"

The second wolf inclined his head to her politely before Tink waved and zipped past them into the cavern. Knowing the many passages by heart, she hurried along chambers with smooth and polished walls, each one lit by numerous lanterns and the occasional opening in the ceiling designed to catch the sunlight. Many generations ago, the bears of Clan Ardal had used their magical stonecrafting talent at the behest of Conall's ancestors. They'd carved out multiple levels of chambers into the rock, and even located the perfect pocket below the earth capable of producing a hot spring. Water from Lake Arweg created a magnificent grotto in Conall's personal level of the den, although many of the pack members visited for a soak.

The aroma of roasting venison reached Tink's nose before she picked out the small gathering of people in the receiving area. Cool water from the lake lapped against the stone ledge, and in the distance, Lake Arweg glittered beneath the afternoon sun. Magical enhancements guaranteed it never flooded the burrow, and despite the open ceiling above them to release

VIVIENNE SAVAGE

smoke from the cooking fire, rainfall never dampened their furnishings. Most had been carved from wood or stone, lightly cushioned with furs or padded seats. The rugs and tapestries were all earth-toned shades, such as russet red, rich golden brown, and mossy green.

Her best friends occupied one of the benches, Conall resting beside his wife with both of her feet in his lap.

"Hello, Tink," Sorcha greeted her warmly, eyes twinkling with happiness. She held the swaddled baby to her breast while her husband, fascinated and ever devoted to his new family, rubbed her feet without complaint. The smile hadn't left his face since Kendric's birth; in fact, he'd endured Sorcha's pregnancy-related mood swings with an admirable grin-and-bear-it attitude worthy of praise. Nothing could shake his optimism.

And Tink was quite proud of him for taking so well to the role. She landed on Sorcha's shin and made herself comfortable on the woman's plaid skirt, using the folds as a makeshift hammock.

"About time you reappeared," Conall said. "I thought you'd miss the festivities."

Tink scrunched her face up at him. "What are you talking about? Your guests haven't even arrived yet."

"Aye, that's true. But you're family, and your place is beside us." When she tilted her face up to look at him, he grinned back at her. "The TalDrachs should arrive shortly. Anastasia sent word that they were delayed—Princess Teagan wanted to accompany them and bring a gift of her own."

"Is she still recovering?" Tink asked, her brows drawing inward. Princess Teagan had nearly died during their kingdom's war two decades ago, plummeting from the sky and crashing through the mountains, where she remained comatose for many years and under the care of goblins.

Conall nodded. "Aye, she is. It's taken her a long while to recover the wing strength to fly this great a distance, but I hear the princess looks well."

"Do we have enough to feed *two* dragons?" Tink whispered.

Conall snorted back his laughter. "There are bears coming too, lass. Ramsay and Victoria are coming from the east."

"I better go hide the cheese!"

"Tink! There's plenty of—"

Panicked, Tink zipped away, a bolt of anxious orange darting from the spacious den and into the lower levels where the wolves kept the pantry and wine cellar. She found her favorite wheels of cheese intact. Distrusting Ramsay, after she'd already witnessed the bear shifter's incomparable appetite, she rolled one wax-sealed wheel behind a pile of potatoes.

"There. Stinky won't eat all my cheese this time."

Satisfied with her handiwork, she returned to find that their guests had arrived. A procession of royal visitors and noble clan leaders from across Cairn Ocland made their way down the aisle into the sitting parlor where Sorcha and Conall awaited them.

Thanks to the spacious and open-walled cavern, there was plenty of room for everyone without crowding shifters or forcing them to sit shoulder to shoulder. The den had been designed to hold an entire pack, after all—not that Tink had to worry much. She zipped up to a little niche in the rocky ceiling and made herself comfortable.

As the tallest man in the room, King Alistair caught her

attention first. The regal dragon and his sorceress wife made a matching pair in their green and gold tartan. Anastasia wore her red hair braided in intricate plaits tied with pink ribbon, matching the young girl behind her. Princess Elspeth and Prince Rua walked behind the two adults, the children perfect miniatures of their stately parents.

Princess Teagan approached last with a wolf trailing a short distance behind her. Tink leaned forward and peered at the older dragoness, who could have passed for Alistair's sister rather than his aunt.

More people followed, and the din of joyous greetings filled the open space. Tink recognized a few prominent faces, especially the three bear elders of Clan Ardal. Unfamiliar clan leaders from the griffins, human settlements, and other groups made up the remainder of their visitors.

"Tink!" Conall called, interrupting the introductions.

"What?" she yelled back.

"Come down and meet our friends."

Reluctant to crash the celebration between the big people, she flitted down and settled on Conall's shoulder. Two dozen curious faces watched her, and a few called out generous greetings and welcomes to her as well. She tucked her chin, too shy to respond.

"I know many of you met Tinker Bell during the Battle of Mount Kinros, but today, I'm honored to introduce all of you to Kendric's fairy godmother."

Tinker Bell jerked around to stare at her friend's unshaven cheek. She'd settled too close on his shoulder to see anything more than the edge of a satisfied smile on his face. "What? But… but I'm barely a fairy."

"You're fairy enough for us, Tink. And I trust you with our little one if we ever need you," Sorcha said.

Stinging tears filled her eyes and blurred her sight. "I'll do my very best, I promise."

If only she were large enough to hug them. She kissed Conall's cheek instead before gliding down on her sparkling wings to show the same affection to Sorcha and Kendric.

"Well done, Tinker Bell," Alistair praised her, wearing a broad smile on his bearded face. "Now on to the presents. I had to rein Ana in before she could empty the castle and bury you in gifts. You'd thank me if you knew her plans."

Conall chuckled. "Much appreciated."

Anastasia drove her elbow into her husband's abdomen and cleared her throat. "Don't listen to him. Of all the gifts I might have brought, I find this will be the most use to you. When you first shared news of your pregnancy, I began to stitch protective spells into this blanket. Little Kendric will have only peaceful dreams and calm nights." The queen passed the folded bundle over to Sorcha then winked. "I also have a larger one for the two of you."

Everyone laughed, Tink included.

"And for my contribution, a simple cradle," Alistair said.

Two clansmen carried over the piece and set it down within Sorcha's reach. Dragons, wolves, and sprites had been carved into the dark wood.

"This is lovely." Sorcha leaned forward and ran a hand over the satin-smooth rail.

"It's nothing, really," Alistair said. "No enchantments or special runes."

"Don't be so modest," Anastasia chided her husband. "The

simplest things are often the most beautiful and heartfelt. He made it himself for you. I never knew dragon talons were so useful for art, but once again, he's proved me wrong."

"I posed for the sprites," Tink spoke up.

The queen smiled. "You certainly did, wee one. And you did a fantastic job."

Tink lost track of the gifts at some point, fascinated by the toys, clothes, and assortment of weapons in varying sizes to carry the child into adulthood. She'd never seen a human with such a vast array of arms, let alone one so little.

Afterward, Tink rode Sorcha's shoulder into the dining hall where a massive banquet awaited them all. Roasted venison, steaming fish, gooey cheese dishes, and fresh vegetables covered the formal table dedicated to entertaining guests. A traditional family meal in Cairn Ocland surrounded a round table, but in the case of hosting so many guests, clan leaders opted to use long, rectangular tables instead, placing the guest of honor at the end.

More tears sprang to her eyes when she saw the tiny golden plate and matching utensils set for her at the head of the table, the place setting accompanied by a miniature chair pushed up to the perfect wooden ledge.

They'd made her the guest of honor. A whole huge spot for only her.

"For me?"

"You're part of the family," Sorcha whispered. "Of course we'd have a place for you."

Laughter and stories abounded over the course of the feast as everyone shared tales from their youth or about their own children. It was rare for the clans to gather in such a number, but Tink enjoyed the merriment and hoped for more parties in the future.

By the time she finished stuffing her face, she could do nothing more than crawl onto Sorcha's lap alongside Kendric and bask in his newborn warmth. She fell asleep cuddling her new godson and didn't stir until morning.

As much as Tink enjoyed helping her friends in the day-to-day care of their infant, something vague and indefinable darkened her spirits. She couldn't put a finger on the source of her glum mood at first, until one evening when she settled nearby to watch the happy family. Sorcha played peekaboo with the baby while Conall made funny faces at him over his wife's shoulder.

Kendric's chubby face lit with happiness, his cheeks dimpled, and he giggled for the first time, releasing the most magical sound Tink had ever heard.

It came with a perceivable change in the air, energy flowing through the room like a living, breathing force of nature. No one but Tink noticed. While both parents playfully argued over who deserved credit for their babe's laughter, the golden mist created from his giggle drifted up into the air and toward the den opening. She followed it as far as the middle of the lake before a breeze picked it up and sped it away to the south, far from her view.

A fairy had been born. Not any fae, but a sprite like her. More importantly, it would be a boy, just like Kendric.

She drifted back home in silence, lost to her thoughts.

  VIVIENNE SAVAGE

Would Kendric's sprite find his way back to Cairn Ocland? What would he be like?

As she fluttered down to the cavern opening, her shoulders and wings drooped. Sprites may have been born from a baby's laugh, but they didn't feel a drive to return to the child. She hadn't. In fact, Tink had no idea whose laughter had birthed her. It could have been anyone.

It didn't seem right, she thought.

Around her, life went on. Sorcha set the table while Conall put Kendric to bed. In the lower part of the den, the rest of the pack settled down with their meals or evening games. She watched them and experienced soul-deep envy for the first time since she'd come to live with Clan TalWolthe.

As much as she considered them all family and friends, none of them were like her.

"I'm leaving," Tink declared as she flew over to the table.

Conall glanced up from his dinner. He held a huge drumstick in his hand, a mouthful of meat between his teeth. "Huh?"

"Don't speak with your mouth full," Sorcha chided him.

The shifter chewed a few times and swallowed, while shooting his wife a dirty look. "Then maybe she shouldn't speak to me while I'm eating," he grumbled. Sorcha may have lived among them for years, but they frequently resisted her efforts to instill culture and manners into them.

"Tink, what do you mean you're leaving?" Sorcha asked. "Did someone upset you?" After a pause, she added, "Did *I* upset you?" The only other time Tink had parted from Conall's side had been years ago when Sorcha entered their life. Back then, she'd been jealous, because she hadn't wanted to share her best and dearest friend with the strange interloping human female who had charged into their life.

"No, it isn't you."

As much as Tink wanted to envy Sorcha for having everything she wanted, the truth was that the sprite's desires had nothing to do with Conall. She didn't want the enormous dire wolf shifter and clan leader, and she'd never felt anything more than strong kinship and a longing for his friendship. What Tink wanted was the woman's lifestyle, a mate who adored her, a little one, and a sense of purpose.

Aside from her minor repairs to the den, Tink had no great purpose. She didn't want to spend the rest of her short life repairing weapons in the armory or fixing the pots and pans for the cook. She wanted to *live*. And she wanted to do it alongside someone who loved her in return.

In her dreams, she wanted someone gentler than Conall, someone less prone to moments of growling aggression, and someone who would play the games with her Conall had long outgrown. Because Conall was now a father, and he had no time for such frivolous activities when he was also the all-powerful clan leader of all nine wolf packs.

Conall fixed her with a hard look, a familiar stubborn set to his chin. "Where are you going to go that's better than here?"

"Kendric laughed," she said. When that answer failed to gain any acknowledgment other than a confused wrinkle to his brow, her shoulders drooped. "Did you forget what I told you about when sprites are born?"

"No," Conall said with a little heat. "They're made from a child's first laugh. Contrary to what you believe, Tink, I listen to every word you say."

"I want to go find Kendric's sprite. If I can find him, maybe he'll come with me and we can both live here together."

Tink had no doubt Kendric would grow to be an exceptional young man, which meant a sprite born from his laughter would be exemplary, too.

"I think it's a lovely idea," Sorcha said. "The sprites are always welcome here. I see some in the woods at times, but they rarely venture close."

"They think I'm odd," Tink confessed. She plucked a pea from Conall's plate and bit into it as an excuse to avoid looking at her friends.

"You're nothing of the sort." Conall's voice raised in indignation. "But if you want to go find this newborn sprite, then we'll make an adventure of it."

"Well…" She wiped her face and peeked up. "I want to go alone."

"Alone? Tink, it's dangerous. You'll need help."

"Tink is very capable, Conall. You ought to know that for yourself," Sorcha chided him.

"Yes, well… It'll be dangerous going by herself to—" He blinked and looked down at Tink. "Where are sprites born anyway? Here in Cairn Ocland?"

Tink held her breath and shook her head, shoulders hunched and wings twitching. "I can't tell you that. Or take you," she said. "Our birthplace is secret from all big people."

Sorcha placed her hand over her husband's mouth before he could utter a complaint. "That's more than understandable," she said. "Is there anything else we can do to help you with your trip? Maybe go halfway with you?"

"No. I need to do this alone."

"Then we'll see you off with all our love and support. Won't we, Conall?"

"I think—" Sorcha elbowed her husband. Appearing grumpier by the moment, the wolf scowled in return before murmuring, "Aye, we will. Whatever you need for your wee journey, you're welcome to have, Tink."

The journey south through Cairn Ocland passed as swiftly as a pleasant breeze. Maeval's defeat had returned safety to the kingdom, restored green to the land, and obliterated the remaining Scourge. If any of the wicked fairy queen's abominations had survived, they didn't dare to show their malformed faces.

Tink made good time, crossing to the southern reaches of the kingdom in less than a week by resting only at night. She usually slept in the trees or curled up in a flower, but twice she ventured into a home and received warm welcomes from its inhabitants.

Thick, ancient forests grew on the border of Cairn Ocland and their southern neighbor, Liang. Tink lingered at the tree line and peered into the thick growth. Vines clung to the trees and draped to the leaf-strewn ground. Little light penetrated through the branches, creating a sinister air.

During Maeval's reign, poachers and thieves from Liang capitalized on Cairn Ocland's weakness and began prowling the woods in search of rare ingredients for their alchemical concoctions. They also liked to capture woodkin, as well as any other magical creature they could get their thieving hands on.

Not me, Tink thought, confidence bolstered by the peaceful atmosphere. She hadn't encountered anyone with nefarious intentions since her departure from Braeloch.

Zipping to a low branch dangling above the ground, she settled on a stem weighed down by a scarlet rose hip. She loved the little pods most of all, being the sweetest before they ripened and turned orange. As she sated her hunger with the delicious treat, she eyed her surroundings and noticed a golden glint amidst the foliage to her left.

Skeptical of it, she surrendered to her natural curiosity and flitted down to investigate, only to catch her mistake at the last second. Trap. It had to be a trap. She'd heard rumors from the other woodkin that Liangese trappers placed fairy mirrors in the bushes to lure their kind.

"Ha!" she cried out gleefully as she zipped away. "I'm on to your sinister plans. You can't fool—oof!"

A cage dropped from above her, slamming down to the ground with a sharp crack. Tink picked herself up from the metal floor and glanced around dizzily. Once her eyes focused again, she realized she was trapped, caught in a cage no larger than a breadbox, with fine wire mesh stretched between the bars. She flew at the door and slammed against it, but it wouldn't budge, and a bell tinkled somewhere above her. Each time she tried to shake the bars or pound the door, the alarm sounded.

Footsteps crunched over the ground.

"Ah, look what we have here," a gruff voice said.

Like the rest of fairykind, Tink understood and spoke all languages. Liangese was among the ugliest, full of harsh, guttural consonants and shrill vowels.

"Another sprite," a second voice said. "We have half a dozen already at the market."

"Yes, but I have a buyer in search of one. This little bit will do."

The cage jostling as it was picked up allowed Tink a closer look at her captors. Both men wore shades of black and dark green to blend in with their surroundings. Their brown hair was cut short, cropped close to their scalps, and their faces were smeared with dirt.

"Yes, we have just the place for you," the first man said. He put his face close to the bars and laughed when Tink charged at him. She struck the mesh and bounced off. "Spirited, this one."

The second man huffed. "Let's be gone then, before their patrols find us. I hate venturing this close to the border."

"Help!" Tink cried. If they were worried about patrols, perhaps someone would hear her and race to her rescue. "Help!"

"Silence the pest before its tinkling brings the shifters down on us."

A fine mist filled the cage, bringing with it the overwhelming scent of poppy. Tink pressed herself against the mesh and tried to gasp fresh air from beyond her prison, but the poachers spritzed her face. Dizzy, she stumbled back and dropped to her knees on the floor. No matter how hard she tried to resist, her eyelids grew increasingly heavy.

The blurring world around the small sprite swirled with dim colors as darkness overtook her.

Chapter 2

HEAVY FOG SHROUDED the sea, enveloping the Jolly Roger in a white blanket. James stood on the forecastle with his eyes closed and his face turned into the misty breeze. This early in the morning, with most of his crew below deck, the only sound that reached his ears was the quiet lap of water against the hull.

Peace. A quiet moment before the inevitable hustle of the day.

"We should come upon our prey within the hour, James," Nigel said from behind him, his low voice shattering the serenity.

James opened his eyes and turned to face his first mate.

"Good. Rouse the men, make sure everyone is ready. If those route schedules we intercepted were correct, this will be the largest haul we've captured. The Golden Goose is rumored to be the most prosperous of all their merchant ships, which means there will be a bounty in slaves as well as treasure. Be sure Smee is ready for any children we might bring onboard."

"The berths have been readied, but I'll double check with him."

"Excellent. Let the hunt begin."

James took one final deep breath before abandoning the forecastle and crossing the main deck to the helm. Within minutes of receiving his command, men and women arrived to take positions throughout the deck.

A young man moved up the steps and approached James at the helm. A leather thong bound his long, golden brown hair back from his slim face. "I couldn't have called a better fog myself. They'll never see us coming."

"So long as you can clear it if we have the need," James said. Little Wolf had joined his crew only five years ago and quickly become an invaluable addition. His ability to shape and control the weather with magic kept their pirate vessel ahead of patrolling ships from Eisland and the Ridaeron Dynasty.

The boy's older sister had promised to skin James alive if harm came to Little Wolf while aboard the Jolly Roger. If any woman could follow through on such a threat, it was Tiger Lily, their tribe's courageous chief and leader. Lucky for him, Little Wolf was more than capable of defending himself.

The ship's combat mage joined them next. Callum was the oldest crewmember onboard, at the battle-hardened age of sixty-two. Strands of silver glinted in his auburn hair, though his beard was untouched by age, remaining the same bright copper it had been the first day James met him sixteen years before.

As the thinning fog revealed their prey ahead, the galleon moved effortlessly through the water, white sails taut and billowed outward with the wind. James grinned.

"Be ready, Little Wolf. If they're unable to maneuver to engage us, we'll be spared any cannon fire."

As Little Wolf's magic manifested, the wind current dwindled first to a tender caress then nothing at all, its absence causing the Golden Goose's sails to slacken. From their hiding spot in the mist, James watched as their quarry's sailors

VIVIENNE SAVAGE

scrambled around the deck, but it was too late. The majestic vessel slowed to a complete stop and wouldn't budge despite their efforts.

"Nigel, bring us in closer. Let's give them a true reason to panic. Callum, prepare yourself in the event that our friends are equipped with a mage of their own."

The older man sneered. "They're Ridaeron. *What* mages?"

For some reason, the people of the Ridaeron Dynasty lacked the aptitude for learning magic. James found it a curious phenomenon that affected their entire kingdom, reaching out like magic-negating tendrils to anyone who dwelled on their nation's shores.

"Ah. But let's not underestimate our foe. They're not fools."

"You think they've hired mercenary assistance?"

"I don't discount the possibility," James replied. "Place a wall before a man, and he'll find a way to tunnel below it. You know that as well as I do, old friend."

While they approached the Goose from the rear, avoiding potential cannon fire, a scarlet glow flared from the taffrail of the ship's stern and hurtled toward the Jolly Roger. James stared at the fireball sailing across the distance, and then he turned his head to raise both brows at Callum. "You were saying?"

Callum chuckled. "Just watch."

Distance dampened most of the power from the fireball as it splashed into the ocean, sizzling and sending up boiling water and steam.

"How did you know it wouldn't reach us?"

"The fact of the matter is that no slaver could ever capture any wizard worth his bloody salt, and a jinn couldn't cause harm under direction of a wish. That fireball was launched from a child. Probably a Samaharan half-breed and unable to control their spells. We have nothing to worry about."

"And the child?"

Callum's amusement faded. "A good thing we'll be freeing the poor tyke."

On the typical boarding, James stayed behind on the ship, but he had a score to settle with the captain of the Golden Goose. A somber mood fell over him, the moment bittersweet after years of searching for his prey. He'd wanted to dispense justice to Captain el'Vartellan for years, but the elusive slaver had always wiggled free of the Jolly Roger's grasp.

Not today.

Due to sails augmented by magic and their weather mage stirring the wind to their favor, the Jolly Roger flew on a perfect course to intercept their quarry. Her enchanted sails billowed out and magical glimmers danced around the rigging.

"Cannons, men!" he cried, thrusting his hook in the air.

Suspecting the Golden Goose to be ferrying slaves to Eisland, they'd loaded the cannons with small shot and lead pellets in advance. The pellets wouldn't sink the ship, but they'd introduce their opponents to a world of well-deserved pain.

A chain of explosions boomed, men screamed aboard the deck of the Golden Goose, and then grappling hooks flew.

"Cut the ropes, you imbeciles!" the shrill voice of Captain el'Vartellan cried from the Golden Goose's quarterdeck. "Archers, take aim!"

"Sharp shooters, defend!" came Nigel's responding order. Under his command, a half-dozen pirates charged forward with their pistols and fired, warding off any sailors bold enough to obey their captain. As the panicked sailors dove for cover, James prepared to join the Jolly Roger's boarding party. While he missed having both hands—one to hold his gun and one to swing with his cutlass—he'd decided to save the former for one man in particular.

The action moved fast, grapplers tugging both boats closely together while the initial boarders swung over on ropes from the mast. These men were the most important, tasked with disabling any defensive measures deployed by their prey, such as razor wire and nets. They'd honed the process over the years, fulfilling their duties under fire by slicing cables with magically enhanced, sharpened steel.

Fatima, a young swordswoman from the deserts of Samahara, had joined the crew only four months prior as their newest addition, but she'd quickly earned her place among the men who led the charge. Wielding a scimitar in each hand, she dashed across the planks and into the fray before their opponents could prepare to ward off her advance. Afterward, the rest of the crew surged over.

While their whirlwind of steel cut her swath through the initial defenders, James stepped aboard the ship. At last, it was a day long coming, the most prosperous smuggler of human cargo from the Ridaeron Dynasty would finally meet his end. James parried a sword strike with his hook, Ridaeron steel singing against enchanted metal. Then he ran the man through, kicked him off the blade, and made his way across the deck.

Captain el'Vartellan had disappeared during the commotion, although James suspected the coward to be hiding while the rest of his crew defended him from danger.

Such was the Ridaeron way, a kingdom of cheats and bastards without morals.

Much like the kingdom James had left behind, his love for Eisland waning over the years as tales reached him of the crown's increasingly classless behavior. Apparently Eisland had fallen so low in regard since his desertion, the parents of Creag Morden's esteemed royal family had married their daughters to beastmen nobles in Cairn Ocland.

He would have loved to hear that story in its entirety, but had few ties to either kingdom.

Another sword whistled through the air to James's left. He spun to the side, raised his right arm, and deflected it. As the hook slid over the blade's edge, he caught the hilt and yanked it from his attacker's grip.

"Run, Cap'n!" Captain el'Vartellan's would-be savior cried out for him to flee and save himself while his crew perished at the hands of the invaders.

The blood thundered in James's ears, and fury pulsed through his veins. No leader should ever abandon his men. No captain should ever be among the first to flee a ship. His gaze darted toward the rail where he saw a small group of sailors prepared to protect their gutless captain with their lives. They'd already drawn in one of their longboats for their esteemed leader to flee, and two were tossing in treasure.

Ridaeron longboats appeared to be a fraction of the size preferred by their Eislander allies. While the men had chosen their fates, el'Vartellan didn't deserve their loyalty. Without a doubt, any sailor aboard the Jolly Roger would do the same for James at the drop of a hat, but a vast distinction separated the two captains—James would never allow one of them to die for

VIVIENNE SAVAGE

him. Ever. He'd made the decision long ago to be the last man to go down with the ship if it meant all others could escape harm before him.

With the boarding party from the Jolly Roger occupying most of the defending sailors, James found his route to the rail unimpeded. A magical shimmer wavered in the air around the small boat, the telltale sign of magical enchantments designed to cloak a stealth vessel. Ridaeron had acquired the designs from Eisland, where every naval ship was outfitted with a similar contraption intended for the senior crew and officers to escape.

One of the three men whirled toward James with his sword drawn. No matter the desperation fueling el'Vartellan's guards, the day had come for him to fall. James forced the fury to subside and led with his sword, fending off two assailants with the grace of a dancer. The frenetic pace of the battle rose to a feverish pitch, and then he snuck by one sailor's defenses with a finishing stroke to the chest. Blood splattered across the deck as the man fell, only for another to take his place. James struck with his hook, slashing another across the throat until no one stood between him and his prey.

"There's no one else here to defend you." James flicked the blood from his cutlass and grinned. "It appears that the rest of your crew is quite occupied, my friend. Now draw your sword. I won't kill an unarmed man."

"What do you hope to gain by doing this, Hook?" El'Vartellan drew his blade and held it in a trembling hand. "What's the endgame? Are you so arrogant as to believe you can end slavery?"

"I may be but one voice, but I'll certainly be the loudest."

Belle and the Pirate

"This is bigger than you, bigger than me and this galley of animals. There's no one in the belly of this ship but Ridaeron *trash*, son. These are the worst our society has to give. They're our peasants who turned to criminal acts. The lowborn and poorly bred. The sons of thieves and beggars. They'll never amount to anything, and your kingdom does them a generous favor by granting them homes and honest work."

"Homes tempered by bondage," James spat.

El'Vartellan chuckled darkly and removed a small vial from his coat pocket. He flicked the lid from it with his thumb and tossed its contents into his mouth. He grimaced, but then his shaking hand grew steady.

Liang's reputation for creating alchemical concoctions had earned them the Ridaeron Dynasty's favor when it came to recreational tonics and other brews. Nobles had become their best customers, exhibiting a ravenous hunger for the ivory milk harvested from Liang's poppy flowers. When infused with other alchemical reagents, a potent elixir was made.

"Unable to fight without a taste of your poison?" James asked.

"I don't need poppy milk to send you to Triton, Hook."

They both went for each other at once, clashing swords joining the cacophonous ringing of metal against metal. James ducked beneath another swing then parried and struck, drawing first blood as waves crashed against the ship and sent cool mist washing over their perspiring faces.

El'Vartellan stumbled back and raised one hand to the bloodied slash across his chest, features contorted into a mask of hate. Once their blades crossed again, the Ridaeron threw James back and sent him stumbling three paces. Drugs infused

  VIVIENNE SAVAGE

the slave trader with unnatural vitality unlike anything James had ever encountered before, and before he could regain his footing, el'Vartellan forced him back toward the rail while growling between his clenched teeth. His face flushed red.

"All of this, and for what? You'll change nothing. Imported servitude is the way of the future, Hook."

The way of the future? Memories of Ridaeron cruelty flashed through James's mind, of savagely beaten slaves and little children with whip-scarred bodies. Of women who flinched away from the mere sight of a man.

Fury guided James's aim, and he lashed out with his hook to score the perfect blow, tearing open skin before he kicked his opponent away from him. "Not for as long as I live," he gritted out.

With the finesse and speed el'Vartellan lacked, despite his drug-enhanced stamina, James spun behind the man and slashed his sword in a precise arc, sweeping across the back of both boots. It sliced through tough leather and flesh, ripping the tendons el'Vartellan needed to stand and unceremoniously dumped him on the deck.

Pride and honor wouldn't allow James to stab a man in the back, but he had no qualms about disabling his woeful adversary. Afterward, he sheathed his sword and smiled down at his foe. Where only moments ago there had been complete bedlam on the deck, the ship's crew had been reduced to a few survivors on the verge of surrender. No one came to the captain's aid, despite his desperate attempts to stand.

"A coward never prospers, el'Vartellan. Let this be a moment the sea never forgets, the day the Golden Goose descended from grace."

Captain el'Vartellan twisted on the ground and glowered up at him with hate-filled eyes. "They'll come for you. My countrymen won't rest until you've danced the gallows jig."

"A true captain remains with his crew until the end," James said. He drew his pistol and aimed between his rival's eyes. "I consider this my only courtesy to you."

As his pirates laid claim to the Golden Goose, Captain Hook pulled the trigger.

Tink had been in darkness for a long time, unable to count the days she'd been captive inside the exquisite little house. While she'd never seen a contraption so beautiful before, she wondered if it would be where she met her end.

Would Conall miss her? Maybe he'd forget about her in a year or so, so wrapped up in his little one and new wife that his old companion faded to the far recesses of his memories.

No, Conall wouldn't forget me. She had better faith in him than that, but of course, memories amounted to nothing when they lacked the power to free her from captivity. Alone and afraid, she huddled in the darkness.

It was a perfect miniature of a noble home or castle, both a dollhouse *and* a cage, although the fore wall consisted of gilded bars. She'd been lying upon one of the beds dozing in and out of sleep when something jostled the container and shook her all about. She screamed and held onto a bed post while a noisy clamor occurred outside. Had they entered a warzone?

Some time passed before the muffled sounds of combat diminished and her surroundings quieted. The cage shifted once more, tilted, and then dropped on its side. Tink stumbled backward, unable to regain her footing and forced to hover in place. A man's muffled voice reached her through the gilded prison's walls, and then her cage moved again with the distinctive rhythm of a human's stride. Eventually, the movement stopped and more voices joined the initial speaker. An excited man whooped in the distance until the door clicked shut and muted the extraneous noises.

"Looks like a phoenix," someone murmured. The man's silky voice caressed her senses.

While fae understood the spoken tongue of all mortals across the world, Tink couldn't recall ever hearing this language before. Intrigued, she plastered her body against the golden bars securing the front half of her fairy house and listened.

"Shall we set it free when we reach land?" another man asked.

"Doubt it'll be able to survive on its own now. The Liangese like to hobble them by frost-burning the muscles beneath the wings with ice magic. Brutal business it is, to damage something so beautiful," the initial speaker said. He had a gentle voice, masculine and pleasant to her ears.

"Can I have this one, Captain?" a third man asked. "Always been fond of exotic birds, and as you said, this poor beast won't survive in the wild anymore."

"I'm not sure it's wise to keep a firebird on the ship, Callum," the man with the velvet voice answered.

"As if I'd be so foolish," Callum said after a snort. "No, I'll leave this one back home with Primrose and Calla. They'll take good care of her."

"Go ahead, then," the captain said. "What else do you suppose we'll find?"

"No idea. I feel bad for the bloody tiger, though. The poor thing is cramped in that tiny cage. We'll have to set it loose at once when we reach an adequate place to free him."

"Take your bird to your quarters and help Nigel with the tiger, since you feel so strongly for it. Do your best to keep the animal alive until we reach Ankirith. Joaidane will know what to do."

"Aye, Captain."

Footsteps passed close by her then faded away. A few moments later, three loud thumps echoed from outside the box holding her cage. She flinched away from the sound and jarring impact.

"What's in this box, Smee?" the captain asked. "Is it something alive? I don't hear any movement." He tapped it again.

"No idea, but I've heard it buzzing, so I saved it for last."

Light pierced her prison from above, and then her cage moved, swinging upward. Tink shrank back against the dollhouse wall and prepared herself for the worst. Once her eyes adjusted to the brighter room, her vision treated her to the sight of lavish surroundings. Four diamond-patterned windows ran along a single wall, each one so close together, they seemed to form one larger viewport. The smoky glass allowed in the light but kept it dim. Sumptuous drapes and heavy tapestries hung on the wood-paneled walls. Wealth gleamed from every corner, reminding Tink of her visits to Castle TalDrach.

Was she in a palace?

"Well, would you look at that. It's like a dollhouse and a cage in one. Another bird, you think?" The closest human wore a pair of spectacles on his reddened nose. He leaned in close and pressed his face against the bars. "I don't see anything."

When Smee tapped his nails against the bars, they resonated at a thunderous volume in the tiny space around her. He shook the whole thing, jostling Tink from her hiding spot. She tumbled out and flew around in a panic. "There it is! I've found—"

Tink zipped across the cage and jabbed him with her dagger.

"Ah! It bit me!" Smee cried.

The taller man behind him laughed. "Won't that teach you to poke your big nose where it doesn't belong?"

Smee rubbed his face and glared at her. Only a tiny droplet of blood had welled from the cut. "You should toss it overboard, Captain. It's feral, it is. Look how it glows red, like a wee devil."

Something about the tall man they called "Captain" reminded Tink of Conall. He had kind eyes, bluer than a cloudless sky, and they crinkled at the corners each time he smiled. Messy waves of untamed black hair fell to his broad shoulders, and he wore an unfastened poet shirt tucked into dark trousers. He had become, in only a few seconds, the most handsome man to ever cross her vision.

"There's nothing feral about this poor creature, Smee. See? If anything, you frightened it. I can only imagine how terrified it must be, having been taken from its home and kept in darkness."

The captain raised her dollhouse and set it on an enormous

trunk beside a bed cloaked by heavy layers of burgundy velvet and glossy silk. "I'll keep it in my quarters for now until we can identify it. How's that?"

Smee rubbed his nose again and frowned. "Fine then. It'll be your funeral, and then Nigel will be the one at the helm directing us," the man muttered under his breath. He ambled away, leaving Tink alone with the handsome captain.

"Let me go, you big bully!" she cried up to him.

He chuckled at her. "You certainly sound angry, but I don't believe you're dangerous. Probably a little hungry, but far from dangerous." He wandered away a few paces to a table decked with a place setting for one. Fruit overflowed from a silver serving bowl in the center. He plucked a golden apple up, buffed it against his shirt, and then sliced a small portion from it before returning to her.

"I wonder if you'll eat this…"

Tink eyed the apple wedge and floated back from the bars. Undeterred, the captain pushed it through and dropped it on the dollhouse's wooden floor. Too starved to dismiss food after the long and hungry voyage from Liang's shores, she snatched the tiny morsel and dashed out of sight to hide in one of the only private rooms that wasn't open to viewing from the outside. The mastermind behind its design had actually created a privy that fed into the rear garden. Flowering ivy crawled up the sides of the dollhouse and sprouted violet blossoms.

"There now, that's better." The captain chuckled and moved away. Tink peeked out in time to see him heading toward a door covered in fanciful engravings. Sunlight flooded the room once he opened it, bringing in the salty tang of the sea and the sound of many voices raised in song. He stepped through and

VIVIENNE SAVAGE

closed the door behind him, shutting out all noise.

Great, Tink thought. So much for her big adventure.

Chapter 3

WHAT NIGEL AND the crew found aboard the Golden Goose had tempted James to sink the ship and leave no traces of it at all. In fact, nothing would convince him he hadn't done them an undeserved kindness when the crew of the Jolly Roger left the surviving monsters with only the scraps of spoiled food they'd provided to the slaves imprisoned below deck.

"How is everyone? Settled?" James asked as he stepped into the galley. Eliza chopped vegetables beside Cook at the counter, a carbon copy of her mother minus wrinkles and gray streaks in her golden hair.

Eliza's defined biceps flexed when she dropped the knife and crossed her arms against her chest, both bared by her sleeveless mage robes. She still preferred the attire, even after defecting from the Eisland Navy alongside him. "A few of the youngest have been too scared to eat or drink. Others are starved for real sustenance that isn't some arsehole's leftovers."

"And the mage boy?" James asked.

"Petrified of beatings. It took me over an hour to convince the lad I wouldn't take a strap to him. He'll mend, but I worry for his heart."

"Have you gotten a name, at least?" he asked.

Eliza's shoulders sank, and she shook her head. "Be grateful I got him to accept a blanket. Words and names will come in time."

"What's happening out there?" Cook asked. "This is the second ship this month we've intercepted filled to the brim with slaves. Practically piled three high, not an inch between them. Most had lice."

James grimaced. "Please tell me you've taken care of that."

"I did. Simple enough remedy. You needn't worry about it spreading like wildfire among the crew," Eliza replied. Women of his native country weren't allowed to learn magic beyond hearth and home, although the kingdom did enjoy pressing them into service aboard the naval ships as healers. When Eliza deserted the navy alongside him, he'd gotten one of the best.

"I know they aren't more than annoying pests, but the itching…" He shuddered, much to her amusement. "Will they all survive?"

Her smile dimmed. "Children are resilient, but as for the adults… the ones who won't are comfortable now."

"Good. If you're not exhausted, I'd like you to have a look at something in your spare time. No one else seems capable of identifying one of the exotic creatures we liberated from their cargo hold."

"Ah." Eliza glanced at her mother.

"Go on then. You don't need my approval. I can chop vegetables without you. You're only in my way when you try to help."

After the older woman nudged her daughter out of the workspace, James led Eliza to his quarters. Only a few members of the crew were welcome to step within, fewer granted permission to enter at any time. He considered Nigel, Eliza,

Callum, Cook, and Smee to be among his closest friends, and more than deserving of the privilege to be in his private space.

"Over there. See the dollhou—"

Eliza beelined to it. "Oh! The craftsmanship is lovely." She bent low with both hands on her knees. "Beautiful garden sprouting from the back. And there's a fountain! What a magnificent work of art."

"I didn't bring you up here to admire the bloody cage," he grumbled. "Here, this ought to bring the creature out."

Passing over the apples, he opted for a blueberry and dropped it between the bars. As predicted, the colorful, glowing blur darted out and snatched it.

"Oh!" Eliza crouched down for a better look. They watched for a few moments until the fruit disappeared. "Fast little thing."

"Indeed."

"She's certainly pretty, James."

"Her?" James leaned down and peered closer. The ball of light's tinkling noises grew louder and more frantic. Fearing he'd terrified it, he jerked back and drew his spine straight. "How can you tell?"

"When she stops moving, the light doesn't glow so brightly. The shape is definitely girlish. Like a tiny, flying doll."

"Ah. S'pose we ought to keep her then, instead of setting her free?"

"It might be for the best," Eliza said. "There's no tellin' where she came from. Those accursed Liangese poachers could have taken her from anywhere between Cairn Ocland and Samahara. As for whatever she is, I haven't a clue. Tiger Lily may be able to tell you once we reach Wai Alei."

James sat on the edge of his bed and studied her. He'd never seen such a fanciful little marvel. Disappointment filled him, but he shook it off. It wasn't Eliza's fault. They didn't have such creatures in Eisland, and he'd never seen their like in Wai Alei or the Samaharan ports they frequented.

Perhaps she'd fallen into his possession by fate, and all of his pleas to the gods for a worthwhile companion had been answered after all.

"I promise to give you a good life, little one. As good a life as I can until I discover precisely what you are."

True to his word, James did give Tink a good life, and she wanted for nothing while a guest within his bedroom. He provided two meals each day and no shortage of conversation when he roused each morning and returned to his cabin in the evenings.

In time, she came to anticipate his visits to the bedside, since the human's conversation broke the monotony of exploring her dollhouse. Unlike Smee, he seemed unconcerned with her stabbing him in the nose. And the longer she gazed upon him, the less she wanted to cause him harm.

After all, as far as she could tell, this man meant her no ill will. He could have taken his associate's advice and tossed her, cage and all.

Tossed her where? The subtle rocking motion alluded to a boat, introducing Tink to a new experience. As she mused over the possibility, the cabin door opened and shut. James staggered past her with a rum bottle clutched firmly in his left hand, and then he dropped to the edge of the bed.

"Gods. Why do I keep doing this to myself?" he muttered.

"I dunno. Why do you?" Tink asked, although her question went unanswered. He took another swig then set it aside before grasping the sides of her dollhouse. It was a ritual she'd come to know over the days of her new life, and she clung to the bars while he set her cage aside on the floor so he could reach the trunk beneath.

James never opened the trunk until he was deep in his cups and so drunk he barely moved in a straight line across the cabin floor. She never saw exactly what was inside, due to her poor vantage, only that he'd pull out a silver frame and stare at it for a long while without a single word.

As he started the same process again, Tink sighed and plopped down on a little velvet bench with what tiny bit remained of her dinner. She was tired of fruit, but it was all the captain ever offered.

"Beautiful, isn't she? The most beautiful woman in all the lands."

Tink looked up, startled by his voice. James had slid down from the bed to sit on the floor beside her cage, silver frame in hand. It held a portrait of a young woman with the palest blonde hair Tink had ever seen. Whether true to reality or a fanciful addition by the artist, the girl's hair shone silver.

"I was supposed to marry her, you know," James continued. "Would have been a prince, I suppose. Imagine that, a vintner's son marrying into royalty." He chuckled and exchanged the portrait for the rum bottle. "Not gonna happen now, is it?"

"No one would marry a drunk."

"I wonder what it is you're saying," he said. "You just sound like you're chiming. Ah well, you probably don't understand a word I'm saying anyway. Not that it matters." He finished the last of the bottle and set it aside, reclaiming the portrait before he stumbled to his feet.

"None of it matters anymore," he continued. Tink fluttered to the top of the cage and watched him cross to the windows. One of the panes swung outward when he knocked it with his hook.

"Ah… Rapunzel. I suppose it's quite time to let you go, isn't it?" James tossed the portrait through it. A faint splash followed a moment later and joined the gentle lapping of the waves against the ship's hull.

"You're going to regret that," Tink said, though she knew he couldn't understand her.

James secured the hidden latch on the window and returned to the bed, where he flopped down without putting her cage back on the trunk. A letter fell from the blankets, the paper wrinkled as if it had been crumpled then smoothed out flat again. Despite her attempts to read it, the looping, exaggerated script foiled her efforts. Sprites may have understood the spoken word of every language, but variances in handwriting made text a challenge.

"They've finally written me."

Startled, she snatched her hand back from between the bars where she'd been reaching for the paper, but James hadn't moved. All she saw was his hook hanging over the edge of the bed.

"My family has made it clear, after years of my attempts to reach out to them, that I am no longer their son. They burn my letters. I suppose Mother must have taken great satisfaction in adding that line. I'd always hoped…" He sighed. "I don't know what I hoped. Not this."

Looking at the letter, Tink began to understand a little more about the broken, drunken man on the bed. She couldn't imagine what she'd ever do if Conall severed ties between them. She'd be heartbroken. Lost.

"If my family thinks the worst of me, what horrors must my betrothed believe about me? Or perhaps she was with her father all along. Don't they understand that I do this for the good of everyone? That no man has the right to own and possess the body of another?"

Was he speaking of slaves? Her brows pushed together as she listened. James babbled for a while longer until his voice trailed. He shifted, as if intending to rise, only to collapse amidst the rumpled bed coverings again.

Soon after, the rumbling of his snores became the only sound to fill the cabin. Only then did Tink tug the rumpled letter into her cage, poring over it and squinting for a long hour to decipher the complicated speech.

What she read made her hurt for James even more.

While Tink had only known Captain James Hook for less than a week, she required no further proof to determine he was far too good for Sir and Madam Hook, who claimed to no longer have a child. Far too good for the likes of them.

Chapter 4

ADMIRAL EDWARD TEACH mopped his brow while reading the summons from King Harold. Hook's lawless behavior in the Viridian Sea had reached new levels of inconvenience for Eisland.

He blamed himself for misplacing his judgment in the boy and failing to see he hadn't been prepared to do what was necessary for his king and country. Back then, he'd thought James to be one of their shining stars.

After folding the summons and shoving it within his blue coat, the admiral ran his fingers over his lustrous black beard and made his way into the throne room.

Three crystal chandeliers dangled from the vaulted ceiling and cast dancing rainbows across the room. A cobalt runner ran the length of the throne chamber to the dais, standing out against the pristine white marble floors. Only the finest stone from quarries in the north had been used in the castle's construction. King Harold's ancestors had demanded nothing less.

Of all the kingdoms and castles he had visited, Teach never found one lovelier than Castle Icedale. Not because it was home, but because it truly deserved the distinction.

Sunlight poured in through large windows fitted with flawless glass imported over a century ago from a desert kingdom across the world. Planters carved from obsidian overflowed with white ice roses. They only bloomed in cold weather following a hard frost. Artisans around the kingdom preferred them over tedious embroidery since the preserved flowers became like silk.

But the shining jewel of the room was the throne itself. Carved from a single massive sapphire, it rose higher than the tallest man in the court, providing an impressive backdrop for the monarch.

King Harold stood out in his white and silver finery, a man of average height with fair hair resting around his slim shoulders. He had never raised a weapon in all his life. His baby soft hands, slender torso, and spindly arms created the meek frame of a monarch who hid behind greater men. In fact, he'd been a child king when he ascended to the throne following the loss of his predecessor fifty years prior—spoiled and denied nothing by the court.

"Admiral Teach, you've finally arrived."

Teach bowed. "Forgive me, sire, I only received your message within the last hour, and I was unfit to be in your company."

"Don't give me bloody empty apologies. Tell me what you plan to do about this damned pirate. Do you know how much money was lost when Hook sacked the Golden Goose?"

"I am well aware of the value," Teach replied.

A scarlet flush swept from the king's starched collar, mottling his pale face. "Had he spared Captain el'Vartellan, I would have hung him myself for this abysmal failure. The man was cocky, and his arrogance cost Eisland a small fortune. Thousands of crowns, Teach. Thousands!"

Suppressing the urge to groan, Teach straightened and

clasped his hands behind his back. "Excuse me, sire, but we both know such a deed would have incurred Ridaeron's wrath. No, it's better that Hook killed him. They'll want his blood now in return."

"They've always wanted his blood, but I want it first," the king snarled. "I want to string him up for all to witness. Then they'll see what piracy brings."

Teach dried his sweaty palms against his breeches. "I've done all that I can, Your Majesty. The shipwrights have yet to build a faster ship. Prior to his desertion, his sails were embroidered with the best enchantments to come from the Collegium of Arthras, and now he has the aid of that damned sorcerer from Samahara. In fact, rumor has it he's employed a weather mage from Neverland, too."

"I want more."

"I can speak with the magister—"

"I've already spoken with him, and I have a plan," King Harold said.

"Oh? And what do the magisters say?"

"My son, Joren, heard of our troubles and suggested commissioning a grand weapon from their best enchanters. The price won't be pretty, but the cost will be worth ridding this world of Hook."

Teach chuckled. "I'm surprised such a recommendation came from Joren. He and Hook were quite close at one time."

"I told him his treacherous former friend is to blame for his sister's delirium. Rapunzel hasn't been the same, you know, since the boy abandoned her, and upon discovering he sacked the ship of her newly betrothed, her delicate mind could take no more."

"But Rapunzel wasn't betrothed."

"Joren doesn't know that."

Awed by the king's devious mind, Teach smirked and tipped his head in respect. "A good plan, Your Majesty. You know your son well."

"Joren has always been a white knight when it comes to his sister. It's a shame those bloody Mordenian ingrates couldn't see his potential. Their daughters chose Oclanders over my Joren."

"Beastmen," Teach spit out. "I've heard they lack a proper navy."

"And many other modern conveniences," King Harold grumbled. "My latest spy reports tell me some of them still live in caves."

"No better than common animals, my king."

"Unfortunately, they have grown in power since Anastasia claimed the throne beside the dragon king, and we have no choice but to play nice with them. Morgan pressed me to accept them into the Compact, and they're our allies now."

"Indeed. But what shall we do about the pirates?"

King Harold's smile returned. "Magister Benedict has designed a cannon for the Queen Anne's Revenge, a one-of-a-kind beauty with the ability to draw magic from the fire rubies harvested in the deserts of Crestoli."

"How soon will this weapon be ready to put on a ship?"

"As soon as you can get your ship to Avalon Bay. Joren will assist in outfitting your ship. However, I don't wish for him to join your crew. I know he'll make the request. Refuse him."

"Joren is a fine sailor," Teach began, only for the king to cut him off with a sharp hand slash through the air.

"I forbid it. Until his sister sees reason and understands imported servitude is the way of Eisland's future, he is my only remaining heir. I can't risk him on this mission."

"As you command. Tell me though, Your Majesty, what is the likelihood of Prince Joren accepting our nation's prosperous new commodity? How do you know he won't behave as his sister did?"

"Joren is more pragmatic than his sister. He'll see the advantages to our new way of doing things and the affluence gained through our endeavors.

"And if he doesn't?"

"Then I'll be forced to arrange for an accident to befall his precious sister while placing the blame on the heathens we've imported from Ridaeron. What better way to gain his obedience than by cultivating his bitterness? I don't need a *daughter*, but I do need my son as an heir."

Chapter 5

WHILE OUT AT sea with days until their next destination, James often left Nigel, Eliza, or Smee at the helm. Most recently, however, it had been Smee, since physician's duties occupied Eliza's time and Nigel had taken an interest in Fatima, clumsily courting the swordswoman during his free time. As she'd been accustomed to a wholly different variety of man in her native kingdom, she fell quite soundly for Nigel's awkward pursuits.

Damn. James loathed envying his friend, but he couldn't help but wish some of the same sweet fortune would befall him as well.

"It was bound to happen eventually, I suppose," James muttered to himself. He settled at the dinner table alone, missing the usual company of his officers. A glow at the corner of his eye drew his attention, causing him to turn and glance at the cage set by his bed. The little creature pressed against the bars, bright and serene.

"I have you to keep me company at least, don't I?"

She tinkled at him, a living bell glowing the most tranquil shade of lilac.

A living bell. Belle. At last, a name for her came to mind, a favorite among the noble ladies of Eisland. "Are you hungry?" He turned her cage toward the dining table.

Her glow intensified. Accepting it as an answer, he

chuckled and relocated her to the table along with him, moving the entire cage. Cook had prepared a sweet medley with the remaining fruit from their recent raid, consisting of blueberries, diced melon, sliced apples, and ripe raspberries. Pushing a blueberry between the bars resulted in his tiny friend shoving it back out.

"What?" He frowned. Had she grown tired of them? He didn't know what to feed her, and hesitated to give the creature something disagreeable that would cause her harm. After a moment of hesitation, he leaned closer to her cage and stared back at her.

"I'm going to allow you out of the cage. After all, we've been friends for a couple weeks now, haven't we?" Deciding the worst that could happen was he spent hours chasing her down in his closed bedroom, he released the latch on the front and swung it open.

At first, she lingered in the cage and hovered in the open doorway. When James was positive she didn't plan to leave, she darted out and sped to his plate, where she snatched up a small wedge of hard yellow cheese and beelined toward the cabin's rafters. There she sat, within sight but beyond his reach, and dug into her prize.

Even a tiny winged creature found his company intolerable, it would seem.

"S'pose this means I'm doomed to dine alone after all, but you're more than welcome to anything else from my meal."

He watched her almost sadly, of a mind to let her enjoy a taste of freedom along with her stolen cheese, even if her choice of food did bewilder him. "I hope that doesn't make you ill, little Belle."

Resuming his meal in silence, he cast a wary look toward his door and considered locking it, then quickly discarded the notion. Few entered his room without knocking, and James suspected Smee would slam the door shut if he opened it to see Belle hurtling toward him. The mental picture his thoughts inspired made him chuckle.

Whether drawn by his laughter or hunger, his little friend drifted down to the opposite end of the table. Not a crumb of cheese remained in her hands.

"Come back for more, have you?" he asked in a soft voice. "Help yourself."

If she had any sort of intelligence, surely she wouldn't take something that would harm her. So he waited, hand on the table and hook resting on his lap, body motionless as Rapunzel had taught him years ago. The princess had held an affinity for all winged creatures, and they'd once spent hours in her private rooftop garden as the birds fluttered to and fro, taking nectar from their cupped palms or seeds from the dishes she left out. That fond memory seemed decades ago.

He channeled that patience now while watching his diminutive friend. Colors flickered across her wings, first orange, then blue, and finally a deep red. Then she darted forward and another piece of cheese vanished from his plate, along with a bit of bread. She retreated back across the table with her prizes and took a seat. James counted it as a tiny victory that she hadn't flown back to the ceiling.

"You're very safe here, little one. I wouldn't harm you. I know you can't understand me, but I hope perhaps you can understand something in my voice."

She tinkled, the orange glow returning to her wings. Her

movements restored the smile lost by his earlier melancholic thoughts. How could he feel anything but joy while observing her? She seemed to take her time with her meal this time around, so he returned to his. Cook had prepared roasted fish caught earlier in the day. Between the stores they claimed from the ships they plundered and what they caught from the sea, they never wanted for food.

Thoughtfully chewing the savory morsel fried in sweet butter churned by Cook herself, he studied her then glanced at his wine goblet. "I wonder… You do resemble a little woman. Do you drink like one too?"

While he hollowed a cork with the sharp tip of his hook, she darted forward and stole a chunk of bread, dragging it through the honey smeared on his plate. After pouring a portion of sweet white wine into the makeshift cup, he set it in the middle of the table on a linen napkin. Then he placed more cheese and bread beside it, as well as a small portion of his fish.

"Cook is an excellent chef," he told her. "I've always thought we'd gotten away with the best in Eisland's navy, and my opinion has remained the same. She and a few of my men tend the animals we keep down below. It's how we keep milk, eggs, and butter on the ship for our meals."

Upon seeing the wine, she abandoned her bread.

Now that she wasn't flitting about or surrounded in a bright glow, James was able to distinguish the finer details of her figure. A slender body, pointed ears, and large, glossy green eyes.

"Eliza was right. You are quite pretty." More tinkling from the creature widened his smile. She seemed to preen under his compliment, though he discarded the ridiculous notion as soon as it formed. "In fact, more beautiful than most human women I've seen," he murmured thoughtfully. *Any* human woman he'd ever seen.

The little creature tossed her golden hair over one shoulder. Fascinated by her, he forgot to eat his own meal, and a moment passed before his rumbling belly reminded him to finish it.

Aside from her occasional chimes, they ate in silence. He refilled their glasses, amused when she raised the cork up to him with pleading, moss-green eyes focused on his face.

If he didn't know better...

She certainly appeared intelligent, even if they didn't speak the same language.

Could she have a human's intellect? He dismissed the thought as abruptly as it came. Even a dog had the wit to beg for scraps, and he'd seen Callum's birds plead for treats numerous times. They were no different from feathered children.

"You have good taste. There. I promised I wouldn't harm you, and when I give my word, I keep it."

Cook had also sent up a pie baked with the sweet, pink apples grown in Liang. This was beneath a dish, though the moment he raised the silver lid, the air became fragrant with spice and sugar.

When he sliced into it, her nose turned up, and she pranced around the rim with her hands on her tiny hips.

"No? Aren't you even a little tempted?" He'd expected her to dive face first into the pie, but she'd also choked down so much food and drink, he expected her to crawl into her little bed without moving until morning. "You know, I had considered bringing some sort of animal on board the ship at one time. A bird like Ylis, or even a cat. It'd be nice to have some creature to share my time."

She fluttered away from him and returned to her bread, intelligent eyes never leaving him.

"Where do you put it all?" James chuckled and took a bite of his dessert. "Ah, well, I suppose you'll have to do. A quiet little companion for me, as opposed to Nigel's louder one. I'd almost forgotten what it was like to have a woman's company."

He polished off the rest of his pie and washed it down with a gulp of wine before rising from the table. He had plans to sprawl on the settee with a good book. Appearing almost uncertain, he offered his hand to her, palm up and with limitless patience. Either she would accept the offering, or she wouldn't, although he'd yet to figure out how to wrangle her back into the cage.

Rather than accept his hand as a perch, she took her wine and fluttered in a weaving pattern to the chaise where he kept his book, settling on a nearby ship model. Its size fit her at the perfect scale, and she played at the wheel, spinning it and staggering across the miniature quarterdeck.

He took it as a sign of acceptance and joined her at the chaise. It was all rich and sumptuous fabric, dark wood and plum velvet, one of the original furnishings in the captain's cabin. He sprawled over it with his boots off and opened the book on his lap, only to become distracted by watching Belle. Her wings glittered in the adjacent lantern light, a thousand shimmers blinking all around her. When she didn't glow, she resembled a tiny woman—a perfectly formed woman with the most delicious attributes.

James immediately flushed with guilt for noticing at all.

And I've not had enough wine to think these thoughts.

What's wrong with me? Has it been that long since I've bedded a woman?

Close to a year perhaps, if not longer, but James often tried to suppress any physical urges. He'd have to remedy that once he reached Samahara.

Clearly, the unintentional celibacy was doing something to his brain for him to notice the feminine curves of a tiny, winged woman. She played upon the model ship's deck, oblivious to his observations, flitting from wheel to mast.

James cleared his throat. Conversation with his newly named companion would have to suit in the meantime. "That is a replica of the first ship I ever served on, Rapunzel's Glory," he said. "Named after King Harold's only daughter. I was nine at the time. Started swabbing decks until I caught the captain's eye and was elevated to his cabin boy."

The memory brought back his earlier melancholy. Commodore Teach had been that captain and like a father figure in many ways. He'd never seen the evil in the man's heart back then. Now the man was Admiral Teach, commanding officer of the Queen Anne's Revenge, well-rewarded for his assistance in their wayward king's diabolic plot.

Most of the pirates merely called him Blackbeard though, claiming to see more beard than man through their scopes whenever his ship approached.

Belle hiccupped hard enough to topple onto her backside, and then she burst into giggles—at least, he assumed the high-pitched, tinkling chimes to be giggles.

Gods, she was adorable. He watched a while longer before resuming his current novel, an epic fantasy told by a Liangese author held in renown. Sometimes the story made him long for life on land away from the high seas. Years had passed since he'd had solid ground beneath his feet that wasn't the Wai Alei islands or the desert coastline of Samahara.

After a few pages, James tilted his head back and shut his eyes. He allowed himself to fantasize about the dream life he'd have when he retired from plundering Ridaeron's ships. A small cottage in the hills, a farm, and a beautiful family. He'd always intended to retire to own his own vineyard, but that had lost its allure.

"I wonder if your kind have families," he mused aloud. "Is there a little husband waiting at home for you? Children?"

He sighed and cracked open one eye to see the creature peeking back at him over the edge of the ship. "You probably don't even know what I'm talking about, do you? Ah well. I should have had a family by now, but it seems I am married to the ship. This is my life. My family. But it's lonely, you know. I have friends, but no one I can be open with. No woman to enfold me in her arms and make me forget the burdens of my job. And not much of a friend anymore, either. Though that's a childish outlook to have, isn't it? Nigel *is* here. Merely occupied with chasing a woman."

He hadn't gotten much reading done. Sometimes he imagined when he spoke to her, that she was chatting back. That she even understood him.

"A rather fine woman, I must say. But, as captain, it wouldn't do for me to get involved with anyone onboard. Smee thinks I should ask Tiger Lily for her consideration, and the idea has merit, but… I don't think I could ever love her. Not as she deserves."

He rambled on, talking more than he read and finding

catharsis in the act of getting his worries off his chest. Laying himself bare before a woman who stood no more than three inches tall. "I suppose the island life isn't for me either." No, he missed the snowy mountains of Eisland too much for the tropical archipelago to seduce him. "I'll probably die on the Jolly Roger one day… as is right. The captain should always go down with his ship, and we'll never manage to keep at this forever."

Weariness crept into his limbs and mind. He'd overeaten and become too warm and comfortable. A part of him knew he should try and put his little friend away, for her own safety, but the thought slipped away from him as exhaustion took its toll.

A heavy fist thumped against the door, startling James awake. He jerked upright with his book clutched against his chest before Nigel shoved it open.

"James, you've got mail."

"You awakened me for mail?"

"Important mail." Nigel held it up, revealing the scarlet thread binding it. "It's from the Twilight Witch."

Ziiiiip! A bright ball of crimson light flashed past the two men, streaking for the door. Belle buzzed into the sunlight and drifted up on a salty breeze above the pirates on the deck.

James bolted from the couch and rushed after her. He shouldered Nigel aside, slamming his friend into the wall beside the door in his haste to sprint onto the wooden deck. His bare feet slapped over the rough wood, and adrenaline pounded through his veins. Her shrill tinkling carried to him despite the wind flapping against the sails.

"Don't just stand there, you numbskulls," James snapped at the paralyzed crew as she flew up the mast to the sails.

"What should we do, Cap'n?"

"Catch her!"

There was a man in the crow's nest, but he doubted Cillian had a net to catch their little friend. First and foremost, her safety came to mind. He'd have to drop anchor—have to lure her back. She did love cheese, after all, as he'd discovered the previous night.

Cupping both hands around his mouth, he shouted up to her, "Come down, little one! It isn't safe."

As he tried to call her back to him, men scaled the rigging with fishnets clenched between their teeth. One came near enough to sweep at her, but she evaded him by performing a dizzying spin.

"Ow! She bit me!"

"She does that," James muttered under his breath. He considered joining them, but he never climbed without the benefit of ample time, lest he become tangled by rushing, or worse, compromise them with his hook.

Damned croc. The beast's actions were always coming back to bite him in the arse. Above him, Belle zipped around the others with movements too erratic and swift for them to anticipate.

When it appeared the situation couldn't get worse, a sea hawk soared into view above them, its enormous body a black silhouette against the blue, cloudless sky. The predator screamed and fell into a dive toward James's little golden bell, talons outstretched toward the glowing prize.

He had only a second to act, and a single shot to make it. As the hawk swooped down, James drew his pistol and aimed. The slug tore into the raptor's wing and took it from the air with a fierce report. Blood splashed against the deck as the bird thumped down and flopped in its death throes. Its thrashing wings left crimson smears against wood.

His little friend flew past him, enveloped in a gloomy black haze, the very opposite of her usual glow. She disappeared through the door to his cabin.

Thank the gods. She recognized safety at least.

"Someone put the poor bird out of its misery and give it to Cook," he barked over a shoulder before ducking into the cabin. He shut the door behind him. "Little one?"

A subdued tinkle reached him from the cage, startling him since she'd been so happy to have freedom to explore the previous night. More than anything, he blamed himself. He'd fallen asleep with her roaming free and nearly gotten her killed.

"Stupid," he growled before kneeling beside the dollhouse, overcome with remorse for his failings. "My foolishness put you in harm's way. I wouldn't blame you if you never came out again."

And maybe she wouldn't, although he'd hoped to gain her trust.

With one finger, he drew back the privacy curtain to reveal a small bedroom decorated in floral colors. She'd sprawled across the top of a plush, canopied bed where she wept facedown across the silk comforter, appearing more human by the second.

"I'm sorry," he continued in his gentle voice, before stroking down the middle of her back between both wings. She had wings like a butterfly, and it was easier to appreciate their beauty when she was still, although he would have preferred to touch her when she wasn't prostrate with fear. "I should have kept you safe, but I promise I will from now on."

After another gentle stroke, he withdrew his hand and sighed. Nigel had stepped into the room and shut the door behind him, appearing reticent.

"Sorry, mate. I hadn't realized she was out of the cage when I barged in. You never let her out."

"I thought I'd give it a go last night. I hadn't intended to fall asleep as I did with her roaming free." He rubbed the back of his neck and slumped his shoulders. Her sad little chimes closed a fist around his guilty heart.

"Still, I feel awful for it."

"It wasn't your fault at all, and the damage is done. Now, I suppose we should get back to business. You said there was a letter? Go ahead and open it up. What does Captain Vandry have to say this time? I swear that woman has it out for me."

Nigel chuckled and broke the seal. "Maybe she's after your body, my friend."

After shutting and locking the cage door, James ran his fingers through his disheveled hair. Nearly losing his tiny lady had awakened him in a way that no amount of Samaharan coffee ever could. "That would be a pleasant change," he muttered. "Could you imagine her attempting to seduce anyone? Barking orders for her lover to disrobe while leering at them with that one eye of hers and..." Nigel hadn't spoken again, staring down at the letter in his hands. "What is it?"

"Eisland has declared open season on all pirates...some sort of new weapon. They've sunk two ships in the past fortnight."

"What?" Nigel may as well have dumped ice water on his improving mood. "What sort of weapon? Which ships?"

Of all the kingdoms, Eisland had the most formidable navy, with over a hundred ships at its command. Ridaeron was a close match, while the kingdoms west of the Viridian Sea had little maritime presence beyond their fishing and merchant vessels sailing close to the shore.

"The Black Opal and the Broken Oath are both gone. No survivors from either crew."

"If there isn't a bloody survivor, how does she know what happened?"

"The Twilight Witch was there and escaped on account of Captain Vandry's magical prowess," Nigel said. "Apparently Blackbeard came upon an exchange, a meeting of sorts between the three. The Twilight Witch had just pulled anchor, but the others... How in the nine hells did he manage that one, though?"

Nigel read too slowly for James's patience, however, so he strode across the room and snatched the letter in his good hand. Reading the details didn't help. It just sickened him, his belly plummeting to the ground. "A magical shipkiller. How in this world did they acquire such a monstrosity?"

"No idea." Nigel looked as shaken as James felt, his face pale. "Creag Morden, perhaps? Last word from home was that, even though they didn't arrange a marriage between the two kingdoms, they still arranged trade terms. Isn't that magical academy within their borders?"

"The Collegium? Aye, it sits on the northern coast. Avalon

Bay, they call it. Our original sails were commissioned from the charm spinner of their finest enchanting school."

"That's where the prince went, isn't it? I always thought that was odd."

"The Collegium is neutral territory and not actually a part of Creag Morden."

"So...they could be working with Eisland then," Nigel surmised.

"It's possible. This changes nothing, however. It only means we've got to remain one step ahead of them. Regardless of the weapon in their possession, they wouldn't come within fifty leagues of Neverland." Few ships risked it without invitation, fearing the wrath of the sea witch who lurked in the island's cerulean waters.

"I don't know, James. A magical weapon could be a match for a serpent. We should let Tiger Lily know right away. Maybe... maybe even approach the sea witch directly to warn her, or better yet, ask for her assistance."

"We've relied on her in the past too much."

"And she's kept us all alive," Nigel replied.

Damn. He had a point. He conceded to Nigel's good advice, tipping his head. "I'll write to the others and find out what they've heard. Tell Little Wolf we need the wind with us."

James spent much of the day on the deck afterward to command the crew and navigate. Although he did worry about his gentle creature, he had no time to tend to her when he had the welfare of an entire ship to consider as well.

No escape. She was on a ship in the middle of nowhere, surrounded by pirates and sprite-eating birds. Each shuddering sob shook fairy dust from her golden wings onto the velvet square of gold-trimmed ivory blanket covering her miniature bed.

Long after the two big people left, her heart continued to thunder in her chest. She'd never come so close to death before, even during the Battle of Mount Kinros when she'd helped remove the injured and fallen from the field.

On and off, her mood flipped from terror to despair, and back again, before finally settling into a deep and profound depression. Even if James did return to feed her, she'd have had no appetite for it.

Where was he? What had happened? Sometime during the afternoon, fear for herself became concern for her pirate friend. He'd received terrible, terrifying news, and she'd been too wrapped in her own worries to even notice.

He came in hours later than usual and retired to the privy. While she was accustomed to pipeline water and pumps in Cairn Ocland, she hadn't expected to see it on a ship. When he finally emerged in clean breeches—she'd noticed he always remained dressed, no matter what—her cage was his first stop. He wore his black hair damp around his shoulders, and he shrugged into another shirt on his way to meet her.

"Forgive me, I should have checked on you earlier," he murmured.

Without promises or bribes to coax her from the cage, James opened her door and stepped back, allowing her the freedom to choose whether she wanted to remain or wander out. Tink thought it over for a moment before she darted out and crashed straight into his chest. The pirate startled back, but she dug her fingers into his shirt and clutched him tight, hugging him the only way she could.

"Well now..." The tender touch of his index finger slid down the center of her spine, sending shivers through her body unrelated to panic. "I'm happy to see you, too. Don't be afraid. No one will come in unannounced anymore, and a sea hawk would have to pass through me to frighten you again."

She believed him, certain he would protect her from anything.

While she clung like a burr, James retreated to his favorite reading spot. The placid thump of his heart lulled her into a state of peace. She listened to the serene rhythm with a fistful of his shirt in one hand until he propped a book on his lap.

He'd been reading the same tome for three nights. Too inquisitive for her own good, she dried her face and twisted around to investigate his novel. It was a thick tome of bound leather in caramel brown with a single ribbon dangling from it. And the print consisted of hundreds of tiny little letters in black ink, each one perfect and identical. It must have been created by a machine. Cairn Ocland books were written by hand.

"Hmm? Curious, are you? It's a tale about two women on the run from shadow assassins."

"It looks boring," she complained. Then again, she didn't like reading, since a single page resembled a mountain of words, overwhelming her with the sheer volume of text on each sheet. And there wasn't a single picture. Kendric's books all had colorful images accompanied by a few sentences in large print, easily read without her scanning an entire page.

Curiosity sated, she fluttered over to the table and looked forlornly at the empty space. James twisted in his seat to follow her path with his gaze and smiled.

"Don't worry, Belle, Cook will send over a meal shortly. I asked her not to send any of the sea hawk, though… I wonder about your clothes. Maybe you'd like the cleaned feathers."

"I've never had a feather dress before. I suppose it could be nice. And new. It would be fun to make something again," she mused.

As promised, it wasn't long before there was a knock on the door. Tink hurried back to her cage and peered out from the bars while James answered. Eliza waited with a covered tray.

"How is she?"

"Better I think, thank you," James replied. "She darted into hiding the moment you knocked on the door, and for good reason."

"You let her out again?" Eliza's brows rose, and she leaned in, peering over at the cage.

"She'll never learn to trust me if I keep her locked up. Everyone knows to knock now, so we'll see how it goes."

"Let me know if you need any help, James. G'night."

"Goodnight, Eliza. Oh, ask your mother to set aside some of the feathers for me, will you? Or if she's already given them all to Little Wolf, tell him I'd like a handful."

"All right. Enjoy the meal."

Once Eliza pulled the door shut behind her, James unveiled the sumptuous dinner brought to the square, four-seated table. Trusting him to guard her from dangerous monster birds, Tink hurried to join him across the room.

  VIVIENNE SAVAGE

"Hungry?" He looked down at her and smiled. "Me as well."

James set out a little saucer for her and portioned out small selections from his plate. Tink's tummy grumbled. Instead of a cork cup, a thimble had been set out on the tray for her. It wasn't her golden plate and perfectly sized silverware from back home, but the gesture deserved appreciation all the same.

They ate in companionable silence, and James never once uttered a complaint when she stole additional servings. At the conclusion of their meal, he stacked their empty dishes, set them outside the cabin on the floor, and removed his hook to place it on a case by the bed as part of his evening ritual.

"I do believe I'll enjoy the rest of my reading in bed, but you are free to explore my cabin in safety. Nothing here will harm you. In fact, you're welcome to join me if you like," he said, beckoning her with his left hand.

How could she possibly resist such a heartfelt offer?

Her kind host crawled beneath the sheets with his boring novel and read, murmuring the words in his clear and velvet voice while she listened on the adjacent pillow. Contrary to her initial impressions of the book, she became his rapt audience and found human stories had an unexpected, thrilling edge.

While his lids grew heavy and yawns interrupted the magical prose, Tink came to appreciate the novel. Fascinated with the man as much as the book he read, she watched until his long lashes fell for the last time and the even rhythm of his breaths told her he'd drifted to sleep.

Flitting down to his chest barely caused a wrinkle in his shirt. The soft silk was the finest she'd ever touched, and the buttons had been carved from an unfamiliar dark material, reminding her of black glass. She tiptoed closer and lifted to the air, hovering above his face to see if he really was asleep. He didn't twitch. So she reached down and touched his hair, delighted by the glossy waves.

He truly was the most handsome man she'd ever seen, even more so than Conall, which she thought would never happen. Her werewolf friend was the kindest, most amazing man she knew. But he was no longer the most handsome.

"He fell asleep again. Whatever he does during the day must be exhausting…"

She had no idea how a ship worked. Oclanders didn't venture onto the open sea, and the largest boat she had ever seen had been the raft sailed by Conall and Ramsay during their fishing expeditions. They always left at dawn and returned by afternoon with an enormous bounty of fish to feed the entire wolf pack *and* the bear clan.

Tink slipped the glossy purple ribbon into the novel to mark his place. Although the book weighed more than she did, she hugged the spine with her slender arms before lifting the leather-bound tome away to the adjacent end table. Sprites possessed supernatural, otherworldly strength in their tiny bodies comparable to humans, and she was no exception.

She darted to the foot of the bed, grasped the folded-down blanket edge, and dragged it over his slumbering frame. With everything set to rights, she helped herself to his extra pillow and tugged the blanket corner over her body, too.

Chapter 6

To TAKE COUNT of the days since her arrival on the ship, Tink made hash marks on a sheet of stationery taken from the desk, creating a calendar for herself inside the dollhouse. A single down feather from the slain sea hawk provided a quill for her to write. Before that, she'd counted the nights with petals torn from a flower in the dollhouse garden.

James jerked his attention from his writing in time to catch her making off with a small droplet of black liquid from the open inkwell. "Were you drawing again?" James asked. "You've left little handprints over everything," he muttered.

Tink dropped her head in repentance until he touched her chin with the tip of his forefinger. She blinked up at him.

"Here." He dipped his pen into the inkwell then issued a tiny stream into a thimble. "You always spill a little. Your vessel is far too small for the amount you try to take."

Delighted by his generosity, she hurried back to her gilded home.

Seventeen days. She'd been a willing captive of the Jolly Roger for seventeen days since James had opened her cage door for the first time. He hadn't locked it again since they reached their understanding. She ate each meal with him, but she'd yet to acquire the courage to venture outside and see the deck. Thus far, her adventure had been a complete mess, and each time she seized a moment for bravery, misfortune befell her.

Maybe today, Tink thought, wondering what harm could come to her if she remained within his reach?

"James!" Nigel shouted from outside. He pounded on the door.

"Come in, mate. Good news?"

Nigel entered then shut the door behind him. His gaze darted to the cage. Tink waved. "She's rather smart for a lady-shaped bug, isn't she?"

"That she is. I believe she has some rudimentary understanding of what we speak, at the very least."

"Even a dog has that at times," Nigel said.

Tink stuck her tongue out behind the man's back, unseen by either pirate. Business began as the quartermaster spread a sea chart—she'd overheard them calling it that before while plotting their course—over James's desk and tapped his finger on the blue and beige illustration.

"The Victorious Dowager is off our port bow and riding low. I'd dare to say we're here, not far from the coast of Liang. They may have recently acquired cargo from their friends."

"Merchant vessel, if I recall. Any weapons?"

"They've three cannons on each side, but it's nothing to match our power," Nigel replied. "Small crew. My guess is there's a patrol nearby from Eisland, or the captain was a cocky bastard who didn't realize this sea belongs to us. How shall we proceed?"

James grinned at him. "Tell Little Wolf we've got prey to hunt. We'll need the wind to run her down. If I recall, the Dowager's greatest asset lies in her enchanted sails. Kill the wind. Have the men prepare to board."

"At once, Cap'n."

Tink returned to the desk once Nigel shut the door behind him. With her hands on her hips, she paced across the polished surface and eyed the chart, recognizing the mountainous coastline of Cairn Ocland and the vast aeries inhabited by the griffins. Ramsay had once told her the colossal bird-lions frequently hunted saltwater tuna there. Aside from her single visit up the mountain to find their clan leader for Conall, she'd never visited the aeries. But that one time, she'd seen the vast ocean beyond it with the sun gleaming scarlet over the sapphire water.

Would she ever see it again?

Missing the fresh air and open skies even more, Tink sulked and kicked over a pile of gold coins on James's desk. So much for her plans to explore the deck. She wanted nothing to do with a battle. If anything, the conversation reminded her of one important fact—James was a pirate. He attacked other ships and *stole* from them.

"S'pose I should do my job and go attend," James muttered, rising from his seat. He tucked his pistol into his heavy leather belt then plucked Tink from the desk corner, only for her to wriggle free and buzz around his head.

"I'm not letting you lock me up again!"

"Stop that. I'd feel better if you were secure while we handle this."

Not once since they'd come to their understanding had James attempted to force her into the cage again. She spiraled up into the air above his head, well beyond his reach, and blew a raspberry at him.

"That's not very ladylike," he chided, dropping both arms

to his sides. "Fine then, do as you will."

"Ha!" Tinkling with laughter, she dove down to his shoulder and perched there, pointing to the door.

"What? You want to go with me?" Tink claimed double fistfuls of his shirt, clutching the fine black silk with all her strength. "I'm not sure that's wise. You could be hurt," he began to say while trying to dislodge her again. She bit the offending finger he wrapped around her.

James jerked his left hand away and swore. Apparently, he and Conall had similar tastes when it came to vocabulary. "Very well then. You are your own woman. I won't remove you or force you to remain behind." His path to the door resumed, and once they reached the deck, the worried captain tucked her beneath his ruffled collar. "Please stay there… if you understand anything I say, at least heed that warning."

"You're no fun." Conducting their one-sided conversations had never been as bothersome.

The sunlight blinded Tink at first after the prolonged time spent in the dim atmosphere of James's cabin. His tinted windows never let in the full light. To abide by the unspoken rules of her pirate friend, she crawled into the silken sash securing his gun belt and concealed herself from view, using it as a makeshift hammock.

In the distance, a ship with white sails flew the blue and white flags bearing Eisland's colors. Tink had seen enough of them in James's cabin on keepsakes commemorating him for his numerous accomplishments in the navy. Wind billowed through the Jolly Roger's sails, coasting them over the sea with enough speed for Tink to thrust a fist in the air and whoop.

No wonder he loved standing on the quarterdeck. The

breeze swept her golden curls away from her face and pointed ears, bringing her as close to flying as she'd ever come without using her wings.

"This is amazing!" she cried.

James glanced down at her and smiled. "I take it you're enjoying it. I've never heard you chime so loudly before. Of course, it *is* a fine day for a chase."

His grin broadened before he leaned forward and called down to the men preparing the cannons, "Load iron pellets and silverware into the cannons. There ought to be plenty of it thanks to the Goose."

"Aye, cap'n!"

Silverware? Tink blinked up at him, fascinated by his choice of weapons. For a better vantage point, she darted to his shoulder and hid herself amidst his dark hair instead. She needed to see every moment. Despite limping on a limited amount of wind, the Dowager grew larger, and the tiny specks rushing on its deck became the shapes of frantic sailors.

"Shields, Callum!"

A flash of crimson light flooded over the ship, originating from the bare-armed magician standing at the Jolly Roger's forecastle. Less than a second later, a series of explosions tore through the air between them.

Cannonballs crashed against the side of the Jolly Roger. Tink screamed and grabbed James by the ear for balance, nearly shaken from his shoulder. "Oh no, we're going to sink!"

One of the things James loved most about his Belle was

her ability to surprise him every day. Perhaps she would be his good luck charm, a tiny golden woman to accompany him on the high seas as he raided slave-bearing ships. Once again, she'd displayed an eerie comprehension of the Eisland tongue, and he began to wonder if she truly understood him or if she was merely like one of the enormous birds Callum owned. She certainly showed evidence of enjoying their time together; they had been inseparable since her near death.

Perhaps she's brought fortune to the Jolly Roger, after all, James thought.

The Victorious Dowager lacked any chance of standing against them, and all action taken would purely be to appease their wounded egos. Prepared for the merchants' offensive, James braced himself as their opponents released a triple volley of artillery. Instead of tearing through the beautiful dark wood, the cannonballs rolled down the side and splashed into the sea, harmless as water sliding off a duck's tail.

Belle's scream rang in his right ear. At least, he *thought* it was a scream, her chiming as shrill as it had been the day the sea hawk swooped from the sky to claim her.

"Run a shot across the bow!" James shouted, voice carrying to the crew down below. Anything more would devastate the vessel, and sunken cargo had no value to them. More importantly, he couldn't bear it on his conscience if they drowned the unfortunate slaves in the belly of the ship.

A blast from their cannons launched pellets, forks, and silver spoons at the Dowager's sails. The scattered shot ripped through the canvas in multiple spots.

With Little Wolf controlling the winds in their favor, it became a simple matter of maneuvering alongside their prey and anchoring the two ships together. Grappling hooks flew. For each line the merchants managed to cut, two more took its place. James liked to overwhelm their opponents with sheer numbers, putting on a show of force with a raucous crew of over eighty men.

The Dowager's crew put up a good fight, but they were no match for the Jolly Roger's seasoned warriors. Pirates flooded onto the deck and faced an inexperienced crew.

"Sad," Nigel muttered. "I've seen tots with greater skill."

James chuckled. Not far from them, Fatima stood above one man with her boot on his neck. He wept. "That's enough, men. There's no need to take any lives this day. Which of you is the captain?" James raised his voice until it carried across the deck. "I'd enjoy a word with him."

An auburn-haired man with a close-trimmed beard stepped forward with a cutlass clutched in his right hand. His fingers flexed over the rune-studded hilt as he faced his captors. Despite their incredible defeat, he stood tall and proud, leveling his gaze at James through fearless eyes. "I'm the captain of this vessel, and you have no right to attack us in this manner."

"I'm a pirate, and rights have little meaning on the sea," James said without losing his amicable smile. The crew laughed behind him as he stepped forward and lowered his voice. "However, this doesn't have to become a bloodbath. You're outnumbered and outgunned. Tell your men to stand down, and no one will be harmed. There's no shame in surrender, but if you desire a challenge, I'll have my men cut down every sailor aboard this vessel. Do you understand me?"

The captain of the Victorious Dowager stared him down

in silence for a long minute, and then he gave a curt nod. "You heard him, men. Weapons down."

The Dowager's crew laid down their weapons and stepped back with their hands behind their heads while Fatima and Eliza secured the swords and pistols. Nigel took the cutlass from the captain then ran one finger over the flat of the blade, no doubt impressed with the quality and magical glow gleaming within the metal. He'd probably already laid claim to his share of the spoils.

"Wise man. Now I invite you to join me in my cabin, Captain, while we discuss what's to become of you and your crew. Nigel, report to me once you've done a sweep."

A brief stroll led the two men from the deck of the Dowager to the Jolly Roger. It wasn't until the cabin door shut behind them that Belle emerged from hiding to investigate their guest.

The other ship's captain gazed up at her with thinly veiled wonder despite his otherwise stoic demeanor, and James admired the man's composure during a time when other men often fell before him, blubbering and pleading for mercy.

"Your name, sir. I'd like to know who I'm dealing with."

"Morgan Hawkins."

"A pleasure to make your acquaintance, Captain Hawkins. You know who I am?"

"Aye. You're Captain Hook, the Eislander traitor."

James's mouth pressed into a thin line. "So they say." His fingers drummed against his left thigh as he regarded the solemn captain. Belle drifted closer to Hawkins and circled around his head. The melodic notes of her inhuman voice filled the air with music.

"My friend seems to like you. A point in your favor, sir,"

James said as he crossed to a cabinet and pulled out two glasses and a crystal bottle. "Brandy?"

"I... How did you come to have a fairy in your possession?"

"A fairy?"

Hawkins gestured to Belle. "Fairy. Sprite. I've seen their like before in Cairn Ocland."

James passed over a glass, which Hawkins took but didn't drink. "Oh? And what, pray tell, brought an Eislander to such an inhospitable place?"

A red pulse flashed before James's eyes as Belle flew up into his face and shook her tiny fist at him. The captain of the Dowager chuckled into his hand as her chimes grew loud and discordant.

"I don't think it much likes you disparaging its home."

"I suppose not. From Cairn Ocland then, are you, little one?" He offered Belle an apologetic smile and his hand. She sniffed, put her hands on her hips, and then turned away from him as a scorned woman would. Determined to make it up to her later, he looked back to his guest. "You were saying, Captain Hawkins?"

"I went once with a convoy from Creag Morden to Cairn Ocland to negotiate trade between our countries."

"And were you successful?" James asked.

Hawkins shrugged. "Not so much. But this has nothing to do with my ship, Captain Hook. What do you intend to do with my ship and crew? Rob us? Kill us?"

"That depends entirely on your cargo," James replied. He sipped from his glass and leaned back against his desk.

"My cargo?" The man's brows shot upward. "If its riches you're after, then take what I have. I only ask you spare my men.

Spare my ship. I value lives above goods and merchandise, and I'd rather part with the commodities we carry than lose a single sailor." He set his untouched glass aside, and Belle drifted down to sniff at it.

A heavy knock sounded against the door. James called out for them to come in, and Nigel stepped through.

"Have you made a thorough accounting?"

"Smee is finishing that up now, but I did a thorough walkthrough of their ship."

"And?"

"No slaves below deck," Nigel reported.

Captain Hawkins stiffened. "We are a merchant vessel hired by Eisland's finest purveyors of Liangese silk. I assure you, I've never in all of my life had any dealings with flesh traders."

James had never seen a man more insulted. He studied Captain Hawkins, taking in his blazing eyes and rigid spine. It wasn't often anymore that he came across a good man, but this was one of those rare times, he was certain.

"Would you ever?"

Hawkins bristled. "Of course not."

"Because it's illegal in Eisland?"

"Because it's wrong."

James pushed away from the desk, rising to his full height, and stared the other captain straight in the eye. Hawkins met his gaze without flinching.

"Return to your ship and leave."

"What?" Hawkins's voice rose in surprise.

"Return to your ship and leave," James repeated. "You have nothing that warrants taking, not even your fortune in silk.

He'll need his blade, Lieutenant Gaumond."

Nigel relinquished the sword, appearing torn while Hawkins studied them both with distrusting eyes.

"What sort of ruse is this? You let me go and then sink me?"

"No trick. Despite what you've been told, murder is against our code of conduct. As you pose no danger to the Jolly Roger, it would be an act of cowardice to fire upon a weaker foe. Consider this to be your lucky day, Captain Hawkins. May you always be the noble and proud man you are today."

It was only afterward, once the ship had set sail, that James came to one startling realization.

Belle did understand him after all. Every single word.

"You've understood *me*?" he demanded, while he thought of the numerous clues she'd given him to that effect. He groaned and rubbed his face with one hand. How many nights had he lain in bed beside her dollhouse while prattling about his mother and father or reminiscing over the old days in the navy?

His brain didn't want to comprehend the fact that he'd uttered the most ridiculous and inane things in her presence, but he was comforted by a single fact.

Belle spoke the language of fairies, and that meant his secrets were quite safe if no one could ever understand her in return.

Some of the crew had muttered when he let the Dowager go free without a single item claimed from the ship, but James had reminded them they weren't bloodthirsty pillagers. Any man or woman who wanted a more traditional pirate life was welcome to leave and hire on with another crew.

No one accepted the offer.

"S'pose I'll go get dinner…" Belle had taken a nap after the excitement of the morning, so he ventured down to the galley, conversed with Cook, enjoyed a drink with Smee, and meandered back to his cabin with their tray. Their ship's repairman, Patrick, had fashioned three tiny silver plates, a bowl, and a polished silver goblet for Belle along with miniature utensils to accompany them. Upon these plates, Cook had arranged the portions of a three-course meal.

In the years since Patrick joined their crew, James had never seen the kid expend as much effort. He claimed the sight of Belle had inspired him, however, and it had been worth the effort.

Balancing dinner upon the crook of his right arm, James opened the door to his cabin and stepped inside, using a heel to shut the door behind him. Belle waved to him from her cage where she reclined on a leaf hammock strung between two plant stems.

"Hello, lovely," he greeted her.

"I'm really tired of blueberries. Can I have some of that cheese you brought up for your dinner?" a tiny voice called out when he removed the lids.

James stumbled back against the far wall, striking his head on a bookshelf. It smarted, but he dropped his hand to his sword hilt and searched the room with wide eyes. "Who's there?"

"It's me, silly!"

"What?" He searched the empty cabin, gaze darting from the unmade bed to the settee and finally the enormous wooden trunk supporting Belle's cage. She'd moved, relocating to the table and cupping both hands around her mouth. A dim glow highlighted her without obscuring her doll-like features.

"Hi!" she called again.

James blinked and mentally recounted everything he'd consumed throughout the day, alcohol included. Perhaps Smee had added something interesting to his rum. Left hand still on his sword, he took a step forward and lowered to one knee. The tiny creature put her hands to her hips and huffed.

"Well? Can I have some cheese?"

Positive she wasn't a danger to him, he released the weapon. "You can talk."

"I've always been able to talk. You didn't know how to listen."

And he did *now*? His stomach tightened and a lump formed in his throat. So much for that hope.

Not only did this tiny thing know his deepest thoughts, but she'd developed the ability to share them—and blackmail him if she chose. While he trusted Nigel and the rest of his crew, he didn't underestimate the human capacity for greed if he showed weakness. A wise man would abolish any risk of it by eliminating the problem, but the longer he gazed upon her, the sicker that idea made him feel. He couldn't do it.

"I see."

Mellow, golden light bathed her as she giggled. It was the prettiest of her colors. "You're worried about the things you've said to me."

"A little," he said in a quiet voice.

"I won't tell, I promise."

"My thanks." But could he trust her word? He hoped so. "What do I call you? Have you a name?"

"Tinker Bell. And you're Captain James Hook," she informed him in a matter-of-fact voice.

Tinker *Bell*? He tried not to grin at that, although it didn't take long for the amusement to dim. Sitting at the table brought them to a conversational level.

He'd long ago begun to admire her, especially on long nights while he lay unable to sleep in his bed. Weeks ago, he'd have gone out to the deck and watched the waves crash against the boat, studied the stars, sought company among the crew for idle conversation, or even read a book by candlelight, as he had dozens of them in his personal library.

Now he spent his sleepless evenings pouring his heart out to a miniature woman, one whom he'd been positive couldn't understand a word he spoke.

"Aye, that I am, little one. Though you may call me James."

"James," she repeated, as if testing the single word on her tongue. Her voice still reminded him of bells, mellifluous and charming enough that he could easily listen to her all evening.

"Yes. Now are you going to tell me how you came to be in such a contraption?"

Tinker Bell began at the top, and by top, that meant her story had nothing at all to do with her captivity. "And there were awful creatures called the Scourge created by a mean big fairy who was cruel and malicious enough to curse our entire kingdom. One of her monsters killed my friend Conall's kinsmen, so we went on an adventure and met Sorcha—she's his wife—and now they're married and they had a baby."

The story went on, never spanning chronologically, and always spoken so rapidly James couldn't determine if it was her natural manner of speech or enthusiasm for having someone who could converse with her again.

"So, you went on an adventure of your own and were taken by poachers," he surmised at the end, once he placed the events in order.

"Yes." Her wings drooped. "Conall will say 'I told you so' when I get back home."

He chuckled. "Well, it wasn't a complete loss, now was it? You've traveled and learned something new about the temptation of shiny things."

She harrumphed and stomped one little foot against the cage floor. James bit back his laughter, positive the adorable creature wouldn't appreciate amusement at her expense. "Are you going to let me go home or not?"

"I can try to return you to your homeland, but I cannot promise how long it will be before we make sail to the north again. Cairn Ocland has a rather inhospitable coast, and we'd dash the ship to splinters if we approached."

"I can fly!"

"And land in another net, no doubt."

She scowled at him, scrunching her entire face and glowing a bold scarlet. "I will not!"

"Just the same, I'd feel better if we could perhaps send word to this Conall and enlisted his aid to return you safely home."

The red faded, overwhelmed by melancholy blue. "No… He has a baby now, and he can't be bothered with taking care of me."

"Has he said that to you?"

"No."

"Then you shouldn't assume or speak for him, Belle."

She lifted off her feet, hovering toward the top of the cage. "Why'd you call me that?"

"Belle? Isn't that your name?"

"It is."

"Which would make 'tinker' your title of sorts, yes, just as 'captain' is mine?"

Her enthusiastic nod preceded another giggle. "Yes! You're the first human to ever realize that."

"Really?" It had seemed obvious to him, but he wisely kept his thoughts to himself and smiled. Then it occurred to him that she wasn't a mindless exotic possession to admire. He returned to her cage and with a few maneuvers of the metal, managed to remove the door. "Apologies, little one. I'll never cage you within this contraption again."

"I can come and go as I please now?"

"It would be unforgivable of me to keep you caged for even a second."

"Can I leave the cabin?" she asked.

"If you'll take care. As you've already learned, there are predators who would make a snack of you, and I must also ask you never to float above the surface. The sea is treacherous here, filled with many sinister creatures who would emerge from the water to claim you as a treat."

"I'll stay close. Can I explore the rest? It's a very pretty boat."

"Ship," he corrected gently. "And…if you promise not to disturb anything, yes, you may explore to your heart's content."

"Tinkers don't break anything unless it's on purpose."

James wasn't sure whether to be reassured or uneasy about her statement, but he hoped, for all their sakes, that her word was good.

The moment the doors opened, Tink darted into the middle of the main deck and spiraled into the air before releasing a joyous whoop. At last, she was free to roam. Every working man on the deck stopped to stare at her while James hung back several paces with his arms crossed while she explored.

The air had never smelled so fragrant before, full of freedom and warm light. The man Tink had identified as James's second-in-command stood beside another pirate near a vast opening in the deck, spouting orders and gesturing toward the front of the ship. Upon seeing Tink, he froze.

"Don't move, mate. Blasted thing got out again. I'll get her, Captain!"

"No need, Nigel," James called over. "Madam Belle is a guest aboard our vessel and to be treated with respect."

A boyish grin spread across his handsome face. He was *almost* as attractive as his friend, but Tink preferred the captain's longer hair. "Finally named her, did you?"

"No, she had her own name and shared it with me."

More than a few crew members gave their captain looks in varying degrees of concern, and two of them began to mutter amongst themselves. Tink bit her lip. That wasn't very nice of them at all.

"Hello," she called out, flying over to the whispering crewmen first. She shook her finger at them, and then she darted over to Nigel and fluttered in front of his face. "I'm Tinker Bell."

He squinted at her then slanted another glance at his captain. "Her voice is rather musical, isn't it, but not a word of that sounds like any language I've ever heard. Are you feeling quite all right, James?"

"I'm bloody fine, you nitwit. She speaks the language of sprites, but she understands everything we say to her."

"Then how do you know her name?"

"Apparently I understand her now."

"I… think you spent too much time in the sun yesterday, and some rest in your cabin would do you a world of good."

"What's everyone making a fuss about?" Eliza asked, moving to stand between the two men. She shot each of them a dirty look before she noticed Tink hovering in the air. "He's finally brought you out for some fresh air, has he? Good."

"Hi, hi," Tink said to the blonde woman. "He finally let me out, and now I can talk to all of you. I'm Tinker Bell, and you're Eliza, and I'm so glad to meet you now." Of all the crewmen, Nigel and Eliza visited James in his room the most, among the small handful of people he seemed to trust with his privacy. But, of the two, only Eliza stopped to speak to her and sometimes smuggle in tiny offerings from the kitchen.

Eliza's eyes flew open wide. "Oh! And how very lovely to meet you as well, Madam Belle."

James shot Nigel a smug look. "See."

"She could be humoring you—"

"You know damned well I've never humored any of you,

Nigel. If you'd pull the stick out of your arse, perhaps you'd understand her, too. Honestly."

Tink doubled over in laughter, hands on her stomach.

"Now that we've become acquainted, perhaps Belle would appreciate a decent meal that doesn't consist of this lubberwort's leftovers." Eliza offered her palm.

"I would! He never gives me enough of his cheese. He's so greedy sometimes," Tink blurted out as she landed on the woman's open hand.

"We'll have to fix you up, then. Come along and meet my mum. Everyone calls her Cook, even me most times, and if anyone else can understand you, it'll probably be her."

Eliza carried her away, but Tink peeked back at James's slack-jawed face and experienced a tiny surge of guilt for exposing him as a greedy cheese hoarder, even though it was quite true.

With each step of their adventure below deck, Tink's new friend introduced her to another area of the ship. "This is the berth and gun deck, where most of the crew sleep."

Many hammocks had been strung between the enormous black cannons angled out of holes in the ship's hull. Eliza explained the purpose of the gun ports and then continued along a narrow plank above a deep hole in the center of the floor.

"What's down there?"

"The cargo hold where we keep most of our unclaimed loot for the markets of Ankirith. It's a port city in Samahara, our next destination. Once there, we unload these goods and James divides the profit."

"James has lots of pretty things in his room."

"As captain, he gets first pick amongst the treasures, it's true. He has the better booty, but he's fair about spreading it around. Everyone gets a pick among the goods." Eliza's hazel eyes twinkled. "He chose you from the Golden Goose."

Something about that sent little flutters through Tink's chest. James had thought of her as treasure, an object of worth to be valued, long before he knew her to be an intelligent, sentient creature.

Bewildered by the emotion overtaking her mood, Tink cleared her throat and changed the subject. "Where's your room? Do you sleep in a hammock too?"

"Certainly not. I value my privacy too much. As we were among the ranking officers of the original crew, Nigel, Callum, and I each have a small cabin below the captain's quarters. Smee has the room abandoned by the original boatswain. Come along. I'll show you the galley where my mum prefers to sleep. It's her domain, and you'll find she's the absolute queen of all that happens to the food here."

They passed through a narrow hall into the rear of the ship while Eliza explained the unfamiliar nautical terms often thrown about by James and the other pirates. "The infirmary is aft of my personal quarters on the starboard side. That's left as we're facing now. Portside is the ship's proper left, while facing the front—the bow."

"It's confusing," Tink complained.

"It can be until you've grown accustomed to it. And you will in time."

The delicious aroma of cooking food wafted out to Tink before they reached the opening. Inside, a slender woman with silver-streaked blonde hair moved about the kitchen with the energy of a maiden half her age. A pot bubbled above a pile of magical stones, and bread baked in a brick oven, releasing the aromatic scent of fresh herbs.

"I've brought a visitor to try some of that special cheese we nicked off the Goose, Mum. The one you claimed for yourself."

"If I've said it once, I've said it a hundred times, goat's milk makes the best cheeses, but James lacks the palette for it. I—oh, who's this then?" Cook leaned over and peered down at Tink with clear hazel eyes.

"I'm Tinker Bell."

"My stars, she speaks."

Eliza laughed at her mother's amazement. "I had a feeling you'd understand her. Tinker Bell says James hasn't been generous with his dinners."

"We'll certainly have to fix that."

In a manner of minutes, Cook prepared a buffet feast fit for fairy royalty, using a teacup saucer for the miniature banquet. As Tink watched, the woman set down cured pork slices, diced fruit, and small cubes of wine-soaked goat cheese with a plum-stained rind.

"Enjoy," Cook said, pouring a thimbleful of clear liquid to set beside it.

Tink sipped from the thimble first. Cook had to have given her the sweetest water in existence. While she stuffed her face with the pork and a generous portion of cheese, the smiling chef returned with a slice of steaming bread fresh from the oven. "Take care with this. It's very hot."

"This is delicious."

"I'm pleased you like it so much. Here, I'll slice off a wedge for you to take back."

"So, where do you come from?" Eliza asked. She snuck a bit of cheese from the wedge while her mother's back was turned.

"I saw that."

"No you didn't," Eliza replied, although she winked at Tink.

Tink giggled and took another bite from her meal. "My land is called Cairn Ocland," she said between bites.

"Isn't that the place where they say men turn into beasts?" Cook asked.

"It is!" Unable to help herself, and thrilled by the promise of having a conversation with people who could understand her again, Tink shared the story of her friends' victory over the wicked fairy Queen Maeval.

Cook settled beside them with a cup of tea and remained her enthralled listener. "Dragons. I've heard stories of dragons from faraway lands across the globe, but never had I realized any lived so close to us. I thought the stories of a dragon king in Cairn Ocland were merely tall tales to scare adventurers."

"There are dragons across the globe?" Tink asked.

"My late husband, bless his soul, sailed upon many ships beyond this sea. He once told me of a great ocean many thousands of leagues away with a continent occupied by monsters and winged beasts. They call it the Eternal Realm and say it's ruled by black dragons."

"I've never heard of it," Tink said.

"I'm not surprised. It's on the other side of the world, and of the half dozen exploring ships sent by Eisland over the years, only two have returned."

"Wow, more dragons. King Alistair thought he was the last

one until they found his aunt. He'll be so excited." And Tink couldn't wait to share the news. But how could she tell him if the Jolly Roger had taken her hundreds of miles away from home? Her wings drooped as the depressing thought took hold. "If I ever get to tell him."

"Don't worry," Eliza said in a gentle voice. "If James has promised to try and get you home, you can trust he'll keep his word as soon as he's able."

"A man of honor, he is," Cook agreed. "I wouldn't have given up my life in Eisland for any other captain."

Tink couldn't imagine a more genuine endorsement regarding James's character. His crew admired him, appearing to follow him out of loyalty, rather than fear. They'd left behind prosperous and happy lives, as far as she could tell.

"Ah, but what's this?" Cook said, looking past Tink. "I see a little mouse peeking into my kitchen."

"What? A mouse? But mice eat cheese!" Tink twisted around, ready to fend off the intruder after her precious snacks. Instead of a furry mouse, she spotted a pudgy boy with light brown curls at the doorway to the galley.

"Hello, Tootles," Eliza said in a soft voice. "Would you like to join us?"

Understanding dawned upon Tink before she could question the boy's presence on the ship. Hadn't James mentioned rescuing more than a dozen captives from the Golden Goose?

The poor boy. Every time she thought of what Ridaeron did to their little ones, it made her chest hurt with unfettered rage. No one should ever hurt a child. They were to be loved, snuggled, and cuddled.

He made fleeting eye contact, his pale gaze moving from Eliza and Cook to Tink before dropping to the floor. He shuffled his feet but came no closer, remaining in the doorway.

Fine then. If he won't come closer, I'll have to lure him over.

After claiming a wedge of fruit from the tray, Tink flew over and offered it to him. "Hello, you want to join us?"

Tootles took the orange piece and peeked up at her. "You're pretty," he whispered. Then he turned around and dashed away.

Baffled by the boy's behavior, Tink returned to Cook. "Did I do something wrong?"

"It's not you," Eliza assured her. "He was rescued from the same ship you were, and they treated him poorly. He's barely said more than five words since he's been here, and two of those were to you just now."

"I'll fix him a treat and see that he's okay," Cook said. "But it seems he likes you, Belle. Perhaps you could make a friend of him."

"I can do that," she said. She liked children, and making friends with Tootles might help break up the monotony of her new life at sea. Without the magical ability to teleport home, Tink had no choice but to make the best of her time on the ship.

When I return to Braeloch, I'll have a tale worthy to share with Kendric.

Chapter 7

THREE PLEASANT DAYS aboard the Jolly Roger afforded Tink the chance to learn the ship and meet each crewmember. She also discovered a small handful of the sailors had enough whimsy in their hearts to understand the fairy tongue.

That had startled her, one pleasant surprise among many. She'd expected James, Eliza, and Cook to be the only ones capable of communication.

Usually when James roused before Tink, he left the door ajar for her to flit between the crack and onto the deck. Instead, she found it wide open and one of the crew's repairmen sitting on a stool while he drilled a hole into the thick panel.

"What are you doing?" she asked.

While none of the pirates struck Tink as outright mean, she'd met some surly ones with no patience for her questions. Patrick grinned up at her instead, one of the most amiable when it came to satisfying her curiosity about their duties. "Drillin' a hole for the captain. He wants me to make a wee door for you."

"A door for me?"

"Yup. Figure it's about time, eh?" A leather sack filled with an assortment of tools lay on his lap, along with a little round door. "Now this, I'll fit this into the hole and nail it in place. It'll swing open and shut like this," he explained to her.

"You're like a tinker!"

"A what's it?"

"A tinker. We create and repair things."

"Ah. Is that why you're called Tinker Bell then?"

"Yes!"

"S'pose that makes me Tinker Patrick."

Giggling, she settled on Patrick's bag of tools to watch him work.

"You know, if you're any good with repairing things, we ought to have you helping us. There's no shortage of bloody things around this ship in need of repair. Knives to be sharpened, pots to mend for Cook, guns to maintain. Bloody things are prone to misfire when they're not kept up, and you can't trust these blokes to care for their own weapons."

"I wanna help!"

"Then tell the captain you're ours for the day and meet me below deck in the workshop within the hour. You know where to find the workshop, right?"

"Beside the crew's quarters, near the bow."

Patrick nodded.

James was never hard to find on the ship. She zipped up the mast to get a view of the entire deck, spotting his red coat at the front end. Giddy with anticipation, she flew down and danced around him.

"Slow down there, sweet little Belle." James laughed and offered his palm. "What has you so happy today?"

"I'm going to help Patrick fix the ship and everything on it."

"Oh?"

"I mean, if you don't mind. I like to fix things, and he says there's lots I can do to help. Oh, and thank you for the door."

"My room is your room. You should have a way in and out on your own without relying on the door to remain cracked open. Is Patrick nearly finished?"

"Almost." She paced across his hand with her hands clasped behind her back.

"And what shall you be repairing today?"

"Guns." Although she was giddy enough to clap her hands together, Tink showed restraint.

"Er… Do you know how to fix a gun?"

"Well, no." Nor had she ever seen one until the day James drew his pistol and shot the hawk hunting her on the deck. Ever since, she'd admired the sleek weapon from afar while lacking the courage to investigate it up close. "But Patrick will teach me. Then he won't have to do so much on his own."

"In that case, enjoy your work. Though, if I might make a suggestion?"

Tink fluttered up off his hand and hovered in front of his face. "What is it?"

"Perhaps start with Cook, if you're able. She hasn't said anything to me officially, but as I passed through the galley, I overheard her muttering about a deep dent and scratch in her favorite pot. I think she might appreciate the gesture if you were to fix it."

"Say no more!"

Tink zipped away and dove into the open cargo hatch, spiraling to the rear of the ship and into the kitchen. Cook kept a tidy galley with everything in its assigned place. The woman herself was absent, but it didn't take Tink long at all to find her special project. A large stewpot hung from the overhead on a hook.

"Did she hit someone with it?" Tink whispered to the empty room, aghast. The large dent matched the rounded shape of a man's upper skull.

Tink sprinkled fairy dust on the pot and buffed it into the tarnished, misshapen surface. A little of a sprite's magical essence worked for any material, making metals pliable and fabric soft as putty to mend the smallest torn threads. If the Liangese cared to learn more about her kind beyond selling them as pets or using their wings in alchemical concoctions, they'd probably abduct fae in even greater quantities.

Whistling as she worked, Tink coaxed the bottom into proper shape. Then she noticed that the repaired portion contrasted the rest, so she scrubbed the entire thing until it shone as bright as a newly minted coin.

"Perfect."

Too excited to wait for Cook to discover the surprise, she darted away to undertake her next mission. There was a saying among the sprites, that a fairy was happiest when allowed to fulfill their purpose. Tinker Bell had been denied hers for far too long. With a renewed sense of self-worth, she passed through the berth while filing other minor repairs away for later inspection. Fraying ropes and torn clothes could wait until after the guns were finished.

She wound her way to the workshop and landed on Patrick's work table, where she admired the assortment of tools strewn over the hard surface. A dozen sheets of parchment hung on the walls in the small room, each one displaying a different ship design. Like James, he built miniature ships from tiny, hand-carved components. An unfinished masterpiece occupied one corner of the desk, a beautiful representation of a double-masted ship with numerous sails. None of those had been attached yet, but the intricate work impressed her.

"Well, it certainly took you long enough, little one."

"I had to help Cook with her stew pot."

The young pirate's eyes twinkled when he grinned. "In that case, you're all forgiven. I'm fond of eating on time, and I imagine her needs were greater. Now, shall we begin?"

"What are we fixing?"

"I'm going over all the firearms. I like to check them once a week, at least, and as we're soon to reach land, I'd prefer if everyone is armed with functional weaponry."

"Why so often?"

"The damp," Patrick said. "Out to sea as we are, you can never escape it. Sometimes the vent is clogged with rubbish or moisture gets into the primer."

After naming each component of the weapon and describing its purpose, he walked her through the cleaning process. She watched him for the first gun, then assisted with the second and third, before trying to handle the fourth all on her own. They discovered she was small enough to crawl into the barrel and drag a piece of cloth along with her.

Tink emerged and coughed a few times before wiping her sooty face. She smelled like gunpowder, but the pistol gleamed beneath the lantern hanging above them.

"It looks brand new. How'd you do that?"

"It's what tinkers do," she replied in a matter-of-fact voice. "Weren't you listening?"

"Aye, but how? Even I've never gotten a weapon so clean. It looks as new as the day it was crafted."

"Magic."

"Huh. Well then, I guess I'll just have to work harder to keep up with you. But seeing as how you performed a miracle with this, I wonder how you'd fare with the cannons." He stroked his unshaven chin and gazed at the open arch leading into the gun deck.

"Oooh, what do they need?"

"A good cleaning and a fresh coat of wax to protect 'em from the saltwater. Of course, we won't do those until we pull into port."

"Then what else can we do?"

Patrick gestured to the remaining firearms. "If you can handle these for me, I'd be grateful. Then I can get to work on the leak in Eliza's room."

"I can do it!"

"Oh no, I've got that one," he said with a quick grin, voice insistent. "It's only a small matter, and I'll be back in a jiff."

"Okay!"

The time passed swiftly, but Patrick didn't return. Tink finished up the last flintlock then wandered off in search of more to do. She repaired a torn fishing net and pile of bent fishing hooks before losing interest in simple tasks and ascending through the cargo hatch.

"Land ho!" Randall shouted from the crow's nest.

A boisterous round of applause and exuberant cheers filled the air, and then the deck exploded into activity as the many pirates hurried to fulfill their duties. For a while, Tink was lost, hovering above the hatch. She'd never seen them so excited before.

"What's happening? Where are we going?" she cried, catching a hold of Eliza when the woman stormed past, face flushed red and mouth pressed into a tight, joyless line.

"Hmm?"

"Where are we going? What land?"

"Samahara, of course. Hasn't James told you anything?" the healer asked while offering Tink a palm to rest upon. Livid red marks and bruises stood out upon her knuckles.

"He told me after the ship has made all of its rounds, he'll take me home to Cairn Ocland."

"So, you'll be leaving us then?"

Tink dipped her chin. "I have to go home. I'm a fairy godmother now, and there are people counting on me. So, did Patrick fix your leak?"

Eliza's blinked. "My leak?"

"He said he had to repair a leak in your room."

"Is that what he said?" The scowl intensified, carving deep furrows between Eliza's fair brows.

"Isn't that what he did? I fixed all the guns while he helped you."

The mage set her free hand on her hip and huffed out an exasperated breath. "I'll just bet he did, the lazy loaf. He came to my room because he wanted a shag."

"What's a shag?"

"It's… I, ah… How old are you, little one?"

"Adult."

"I mean in years."

"I don't *know* how many years. Why?" Her head tilted.

"Because I'm not about to talk about sex if you're not old enough for it."

"I'm not a child. I know all about mating!" Tink snapped, although a surge of heat flooded her face. She especially knew to announce her arrival before entering any room occupied by Conall and Sorcha for more than five minutes. The pair were insatiable.

Eliza's scowl broke and laughter spilled from her lips. "Mating? Is that what you call it?"

"What else do you call it?"

Eliza repeated a bad word Tink had heard Conall say before. Plenty of times. Her eyes flew wide open. "You're not supposed to say that. It's a naughty word."

"Yes. Yes, it is." Eliza's brightening grin crinkled her hazel eyes.

After conducting a brief search of the ship, James found his fairy perched upon Eliza's shoulder when the woman emerged from her cabin.

"There you are. I've looked everywhere for you."

"Eliza was telling me about Samahara."

"Perhaps I can do one better by *showing* you Samahara." James performed an elegant bow before offering his left arm to Belle, palm up for her to land. Upon discovering she possessed equal intelligence to a human woman, he'd endeavored to treat her no differently from Eliza or Cook, lavishing her with the utmost respect at all times. "Would you like to join me ashore?" he asked, following a wild impulse.

"Really?" Belle flitted to him, bypassing his hand in favor of landing on a shoulder, instead.

"I see no reason why you shouldn't. So long as you remain with me, no harm will come to you. I thought you might enjoy seeing a new place, or…" He paused, brows drawing inward as he thought back to her long tale about her homeland. "You haven't been here before, correct?"

"No, I've only heard tales. Father Bear and his mate rescued an ifrit once for his mate. They really appreciated it, because they thanked Victoria with a pretty gift and burned away our cursed forest. Now it's beautiful and thriving again. All of my fairy friends went to help."

She never ceased to surprise him with her stories. "Djinn are quite rare. Your friends must be special indeed to have earned the favor of one."

"In that case, I suppose I'll prepare to disembark alone as you two lovebirds plan your visit," Eliza said dryly. James had forgotten she was there at all.

"Sorry. You're welcome to join us."

After waving him off, she stepped around them and made her way to the main deck where men were lowering a smaller boat into the water.

"Why are we staying way out here?" Tink asked. Samahara's shore gleamed pristine white in the distance.

"Docking at the pier takes effort, and we're at the mercy of the winds when we wish to leave. Well, most ships are, at least. We're lucky to have Little Wolf, who can conjure an acceptable wind whenever we need it, but it's easier to moor here and row in unless we need to move large, heavy cargo. Nothing we took from the Golden Goose will require much more than a trip or two in the longboat."

"I suppose that makes sense. So, since you're the captain, do you get to go over first?"

"Unless I let Nigel go to handle the business end of things," he replied with a grin. "Do you need anything before we go?"

"I'm ready now," she exclaimed. "But…"

"What is it?"

"Won't someone steal your ship if you leave it out here?"

The absurdity of the question took him by surprise. "Never you fear, Belle. No one would dare steal the Jolly Roger from me. Besides, Callum will be onboard, as will Smee and several others."

"But what if they steal it?"

"She won't be stolen. I'd say that's only a danger if I've done something absolutely awful to warrant mutinous behavior."

Her green gaze searched his face and held eye contact, expression solemn in her tiny face. "Okay. Because I'd be very sad if I had to fly home to Cairn Ocland from here. The people in Liang aren't very nice to fairies."

"That, my dear, is an understatement."

A crewman rowed them in the longboat to Samahara's most prosperous port city, allowing James to leave the Jolly Roger for the first time in nearly a season. He'd forgotten how much he missed dry land at times, how good it felt to have solid earth beneath his boots. With Belle on his shoulder, he made his way through the crowded docks.

"Where are we going?"

"We are going to pay a visit to Grand Enchanter Joaidane."

"Who's he?"

"You would call him the governor of these parts, I suppose. He protects the coastline from Ridaeron invaders and pirates of the more lawless variety."

"Aren't you lawless pirates, too?"

"Not entirely. Contrary to what I said to Captain Hawkins,

we follow most laws of sea and civilization."

"Most," she echoed. Her frown scrunched her entire face and put a wrinkle between her small brows. He'd come to learn she was quite expressive in features, as well as her glows, and it helped him to memorize the meaning of each color. She tended to become a deep, serene blue while thinking, but when speaking of how much she missed home, the color became a pale shade closer to gray.

After a quiet chuckle, he navigated the narrow paths and walkways leading from the docks to the adjacent mercantile quarter.

"Look, James, look! They're making glass." Aglow with golden color, her bare feet lifted from his shoulder and she zipped around him in a circle before pointing to her object of interest. Nearby, a glassblower had drawn a crowd near the front of his shop as he twisted a piece of molten sludge with his tools and manipulated it into a horse with a flowing mane and tail.

"He does that several times a week and often makes figurines on demand. He's quite talented."

"I wish I had money," she murmured. Then that soft, dismal blue color spread over her from head to toe.

"But you do."

"Huh. What are you talking about? I don't have any money."

James displayed his skill with sleight of hand by producing a coin for her, making it appear to come out of thin air.

"You know magic," she breathed, becoming a miniature sun.

"Not exactly, but this silver should cover his fee."

Amused by her rapid change in emotions, he watched her dart into the queue with the silver bit. She waited her turn with surprising patience, and when the glassblower turned to address them, he marveled over her tiny size, too.

"What a dazzling creature you have with you this day, Captain Hook."

"I seem to have a talent for making unusual friends. If you're not in a rush to leave for the day, she'd like you to create one of your marvels for her."

"Certainly. What would she like?"

"Me!" Belle cried upon landing on the work table. Her glow dimmed with the stillness of her wings. "Oh, wait. That's boring."

"She's undecided," James said.

"Then she may have a moment to think. I'm in no rush to leave."

While the sprite pondered over what she wanted, James crouched beside the work table and brought himself to her eye level. "Why do you think a glass figurine of you would be boring?"

"I already know what I look like, I don't need a replica of myself," she pointed out. "I guess I don't know what I want."

The glassblower glanced at them, a hint of a smile playing at the corners of his mouth. "Has she decided?"

"No. She initially wanted you to sculpt her in glass, but she believes it would be dull."

"I see." The glassblower leaned closer to Belle. "If a sculpture of yourself is what you desire, may I have the creative freedom to instill life in your piece, little one?"

"Yes!"

"She agrees," James translated.

Chuckling at Belle's enthusiasm, the man straightened and returned to his work. He removed the molten ball of glass from the furnace and before their eyes, years of talent manipulated the shapeless blob into two distinct pieces connected by a single point. He rolled it against the metal table surface, hammered and twisted with his tools, and the vague shape of two figures emerged from the raw material.

Belle never glanced away, gaze fixed on the artist's deft hand movements. He added dots of color and tapped glittering pearls into pieces of glass before tugging and elongating them from the figure's back. Within minutes, the glass silhouettes revealed the shape of a pirate and fairy in dance. The pirate had only one hand, the other ending in a glossy hook with silver glass. The sprite's wings glittered with luminescent, golden sparkles over each edge.

"Do you like?" the man asked as he extended it toward her for closer viewing.

James struggled to discern her mood through the rapidly shifting colors. Green then yellow, gray-blue to sapphire, and back to pink again. At last, the turbulent wave settled on a sunny, lemon shade. "She loves it," he said, although Belle had said nothing at all.

"Return tomorrow and this will be ready for you. Good eve to you both, sir and madam."

Jarred out of her daze, she glanced up at the glassblower. "Thank you."

"You're very welcome." And after a moment of pause, he asked, "She did thank me, didn't she?"

"Yes. A sentiment I will mirror for your kindness." James

placed another silver piece on the table for the man's work then lifted Belle from the table. "Thank you."

She spoke little once James returned her to his shoulder, and a thoughtful silence fell over the gentle creature.

"Would you like to see any of the other traders? They'll all be closed soon."

"Are there other places with pretty things?"

"The market is full of wonders, I'm sure."

"Then yes, please."

Perfect. The market would make an ideal distraction. Eager to restore her cheerful disposition, James veered from his intended course and headed deeper into the mazelike bazaar. With each stand or shop they passed, Belle's deflated mood brightened, both physically and metaphorically, until she lifted from his shoulder and dashed forward to a red and purple striped tent.

"I love candles!" She zipped around the display, flying from one fragrant taper to the next. Some had been dyed in beautiful colors and others carved to resemble fantastical beasts. One looked like a dragon, the wax infused with sparkling blue motes and a scent reminiscent of cinnamon and smoke.

James had never taken the time to truly shop before, but Belle's infectious enthusiasm changed his perception of the traders' district, and he found himself studying the artistic offerings with genuine interest.

"Oooh, I like these." Belle circled around a bundled set of tapers in varying lengths, nearly knocking them from the shelf. At first glance, they appeared rather ordinary compared to the rest, made from plain beeswax without any added colors at all, but closer inspection revealed the silhouettes of wild horses and floating jinn carved into the columns.

"Please forgive my companion," James said to the nearby shopkeeper. The woman lingered nearby with her gaze focused on Belle. "She seems to like your wares quite a bit."

"How much for the lovely creature, my friend? The tinkling sound is quite beautiful, like many wind chimes in a gentle wind. My daughter would love such an exotic mystery."

Belle abruptly spun to face the shop proprietress, fury turning her into an ember-bright ball. "She isn't for sale," he replied, wincing. Hadn't the woman heard him call Belle a companion?

"All things have a proper price. How much for her ownership?"

"I'm not for sale, you big turdlet!"

"She says thank you for the compliment, but she's quite happy to remain with me," James translated.

The sprite shook her fist at James. "That isn't what I said."

"I will offer you three golden rubles for her."

Three gold coins, the equivalent value of a healthy horse or three goats, may have taken the candlemaker a week to earn. "Thank you, but no. Belle is no pet of mine, but an intelligent and thinking companion with desires of her own, madam. Think of her as a jinn, but much smaller."

Recognition and understanding dawned in the woman's gray eyes before she dipped into a low and humble bow. "Ah, forgive my mistake. I hadn't realized. You both have my deepest apologies." She removed the candles from the shelf, wrapped them, and offered the package to James. "Please, take these with my blessing for your tiny friend, since she enjoys them so much."

James bowed. "Your kindness is most gracious." When he slanted his gaze to Belle, he saw her gazing back at him with wonder in her eyes.

"You fixed that quickly."

"The Samaharan people revere jinn and their kind, seeing them as benevolent spirits," he explained. "She meant no insult to you."

"A benevolent spirit?" Her brows drew pinched together. "Oh, I see! Well, thank you then," Belle trilled to the woman. Before James could translate for her, the little sprite flew up and kissed the startled shopkeeper's cheek.

When they walked away, James glanced over a shoulder to find the starry-eyed candlemaker still watching them. With one kiss, Belle had made the woman's day.

"They're going to look so pretty in the den."

"I'm certain they will."

The trip took twice as long as planned, thanks to the sprite's inquisitive nature. She flittered from shop to shop, perusing the wares that James usually passed without a second glance. Seeing Ankirith through her eyes brought him a new appreciation for the bustling port city on Samahara's northeastern coast.

Only after the shops began to close did they finally make their way back to the path that led to their original destination. James glanced down at the various packages tucked into his satchel and chuckled to himself. Between the two of them, they'd bought several treasures and small bags stuffed with treats.

"Where are we going now?"

"There." He raised his hook and gestured to the white

tower at the edge of the city.

The Opal Spire never failed to awe him, despite his many visits over the years. James thought it surpassed the beauty of Eisland's throne room a thousand times over, rivaled only by the nearby section of desert known as the Jeweled Garden. He hoped to ride out and show Belle the gemstones growing from the sand like flowers before they set sail again.

"Your friend lives here?" Belle asked from his shoulder.

"That he does. As I said, he is the protector of this area, and a mage of some renown."

"It's so...tall. It's taller than Benthwaite Castle where the king and queen live."

"It must be tall so Joaidane is able to hurl magic at invaders approaching from the sea." Her little gulp made him chuckle. "Never fear, he's as nice as they come for his kind. Unless, of course, you do something to incur his wrath. Then, I hear, he can become quite terrifying."

"Right," she muttered under her breath.

James hid a smile.

They passed through the open gates into a fragrant garden where an older man knelt beside the flowerbeds.

"Good evening, Orrin," James greeted. "Is he in?"

The friendly retainer raised his attention from the flourishing desert roses and smiled. "He's been expecting you. Probably pacing the study if he hasn't seen your approach—"

The doors slammed open to frame Joaidane, a stern-faced man adorned in a cerulean blue, knee-length coat over matching trousers. He strode toward them, radiating the kind of confidence expected from a wizard who could crush the Jolly Roger with a few magical words.

James bowed. "Greetings, friend."

Joaidane glowered. "You're late for dinner."

"Forgive me," James said. He shrugged despite their host glaring daggers at him. If looks could kill, he would have melted into a puddle of molten goo. "I showed our newest addition the markets, and, well… I lost track of the time. But I *did* bring that Ridaeron rum you favor."

"Uh-oh. Did I get you into trouble?" Belle asked.

"Of course you didn't."

Taken back by the appearance of Belle, who had been hovering nearby to admire the roses, Joaidane's brows rose. "You brought a sprite." The murderous glare vanished. Leave it to Belle to simultaneously get him in and out of trouble.

"I figured, if anyone knew what she was, you would. Of course, I discovered it myself only a short while ago."

"I had no idea you traveled in such magical company, my friend. It's a shame my family isn't present to meet her as well. The little one would be especially enchanted, but they've traveled to visit relatives." The noble magister smiled and offered out his hand, palm up. "What may I call you, little fae?"

"Tinker Bell," she answered in the same moment James replied, "I call her Belle."

Joidane's amber eyes brightened until they resembled plumes of golden flame. "A pleasure, Tinker Bell. I am Enchanter Joaidane, and I welcome you to my home."

"You understood her?"

"Indeed. Her language is not much different from the ifrit who roam the desert. Consider me impressed that you were able to learn it at all in such a short time. They say only a deep bond allows an older human to communicate with fae.

Children and adults with light hearts usually have a natural gift for the language, but for a man of your age with your history…"

"Really?" Belle asked. Won over by the smooth-talking mage, she moved to Joaidane's waiting palm and settled on his fingers. "My friends met an ifrit once in Creag Morden. They helped an old enchantress rescue her true love from a vile fiend named Aladdin."

The corner of his mouth raised. "You are friends with Victoria and Ramsay?"

"You know them?" Belle asked, becoming a beautiful shade of purple.

"Indeed, little one, for the enchantress they assisted is my mother."

Belle clapped her tiny hands and danced around. "See? I told you that story."

"So you did," James agreed, turning to regard his friend. "It would seem our large world is actually rather small."

"It does appear so. I imagine the tale of how you two came into one another's company will make for an interesting story over dinner. Then you can share the latest news of your fellow pirates and Ridaeron's transports."

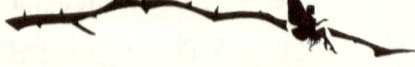

Tink had never realized a visit to another kingdom could hold so much excitement. She awakened before the dawn and tugged on James's ear for him to get up as well, but he blearily shooed her away. She put her hands on her hips and blew a raspberry at him.

"That's what you get for staying up all night drinking rum."

"It's what we men do," he mumbled against the pillow.

"C'mon," she wheedled. "We have to get my glass sculpture."

"Fine. Just please give me a moment to get ready."

Pleased with her victory, she darted in beneath his hair and kissed his scruffy cheek. Then she hurried out to give him privacy. Unlike James, Joaidane greeted her with a fresh face and smile, animated despite their long night of catching up. She found him in the dining room with a variety of Samaharan breakfast choices laid on the table beside a steaming pot of black coffee. Ramsay, Conall, and Victoria had all taken a liking to the strange brew, but Tink and Sorcha didn't care for it. Too bitter.

James's requested moment became an hour by the time he joined them, smooth jawed and dressed in unwrinkled clothes. He accepted the coffee Joaidane slid his way and chugged it down at once.

"Perhaps this will teach you the folly of attempting to out drink me," Joaidane said. "Now, where are you both off to this fine day?"

"I've promised Belle a tour of the Garden. Do you mind if I borrow a horse?"

"Not at all. Enjoy your visit to Ankirith while I enchant these guns Smee and Patrick have brought to me. I've never enhanced a flintlock pistol before or its ammo, but there's a first time for everything, no? Bring yours to me later, and I'll do the same for it."

James grinned. "I thought you'd feel that way. Thank you for doing this."

"I appreciate the challenge. It may consume most of my day, but it'll be time well spent. Perhaps my beloved will have returned by this evening. With her brother out of town on business, his wife needed help with their little one."

"A baby?" Tink asked after swallowing a mouthful of honey cake. "I love babies. Will the baby be here, too?"

"Perhaps." His eyes twinkled with amusement.

Her ever increasing anticipation led her to pull James out before he could finish his meal, while Joaidane howled with laughter at her antics. James stumbled behind her, drawn forward by her grip on his hook.

From that moment onward, the day was hers. James rode out from the city on one of the finest horses Tink had ever seen and took her to a place straight out of a dream. The Jeweled Garden was aptly named. Crystalline spires rose from the dunes at varying heights in every color imaginable.

"How are they growing like this?" she asked.

"Magic. Legend says a powerful ifrit created this place for the love of his life when he was attempting to win her heart."

"Did it work?"

"It must have, since Joaidane is the product of that union."

"It's so romantic."

"You think so?" James asked.

"Well, yeah. He made something for her that no one else ever could. It's unique and special."

"It's a bit showy, don't you think?" A playful gleam shone in his eyes. "What do the people in your land do when they ask a woman to be theirs?"

"Sex."

James's eyes nearly bugged out of his head. "Er…" The

pirate cleared his throat. "Far from what I expected to hear. That's how your people propose marriage?"

"Well… It's how the Oclanders propose, and shifters don't have weddings. They find their mate and spend time hunting together. At the end, if they agree to be true mates, they have sex and they bond. I don't really understand the specifics. Sprites don't marry, either. We just find someone we like and hang around them all the time."

"I see."

"What do they do in Eisland?" Tink imagined something elaborate and expensive. James had a fondness for velvet and silk to rival Anastasia's tastes in wardrobe.

"The man presents the woman with a gift of jewelry. Usually a ring, but it can vary. Always shiny, though. Sapphires are a traditional favorite."

"But blue is a sad color."

"Oh? What color do you favor then?" he asked.

"Pink! Or yellow. Anything else isn't a very happy color to commemorate your love for someone. It should *always* be happy, especially if you want to live the rest of your life with them."

"A fair and wise point."

They remained for a while longer, exploring the vast garden of living jewels. Tink discovered no two flowers were alike, each one a different masterpiece of gemstone in varying combinations. Turquoise stalks led to topaz flower petals, and ruby vines trailed across the sand with diamond blossoms. James told her he'd once wandered for hours after sunset to enjoy a break from the Jolly Roger.

Afterward, they returned for her figurine. James paid a

messenger to deliver all their purchases to the pier where he said Smee would arrange for the things to be brought over to the Jolly Roger.

Tink rested on James's shoulder and stretched out her arms, tired after their long day. He made the perfect perch, his tall height giving her a clear view of the streets and people around them. Everywhere she looked, she saw something new, until her gaze skimmed over a man with a thin mustache beneath his long, hooked nose. His braided beard reached a chest inked with the black tattoo of a fire-breathing reptile with a slim, serpentine body. She'd seen him earlier in the day, she was certain.

"James," she whispered in his ear. "I think there's a man following us. A creepy man."

"Keep an eye on him and let me know if he leaves," he murmured in a low voice while turning left into the next alley. Tink twisted and parted James's dark hair with both hands to see behind them. The stranger made the same turn.

"He's still there."

After another two turns, goosebumps covered Tink's arms. It couldn't be coincidence. Dread formed a tight ball in the pit of her stomach when James veered left into a narrow alley without an exit. He swore under his breath.

They had been herded into a trap with no means of escape. Two additional men had joined the first, and the trio wore matching smirks on their faces.

"Gentlemen, I suggest you allow us to pass," James said, putting his hand on his sword hilt. Tink tensed and clung to his collar. A fourth swung down on a rope behind them, entering the alley from the rooftop of another building.

"You've a price on your head, pirate, and we aim to collect," the bearded man said. He pulled a large, curving blade from the sheath at his waist.

"Ah. Bounty hunters from Liang. I suppose I should have expected this. How much are they offering you?"

"The emperors of Liang and the Ridaeron Dynasty have offered fifty thousand rubles and our weight in jewels for your head... and your hook."

Without wasting any more words, the bearded man lunged forward with his heavy sword. Quicker than she could blink, James blocked with his hook and pulled his sword in the same movement, slashing out with the razor-edged blade. The second attacker had two curved scimitars engraved with runes.

"Belle, flee while you can!"

Flee? What did he take her to be? Refusing to abandon her friend to the ruffians in the alley, she held her ground and zipped between James and the aggressor coming up on his rear. They had him outnumbered four to one. While she had seen him spar with the other pirates on the deck, those had been friendly practice matches.

These men wanted nothing less than his neck.

"You leave my friend alone," Tink seethed, too furious to see anything more than red. It surrounded her in a haze of livid energy, and she glowed brighter than she ever had before.

"What is this? A sprite here, of all places?"

"Don't damage it too badly. Its wings will fetch a good price when we return home," one of the others said.

James lunged forward with his cutlass, drawing the attention back to him. "I mean it, Belle. This isn't any place for you to be," he called back to her. Blades touched, and the edge of a sword sang as it glided over James's hook. He ducked and pivoted to block, still three against one in a battle where no one appeared ashamed for teaming up against a one-armed pirate. "You won't harm a hair on her."

Evading the open palm attempting to grab her out of the air, she channeled her magic into a cloud of flames. The fairy fire became a rush of embers, and wherever they touched, it quickly caught fire, despite her target's desperate attempts to pat the fires out. Within seconds, the panicking man was ablaze and running in terror.

"He has a feisty one. Forget the wings and smash it!" the bearded man called out.

"Oh no, you don't!" No one was going to smash her. Triumphant in her first victory, Tink turned her fiery attacks on the man who had ordered her death.

The bearded man swatted at her with the flat of his blade. The wind current knocked Tink off course, and she tumbled through the air, head spinning, and narrowly missed crashing into the alley wall. Once the world stopped moving, she rushed back, drawing once again on her flagging strength for another wave of fairy fire. Her attacker blocked the flames with his open palm. The ring around his index finger blazed with power and absorbed the spell.

In that moment, she provided the distraction her pirate needed. He thrust forward, claiming one assailant's life. "Good one, Belle!" he called to her in approval, although two enemies remained.

Energy depleted, Tink tried to think what else she could do to help. She swerved up beyond the bearded man's reach then became a blazing bolt of furious light, a red streak charging toward him with her dagger held like a spear. Evading his hand at the last moment, she swerved on course again and plunged her weapon directly into the flesh of the mercenary's ugly hooked nose.

"Ah!" He cried out and stumbled back. Taking advantage of his disorientation, she charged in again and bloodied his eye. It only took one jab from her thorn-sized dagger. The bearded man screamed in pain, his sword dropping to the ground as he reached up to his face. Leaving her weapon in his eyeball, Tink watched him run off like the coward he truly was.

Behind her, James put up a ferocious effort against the last bounty hunter, despite the disadvantage of having only a single weapon. The Liangese mercenary's swords gleamed with magical luster, enabling him to perform one effortless parry after the next. He and James met each other stroke for stroke, two skilled men fighting for their lives.

For years, Tink had watched Conall adapt to battle by using his sword or werewolven body, but she'd never felt compelled to admire the beauty in his fighting form. James was different, maneuvering the sword with finesse. As he found an opening, he kicked with his boot into the bounty hunter's thigh, causing him to stumble, and then James dropped the cutlass on the ground.

Before Tink could question why he'd abandoned the weapon, James drew his gun and fired the round pointblank, burying the slug into his opponent's unarmored chest. The man jerked back and staggered, with a hand to his bloodied torso, mouth forming a small "o" and eyes wide open.

Unconcerned with the dying mercenary, James holstered

  Vivienne Savage

the gun in his belt and swept his blade from the ground. He spun to face her with worried blue eyes slit against the perspiration trickling down his brow.

Had the fight truly lasted so long?

"Are you hurt?" he asked.

"No. Are *you*?" She scrutinized him from head to toe. They hadn't even cut him once, and throughout the fight, he'd handled the cutlass with endless grace.

"Far from it. I was more concerned for you, but now I see you're as fierce as you are tiny, little one."

How could she remain angry when he'd paid her such a wonderful compliment she'd never heard from her friend Conall?

"If it wasn't for their sneaky traps, they'd never have caught me to begin with."

"I believe it." He wiped his sword against his pants, the blood indistinguishable on the dark fabric.

"What now? Two of them got away."

"True, but they're wounded, thanks to you. Joaidane won't be happy about Liangese bounty hunters poking around his city. He's kicked them out in the past," James said. He sheathed his blade then moved over to the groaning man on the ground.

"Who hired you?"

With his last breath, the mercenary spit at James.

Tink wrung her small hands together and returned to her pirate's shoulder, wings drooped behind her. "Do you think there will be more?"

"Doubtful. At least, not this soon, but we'll probably set sail as soon as supplies are gathered rather than spend any extra time here."

"I'm sorry."

James blinked and turned his head to look at her. "Whatever are you sorry for, Belle? This isn't your fault."

"But your vacation from the sea is ruined."

"Is that what you think?" He scooped her from his shoulder and brought her in front of him. "I'll have you know, today is no worse for having battled alongside you. Not only are you tiny, but loyal and dependable in a fight, little Belle. I would have you beside me in battle over my choice of pirates."

"Really?"

"Really," he confirmed, solemn features filled with truth. "Now, let's pay a visit to Joaidane and tell him of our two friends here, shall we? He deserves to know there are mercenaries in his backyard, and I doubt he'll be thrilled to know they were sent by the Emperor of Liang."

Chapter 8

ANOTHER BEAUTIFUL SUMMER day dawned in Cairn Ocland when Conall carried Kendric outside for a breath of morning air. Sorcha had predicted Tink would arrive any day now with her new little friend in tow, so he patiently waited for her to buzz into his face, full of giggles and laughter.

It had been funny, at first. When she failed to return after the first month, Sorcha had suggested the two sprites were becoming acquainted on a personal level.

"You're not suggesting… Tink? There's no possible way my Tink would… Don't even suggest it," Conall had growled.

"Why not?"

"Tink isn't interested in mating. You heard what she said. Sprites do no such thing."

"You don't know what Tink is interested in doing, and, for the record, I asked her about it. They do. They do it plenty, if and when the urge is there," his wife had told him with triumph ringing in her voice. "There's no wee ones created from the act, but they have a hearty enjoyment of it when there are male sprites about to satisfy them—"

"I don't want to hear anymore."

Sorcha had relented, laughing at him all the while he sulked because he loathed the idea of his little Tink knowing anyone on an intimate level. She had become, in a way, like his first child. A daughter more than a friend. Or even a close sister.

As they approached the third month, Conall feared for his little sister's safety.

"Where could she be?" he murmured while scanning the trees with his son in his arms. He ventured forward and stroked Kendric's back when the fussy baby made a disagreeable noise.

"Conall?" Sorcha's voice disturbed the peaceful forest. "What are you doing out here this early in the day?"

"Still no sign of Tink. I was thinking, if I head south, I may be able to find some sign of her. Perhaps someone has seen her in one of the other villages."

"She's having the time of her life with another sprite. Give her time."

"It's been close to three months since she left on this blasted journey, Sorcha," he snapped without meaning to raise his voice. "*Three* months. I don't care what you say, I'm going to find these birthlands and bring our Tink home where she belongs. She can play with her new lad here to her heart's content if that's what they're up to."

"All right."

"All right?"

Sorcha nodded. "If you're to go look for Tink, then I will go as well, Conall. She's my friend as much as she is yours."

"Your place is here with Kendric."

"*Our* place is together as a family. Do you believe for all the time my parents traveled with us that they ever separated? That Mum gave up her way of life and went home to the villages once she became pregnant with Egan and me? Never." With a few deft movements of her hands, she fashioned a loop of fabric into a sling then took their infant and nestled him within it. Content with his mother's warmth, Kendric snuggled against her. "I'll fetch my bow. You inform the wolves of our plan to leave."

He sagged with relief. Too wise to argue with his wife, he nodded and dipped down to kiss her instead. "Thank you."

"No need to thank me. She's my Tink, too."

By the time Sorcha emerged in her armor with their travel gear, he'd already alerted their clansmen of the plan and mailed a letter by eagle to the king and queen, asking if Anastasia would gaze into her crystal ball to lend them any clues.

"I can't believe we're taking the wee one with us on a journey south."

"It'll be educational for him," Sorcha replied. "Besides, we're in safe times now. There are no Scourge, no dangers."

Within seconds of Conall undergoing his transformation from two-legged man to four-legged beast, Sorcha climbed astride him and claimed a handful of the fur on his withers.

They rode to Calbronnoch first and asked if anyone had seen their little friend. Conall visited the few clan members who had chosen to live in the city while his wife spoke with her family.

"Anything?" Conall asked when Sorcha rejoined him.

"No. She didn't pass through this way, which means we should start southward. I can't imagine her heading west without stopping to grab some of Gran's honey cakes. Gran would have told us if Tink visited her."

He swore under his breath and shaded his eyes against the sun while gazing toward the southern road. "We should send a bird east to Ardal, just to be sure."

"Egan is going that way himself," Sorcha said. "Mum and

Dad are going to ride west to Frosweik to search along that route. They'll alert every hunter they pass to be on the lookout for Tink. She's so well known, after all. That leaves the south to us."

Admiration for his wife flooded through Conall. He pulled her close, mindful of Kendric between them, and kissed her brow while thanking the stars for the day they guided him into her life.

"Did you want to stay here for the night?" he asked once he released her.

"Only if you need the rest. Otherwise, Kendric and I are good to set out."

"Then let's get going."

For three days they ran south, but discovered no word of their little friend. No one had seen her, but everywhere they went they found volunteers to expand the search. It didn't matter that none of them personally knew Tinker Bell. They were glad to help one of their own.

That was the Oclander way, a kingdom of selfless neighbors who looked after one another.

On the fourth day, the bleak clouds of an unforgiving summer storm chased them into shelter. As much as Conall wanted to press on, he would never put their child's welfare at risk in the rain, and they sought refuge on a cozy farmstead.

A middle-aged woman ushered them inside the moment she opened the door to find them on her stoop. Wrapped within her waterproof red cloak, Sorcha and the baby remained shielded from the weather, but Conall had been soaked to the bone.

"You three look quite the sight," the woman said as she

bustled them inside, where a cheerful fire warmed the home. "I'm Miranda. My husband was caught out in the storm, but he should be along shortly. Have you come a long way?"

"Conall and Sorcha of Clan TalWolthe. We've come from Calbronnoch," Sorcha replied. "Thank you so much for letting us inside."

"Think nothing of it. What brings you all the way down here from the north? There's naught much else but crops and sheep."

"We're looking for a friend of ours, a sprite by the name of Tinker Bell."

"I don't know about the name, seeing as how I can't understand woodkin speak, but we had a sprite stay with us a few months back."

A spark of hope ignited in Conall's heart, pushing away the dread that had slowly been creeping in. "What did she look like? How long did she stay?"

"Pretty thing with blonde hair and green eyes. She made those for the children." She gestured to a pair of pipes resting on the table.

"Tink… It was Tink." A deep relief loosened the tension he'd been holding onto since their departure. "Please, do you recall which way she went?"

"Aye. The little ones wanted to watch her leave when morning came. She flew south from here. I cautioned her to be mindful of the forest, and she kissed my cheek. That's the last we saw of her."

Overcome with appreciation, Conall took the woman by her shoulders and startled her with a kiss to each cheek. "Thank you."

"You're quite welcome, though I did nothing." Miranda blinked up at him owlishly while childish giggles sounded from the top of the stairs.

"You did plenty. You soothed his worried mind and gave him some peace. We've been worried about her."

"This means we're on the right path if she's come this far."

"We'll find her, Conall."

Sweet stars, he wanted his wife to be right about Tink losing track of the time with her new friend.

Once Sorcha had nursed and cleaned the baby, they enjoyed a hot bath courtesy of Miranda. Most of the new farms in the southern reach pumped their water from wells and heated it with furnaces, a wondrous technology spreading northward to Creag Morden thanks to a treaty between Anastasia and her father. Afterward, they warmed in a dry change of clothes in front of the hearth while the farmer's wife served them hearty bowls of lamb stew.

Thank the stars for benevolent hosts. He'd been starving, their rations and what he'd been able to hunt not enough to offset the great amount of energy spent during their travel. Some years had passed since the last time Conall held a dead sprint over so great a distance. Even then, he hadn't carried Sorcha the entire way.

"Anastasia should have attempted to summon us in her ball by now. Do you think she's received your message?"

"Perhaps not. That storm swept in from the west and could have delayed our bird. Try the mirror again. I'll hold Kendric while you do it."

He took Kendric in his arms and smiled down at the dozing boy. He'd be walking soon, which meant his first shift wasn't far ahead. Conall looked forward to the day, but he'd always expected Tink to be present for the occasion.

Sorcha pulled a small folding mirror from her pack then traced her fingertip along the rune-engraved silver frame. The magical communication device only worked if Anastasia was within hearing range of the crystal ball attuned to it. Otherwise, Sorcha would be speaking to an empty room.

"Please be there to hear me, Ana."

"No luck?"

"I guess she must be away—"

"Sorcha?" the queen's melodic voice echoed from the mirror.

"Ana!"

Queen Anastasia's concerned face appeared in the glossy surface. "Sorcha, it's good to see you after so long. Is there any news? Have you found her? I only received your letter this evening."

Sorcha shook her head. "Not yet, but she stopped a night at this farm. Have you looked into your ball?"

"Nothing. I've found nothing at all, so I'm sending Alistair to aid you." Anastasia pursed her lips. "I have an idea of where to find these fairy birthlands. If my suspicions are correct, it may account for why there's suddenly a shortage of wee ones in the forests. In the meantime, I'll continue to widen my net and search throughout Cairn Ocland."

"Please do, Ana. Conall is dreadfully worried. I've never seen him like this before."

He opened his mouth to protest her observations, then thought better of it and wisely remained silent. The truth was, his wife knew him better than anyone, and she was right.

"I understand. Tink is a friend to us all. Take care in your journey and burn the scarlet flare stones each night whenever you make camp. In fact, toss one into the hearth now. They leave a smoke stain against the sky, and Alistair shall have an easier time of tracking you both."

"I'll be sure to warn Miss Miranda and her family that a dragon will be flying over."

After they said their goodbyes, Sorcha put the mirror away. Kendric didn't stir, so Conall gently set him down in the crib Miranda had provided for their use. Then he beckoned Sorcha over and pulled her into his embrace. She softened against him, her arms wrapping around his waist and holding tight.

"At least we'll have dragon eyes to aid us," Conall said.

"Do you have any idea what she means about the lack of sprites?"

"The only danger to them I know of are the poachers."

"Is that why we're headed south?"

"Aye. Tink knows Liang is dangerous, but if she ventured anywhere close by—if their birthlands are near there…"

Sorcha hugged him tighter. "Then we keep heading south to look for her. With the king helping, no one, not even a poacher, would dare harass us."

The silent forests chilled Sorcha, raising goosebumps over her arms. While they were beautiful and verdant with life, it lacked the beautiful song whispering between the trees in the north. There, sprites hummed, and their twinkling lights darted in and out of the branches during their exuberant games of tag.

The southern reach lacked the playful activity, and both times she found little fairy homes nestled amidst trees or swaying branches, they were long abandoned. The fronds above the little roofs had gone brown, the grass walls dry as hay.

"Look, here's another fairy door," Conall muttered as he got down on all fours and peered at it. He tapped the blue door at the base of the tree with his finger, but no one answered. "We mean you no harm, little ones. We desire only a chat. I am Conall, werewolf leader of Clan TalWolthe, and I swear this to you upon honor and blood."

No tiny voice cried out to him from within the hollowed trunk.

"Where have they all gone?" Sorcha asked. "They should be flocking around us by now, especially the baby." Even a few of Tink's shy little friends had stolen brief moments of cuddling with Kendric whenever they picnicked outside beneath the leafy boughs. The sprites would come up and touch his chubby cheeks, inhale his sweet baby breath, and leave little flowers in his curls.

"These woods stink of man," Conall muttered. "I can smell it in the air."

"Poachers?"

"Likely so. I can think of no other reason for them to flee their homes."

They moved deeper into the forest, searching until the sun

hovered at its highest point in the sky, but all they found were more empty homes and eerie silence. After that, they retreated back to the forest edge and made camp. Sorcha tossed one of the signal stones onto the fire and watched the crimson smoke rise into the air. Even in the brightness of the day, the color stood out, leaving a bright stain overhead in the sky. Unlike the clouds, the red smoke lingered despite the breeze.

"Sorcha, look."

Conall's call drew her attention away from the fire to the northern horizon, where jeweled specks glittered against the blue sky like rubies. While Sorcha had expected one dragon to accompany them, what they received were three. King Alistair arrived with Princesses Teagan and Elspeth on his heels. The youngest dragon hadn't yet grown into her frame, and her gangly limbs brought to mind a young filly.

Alistair shifted, trading scales for armor and tartan, but Teagan and Elspeth remained in their dragon forms. From her talks with Anastasia, Sorcha surmised it was due to the fact that Elspeth hadn't yet mastered shifting with her clothes. Few shifters, in fact, exhibited the control needed to do so. Alistair and Conall were among the exceptions. Teagan had a century of experience and wisdom in her favor, much older than her hotheaded nephew.

"Welcome, Your Highnesses."

"There's no need for any of that," Alistair chided Conall in his deep and rumbling brogue. "We're all friends, remember?"

"Aye, we are. And we appreciate you coming to help us get to the bottom of this," Sorcha said.

"Splendid," the dragon king replied. "Now, what have you found so far? I take it from the solemn faces that the little minx hasn't appeared yet."

"We found half a dozen sprite homes, all of them empty. Whether they've fled or were captured, though, we have no idea," Conall replied.

"I pray for the former, but Ana and I suspect the latter." Alistair joined them at the fire and took a seat, then proceeded to empty food and wine from his pack.

Sorcha accepted the fresh bread and wedges of cheese happily, eager to enjoy something more than trail rations. By the time the king was unpacked, they had enough for a hearty stew and a few indulgences.

"You believe the poachers have come this far north?" she asked. "We encountered them once or twice during our travels over the years, but Mum and Da' always chased them off again."

"They grew bold during the Scourge, but I hadn't realized how much. While we suffered, their emperor provided no aid and failed to rein in his people. With safety restored to the land, it seems like they've decided to risk coming in further, knowing our people have yet to migrate to the south again."

"What I don't understand is why Tink would venture so far south," Sorcha said. "Why would the sprite birthlands be in such an inhospitable place?"

"I doubt they choose the place of their birth," Teagan said in her gentle voice. Shifting into her human shape revealed a thick leather cuirass over the green and gold tartan of Clan TalDrach. Of all members of the royal family, Teagan struck Sorcha as the gentlest, a quiet woman with a healer's soul instead of a warrior's spirit. "If it is a fixed location, the sprites have no say over where they appear. Considering that, Ana and I pored over old maps. This entire forest was once Ocland land, stolen little by little by Liang in recent years. With Rua dead and Alistair...out of the way, they saw an opportunity."

A low snarl from Alistair reverberated through the forest growth. "I should have recognized their treacherous intentions. Had I done something sooner, it would never have come to this."

Teagan placed her hand against his arm. "But you didn't, and we can only fault you for so much, my nephew. But now the time comes when you and your wife must make a stand for Cairn Ocland. We cannot abide them taking our little ones any longer."

Sorcha's heart sank into the pit of her stomach, stirring nausea and the taste of bile to her mouth. "Does this mean they've taken Tink?"

"It's possible. Their thieves were always a nuisance to us in the past, but never with such brazen pursuit. My brother needed only soar above our borders, and we would see neither hide nor hair of their ilk for years again."

"I think it will take more than flying over our borders now." Alistair grunted and cast his amber gaze toward the south. "Teagan and I will do what we can without instigating all-out war, but the time has come to meet with the Emperor of Liang."

"While you two do that, I'll scour the forest to the border. Which would be…?" Conall looked at Teagan.

The elder dragon knelt down and drew a map from a case tied to her waist. With Sorcha's help, she rolled it out and traced a few distinguishing landmarks, including a thick blue line.

"The Strath River is the original borderline between our

two kingdoms. My father and Liang's emperor shook on it many centuries ago. While I was young, I still remember their vows to always maintain the peace and honor between the two nations." Her dark eyes narrowed, and her nose crinkled. "Their ancestor would be disgusted."

Conall looked down at the map Teagan had spread out and gave a nod. "Good. I'll have a dozen wolves here within days. We'll sweep our lands and make sure any poachers realize their mistake."

Alistair clapped his hands together. "Fantastic. Now, I imagine they won't be happy to find this land contested and there shall be some measure of resistance from the lads. This may be the proper time to part ways."

"Part ways?" Conall asked.

"Aye. For your wife and little one. Now that our search for Tink has become a rescue mission, it's for the best that Sorcha takes Kendric to safety."

"It's a long way back home to travel alone on foot," Sorcha pointed out. "Unless you brought an invisible horse."

"Sadly, I fear such creatures only exist in Samahara. I thought you might enjoy a quicker and smoother ride. Elspeth is a talented flier. Quicker than I am, for certain, and *I* can cross the kingdom in a day," Alistair said. "Allow her to take you and the wee lad to Benthwaite while the three of us continue our search for the sprite."

The young girl's eyes lit with excitement. "You'll let me take them?"

"If they're agreeable."

"I'd rather go with you to find Tink, but…" As her voice trailed, Kendric wiggled against her and grasped a handful of her dark hair. She smiled down at him. The Liangese were fierce warriors with alchemical tricks few Oclanders could rival. She'd heard stories that one of their assassins had come close to killing Alistair once, before his curse was broken. Could she risk exposing her son to their noxious clouds of deadly gases and poisons?

Her parents had carried her and Egan into danger because there had been no other choice. They could either travel the cursed lands together, or struggle to eke out a living in overrun communities where food was scarce.

Sorcha had more choices than the dismal options available to her mother years ago.

"I'll do what I can to help Ana and coordinate with the other hunters while you search Liang. If Conall takes my mirror, we'll be able to keep in touch to share any news."

The king inclined his head. "I have one of my own, as does Teagan. Apart, we'll cover larger ground while Anastasia serves as our contact."

"Agreed," Conall said. Her wolf stepped close enough to kiss their son's ginger curls. Afterward, he raised her chin with a nudge of his fingertips and kissed her, too. "I love you, lass, and I promise we'll bring Tink home. As for you, Princess Elspeth, you take good care of my wife and wee boy. Keep them safe for me."

Elspeth leaned forward and stretched out her wings, excitement widening her draconic mouth into a grin. "I will!"

As much as Sorcha hated parting from her husband's side, it was the best way to discover Tink's whereabouts. He'd worry less, and she would be useful coordinating their various search parties with the queen's aid.

More importantly, Kendric wouldn't come within a hundred yards of a Liangese trap.

Chapter 9

As James predicted, Joaidane had been livid and apologetic about the attack. Once, James thought nothing could be more frightening than an angry mage. Then he'd met Joaidane and realized a furious sorcerer born of a grand ifrit was absolutely *terrifying*.

A good thing the man was on their side.

"I wish we could have stayed longer," Eliza mused from beside him, watching the horizon. Samahara's coastline was barely a speck of white, and in a few minutes more, it would be out of sight completely. They'd left with the dawn, taking advantage of the favorable winds.

James turned his gaze to the woman on his left and patted her arm. "As do I, but it's for the best. I didn't want anyone else coming into harm's way because of me."

"Oh, I'm not blaming you," she assured him. "Still, I wish I'd been at your side with my sword."

"I came through well enough."

Eliza ducked her head and laughed softly. "Yes, you did, and saved by a tiny sprite of all things. I wish I could have seen that too."

"It was sort of scary." Belle's voice surprised them both, and they turned from the railing at the same time.

"And here's your savior now, James," Eliza said.

"Indeed, she is." He bowed and smiled up at Belle. Her soft

yellow glow brightened and transitioned to pink. The way she shifted through colors fascinated him.

"Tell me," Eliza said, "where did you learn to fight? I'd not expected it."

"Conall and his mate are warriors," Belle answered. "Conall taught me to fight so I wouldn't be defenseless against the Scourge. I've never fought assassins before, though."

"I hope you'll never have to again," James said, offering out his hand. Belle tinkled and circled above his palm in a merry dance before settling down, her wings shining.

"How long until we get where we're going?"

"A few days," Eliza replied. "I think you'll enjoy Neverland."

"Neverland?"

James laughed. "It's what the local call the Wai Alei Islands, since invaders have never landed there. Not in many generations, at least."

"How come?" Belle asked.

"Because it's protected by a giant sea serpent," Eliza said. "Legends claim the sea witch conjured the creature up from the deepest, darkest depths of the ocean."

Belle walked out to his fingertips and leaned toward Eliza. The pink had faded in place of lavender, a color which he still hadn't deciphered. Now he wondered if it meant she was curious, or enthralled.

"So, the serpent and witch protect the islands? Except against pirates?"

"Oh no, they've warded off pirates before. Only those who mean the islanders no harm can pass," Eliza told her. "In fact, the first time we tried to reach the islands, we were stopped by the serpent."

The purple morphed into red, and Belle fluttered up from his hand. She twisted around, green eyes large in her face, and hovered inches away from his nose. "What did you do?"

"We fought at first," he replied. "But then another ship arrived, one hailing from Ridaeron."

"They fired at the serpent, *and* at us," Eliza said, picking up the story. "Worse, they fired toward the island."

"Then what happened?"

"We had to choose, the serpent or the attacking ship. And since the serpent left us to attack them, we decided to give it some help while we tried to make an escape of our own," James said. "Of course, things didn't go quite to plan. We lost a mast in the battle and were dead in the water."

"I remember we were all certain the serpent would come back and drag us beneath the waves the way it did the Ridaeron ship," Eliza continued. "But the serpent had vanished. Instead, the sea witch appeared."

James grimaced at the memory. "Aye, she did. Since we helped bring down the other ship, we were given passage to the island, but with a warning."

"What warning?" Belle asked.

"That if we caused any harm to the people of the island, we would suffer a fate far worse than being sunk by her serpent."

Eliza broke the tension with a soft laugh. "Lucky for us that we're not the sort to cause harm, yes? Ever since then, we've been friends with Tiger Lily and her people, free to pass through the witch's domain."

Belle shuddered. "I hope I never have to see it. Snakes give me the creeps."

"Me, as well," Eliza said with a wink. "Anyway, I'm off to

grab some food and a nap before my turn at the wheel. You two enjoy the morning."

His friend had hours until her watch, he knew, since he had written out the assignments, but he only gave Eliza a wave and watched her head off. The stories had dredged up old memories, ones he'd rather have forgotten, but seeing the fascination in Belle's face eased the discomfort.

"What?" he asked her. "You look awestruck."

"I guess I didn't think there were so many dangers in the rest of the world," she said. "Pirates, witches, and giant sea snakes."

"You have dragons and wolves who take the shape of men," he pointed out. "Surely you didn't think your kingdom was the only one with such marvels and dangers."

Tink drifted down to his palm again, her glow dimmed and a frown on her face. "I never really thought about it at all. Cairn Ocland is all I know aside from Creag Morden. I learned that before they were conquered, Dalborough was an evil, vile place. And I know that Liang likes to steal sprites like me. But I've never been to any of those places before. This… this is my first big adventure."

"While I'm saddened by the initial cause of your adventure, I am glad to have you here with us," James said in a quiet voice. "I know you miss home, and I promise I'll get you there, even if I must take you there myself."

"I know you will." She lifted from his hand and hovered close to his face, where she dropped a tender kiss against his cheek. The feathery touch sent his pulse into a wild gallop and enveloped him in more warmth than stepping into a pool of sunshine. His only regret was that he couldn't return the gesture in kind.

"What was that for?" he asked.

"For being my friend and trusting me," she said. "I'm glad it was you who found me, and I'm glad I was there with you in Samahara."

"Because of all your pretty purchases?" he asked in a teasing manner, to hide how much her words had touched him.

"No, because you could have been hurt or killed, and that would have been awful. Not because you're the one taking me home, but because you're my friend. I don't want to lose my friend, and I think the world is better for having you in it to save little boys and girls, as well as all the other people you rescue."

James swallowed back the lump in his throat and lifted his hand, one finger extended for her to land on. Then he brought her close and carefully kissed the top of her golden head.

"I'm glad you were there, as well," he said once he found his voice again.

Belle's pink glow engulfed her from head to toe. She accepted her perch on his finger in lieu of her usual place on his shoulder. It brought him no end of happiness to have her there with him, and it brought even more joy each time she gleefully assisted with his daily tasks, because it made her happy. His Belle had taken to the ship life like a natural, and he looked forward to each evening when she'd tell him what she'd done for the day before they settled down with a book.

"What do we get to do today?" she asked.

"Today there's nothing special. Smee and Nigel have accounted for all the supplies, we have fresh food and water, and the skies are clear. When we reach Neverland, however, we'll careen the ship and there will be plenty of work for everyone."

"Careen?"

"We unload everything we can then tip the Jolly Roger on her side on shore so we can clean the hull. It's a lot of work, and dangerous if not done properly, but I've never lost anyone in an accident."

"That sounds hard."

"It is. The ship is so heavy it takes every man and woman to help tip her. The islanders usually loan a few barges to remove the heaviest cargo."

"Huh. Well, I can't wait to learn about that. Maybe I can help."

"Maybe you can." As much as she'd done onboard, he had no doubt she'd be an asset when it came to scraping off the accumulated barnacles and seaweed, but he didn't think she'd be able to do much in tipping the ship.

"Hey, James?"

"Yes?"

"What's that sound?"

"What sound?" Hearing nothing but the usual clamor of men talking and working, he glanced down at Belle in curiosity.

"I don't know. A sort of faint...ticking?"

Ticking? Sometimes even the perceived sound of a ticking clock was enough to pound the blood to James's head and put him on edge. After dashing to the rail overlooking the main deck, he roared a command for silence down to the men below.

A dozen startled faces turned toward him, but his crew fell

silent as the grave. At first, James heard nothing but the wind and the lap of water against the hull, along with the creak of wood and the ripple of the sails. Then he caught it, the faintest whisper of sound carried on the breeze. A ticking clock. James had long ago sold or destroyed every ticking clock aboard the ship, save for a beautiful cuckoo clock Cook kept in her private quarters, far away, where it could do no harm.

"Prepare for an attack. Man the cannons and arm yourselves. Croc is coming."

His crew didn't hesitate, and they didn't panic. Every man and woman knew their place and their duty, and they worked together to make the ship battle ready. While some disappeared below deck to ready the canons, others took up spears and pistols before they claimed their places on the rails.

"James, what's happening?" Belle cried.

"We haven't gotten to the story about the crocodile yet," he grunted. "Needless to say, you'll see the monster yourself in a few moments. Stay close, please."

Callum, Little Wolf, and Eliza joined him on the quarterdeck with little Tootles in tow, but James eyed the child. "What's he doing here?"

"An educational moment. Besides, we'll need every bit of magical help we can get," Callum replied before tousling the young mage's hair.

Worrying for the boy's safety, James hesitated to agree with his battlemage. Tootles hung back beside Eliza, his face pale and his hands trembling. "He isn't in any shape for an educational anything, Callum. Look at him."

"I'll stay with him," Belle volunteered. When she flitted down from James to the petrified boy, Tootles loosened his clenched fists. One kiss from the sprite to his ashen cheek restored the color to his face.

Belle was magical. He'd always known her to be extraordinary, but, in that instant, James couldn't respect and adore her more.

"Tootles and I will work together. Right?" she asked.

"Y-yes," Tootles stammered. He drew himself tall. "I want to help."

James knelt to place himself eye level with their young volunteer. "You're a brave young man to be helping us," he said. "Stay up here with Callum and listen to him. He's been in many magical fights and will help you, as will Belle."

As he rose to stride away, the ship rocked on the waves, bumped from below by their unseen foe. A dark shadow moved beneath the water off their port bow.

"Hold your fire, men," James yelled. "Wait until you see it clearly."

They didn't have to wait long. The crocodile surged from the water, propelling itself up and forward with its powerful tail, massive jaws opened wide. The first bullets pinged off its thick hide, as harmless as bubbles.

Wood cracked and splintered as the behemoth struck the side, but the spearmen forced him back before his claws could do more than gouge the rails. Then he disappeared beneath the water and left the crew searching the choppy waves for any sign of him.

"There, I see him!" someone yelled, their voice carried from the cargo hatch.

"Fire!"

A cannon roared, and its heavy iron load sent a geyser into

the air where it splashed in the water. Croc surfaced twenty feet beyond, untouched and angry.

"Blasted beast, go back to your mistress," James muttered. Positive it would be a wasted shot—and precisely what the beast wanted—he held his fire. Seconds later the ship lurched, bucked from beneath. A second bumped rocked them, throwing a few men down to their knees.

James braced for a third hit, but it never came. He searched the water, but the sunlight glittering across the waves made it hard to make out anything. Still, he knew Croc was out there. The clever bastard would never give up until one or both of them were dead.

"Steady, men," Nigel cautioned.

Tick. Tock. Tick. Tock.

James's nemesis shot from the water in an impressive vertical leap, the monster's tail whipping side to side as it propelled itself from the salty water. Over two thousand pounds of vicious reptile landed on the portside rail. Reinforced wood splintered like twigs beneath it and the enchantments carved into them dulled.

Bollocks.

"Guns!" James roared, thrusting his hook-wielding arm into the air.

Pistols fired. Each shot issued streaks of lightning and other magical effects, a cacophony of sorcery propelling the iron balls. Although they scorched and hurt the monster, they weren't enough to penetrate its incredibly thick hide. As the first wave of gunmen scrambled back to reload and the second wave moved forward, a wall of water arose from behind Croc and funneled toward the crew. On top of his brute strength, keen intellect, and endless stamina, Croc also had a rudimentary skill with water magic.

Eliza's shield swept over the front line, although it was imprecise and failed to provide cover for the men in the rear. Water surged over the starboard deck and swept Patrick against the rail. He grunted, pinwheeled one arm, and went over. Before the words "man overboard" could pass James's lips, Belle hurtled toward the surface, faster than a lightning bolt cast from the sky. Seconds later, the tiny fairy floated above the deck again with the man in tow, gripping him by the seat of the pants. Patrick's head and shoulders sparkled with golden glitter.

Somehow, Belle had done the impossible and saved a grown man. She deposited the soaking wet pirate on the deck as he coughed up water.

But James couldn't focus on them, not yet, at least. As Croc scrambled in a desperate bid to climb aboard, James aimed his pistol toward the scarred eye facing him and pulled the trigger to no effect. His weapon had failed him.

Crimson flames snapped across Croc's snout from the quarterdeck. When Callum cracked the fiery whip a second time, Croc fell back into the water, claws gouging furrows in the hull the entire way down.

As the wind picked up into a fierce gale, the water off the ship's portside bow swirled into an ominous sight that never failed to bring fear to a sailor's heart and soul. Spotting the whirlpool at the same time as James, Nigel spun to the crew and issued orders to turn them away. Those who weren't engaged with the crocodile hurried to the sails. Even Croc paused in its efforts, albeit briefly.

Rather than sucking downward, a waterspout shot from the foamy, white-capped waves toward the sky, roaring and throwing salty spray at the Jolly Roger. The swirling vortex moved across the water directly toward the crocodilian behemoth. The ticking reptile tried to swim away, but it was swept into the funnel and tossed about.

James stared, transfixed by the magical display. Around and around Croc went, unable to escape the furious winds. He rose higher and higher until the force flung his spinning body through the open air. Croc landed somewhere in the vast distance with a colossal splash.

The monster didn't approach them again, although the vague silhouette of his enormous body hurtled through the water toward the horizon. Cheers went up from the crew, short lived once they began assessing the damage. They'd been lucky, with mere days until their arrival to Neverland's shores.

"Excellent work, Callum," James called out. He turned and looked over the assembled mages. "I've never seen you use that wind trick before."

"It wasn't me," the older wizard said. He set his hand on Tootles's shoulder and grinned. "You can thank our young friend."

"That was some impressive spellwork." James crouched down and inspected the boy. "You're all right?"

After a vigorous nod, Tootles inched behind Callum's leg. Hopefully, the boy came out of his shell one day, and as much as James wanted to hug the youngster for saving the day, he settled for ruffling his curly hair instead.

"When we get to the island, there are people who can help you train your magic, but only if it's what you want. However,

I think you'd make a fine sorcerer and protector."

"You mean… I don't have to hurt people?"

His heart broke for the boy. "No, Tootles, you don't. Your magic is your own, and I won't tell you what to do with it. That choice is yours alone, whether you wish to learn the healing arts like Eliza, become a battlemage like Callum, something in between, or a completely different mage of your own choosing. Regardless of who you become, it will be *your* choice. In Neverland, no one will ever hurt you again."

Tink delighted in observing Little Wolf at the forecastle with the wind behind him. He had a command for weather magic she'd only witnessed in fairykin like Anastasia. With his gift, the wind coasted the Jolly Roger eastward toward their next destination at a remarkable pace, despite the immense damage to the portside bow.

James said they'd lose too much time by turning back for Ankirith, which meant all repairs had to be made with what material they carried in the hold, which was little, considering they traveled light and lacked the amount of lumber required.

"Let me at it," Tink declared before performing a marvel that left the entirety of the ship staring at her in awe.

She swept up and down the ship's portside sprinkling fairy dust wherever the wood had splintered and left jagged edges. While she couldn't use her fairy dust to create new wood, she made what was there malleable to affix the broken shards that weren't lost to the bottom of the sea.

"Is it glue?" Patrick asked, bewildered. He'd done nothing

but watch and hand her tools as she directed.

"No, silly. It's fairy dust, and it does whatever I want it to do."

An hour ago, she'd used it to make him light as a feather, and now she used it to mend the shattered pieces of their ship.

"Nail, please."

"Oh, yes, of course." Patrick hurried to place a nail against the soft wood. Using his hammer, she drove it in with one stroke.

Once the surprise wore off, the others began to ask how they could pitch in and help her. They sawed wood and patched together the damaged deck until the sun touched the water, and everyone felt safe again. Or safer, at least. There had been no sign of the crocodile since the water spout had tossed it away.

"Go on and eat, Belle. We've got the rest of this. Thanks to you, it'll all hold firm until we reach Neverland," Patrick said.

Exhausted from all her work, Tink retreated to James's cabin and flopped onto the table. Someone had delivered dinner, although it was all hidden beneath a silver dome. As she started to raise the lid for a peek, James stepped in and shut the door behind him. He groaned and rolled his shoulders before kicking off his boots.

"What are we having?" he asked as he approached.

"I don't know yet, but it smells delicious." She lifted the lid and set it aside, revealing bowls of steaming soup laden with chunks of chicken and vegetables. A round loaf of dark bread and a crock of butter accompanied the simple meal, but there wasn't a slice of cheese in sight. Not even a crumb.

"But…where's the cheese?" she whined.

James laughed. "If we have it with every meal, we'll run out within a few days."

"I suppose…"

For a time, they both ate in silence. Tink stuffed herself until she couldn't manage another bite, and then she retired to the ship model near the chaise. She liked to spin the wheel and pretend she was at the helm of the Jolly Roger, navigating the wild and treacherous waters of the Viridian Sea as Captain Belle. And sometimes in those fantasies, James was beside her.

"Do you think that crocodile will come back?" she asked.

"Not anytime soon. We gave it a good bruising, and it won't want to tangle with Tootles's magic again. However, I'm sure it won't leave us alone forever."

"Why does it hate you so much?"

"Did you notice its missing eye?"

Tink's eyes widened. "You did that?"

"Indeed I did."

"Why was it ticking?"

The corner of his mouth quirked. "Because, prior to that damnable croc taking my hand, it burst through a load of expensive cargo we were bringing onboard and swallowed several pricey trinkets. That cargo happened to be comprised of clockwork mechanisms from Ridaeron."

"But… it's still ticking."

"Ridaeron gnomes make *very* good clocks. It's why they fetch such a high price on the market."

"Gnomes?" Trailing sparkles, she darted toward the pirate's face, close enough for his eyes to cross. Tink giggled and drifted back until his blue eyes regained focused. "Sorry. They have gnomes in Ridaeron?"

"They do, though they're few in number, from what I hear. Another reason their goods demand such high prices. You've heard of gnomes? Do they live in your kingdom, as well?"

"Oh no, not in Cairn Ocland," she said. "But Victoria told us a story about a gnomish city once. It was long ago abandoned and trolls had moved in! She and Ramsay had to run for their lives, and they ended up in a gnomish castle with ballista and oil pots." Leaving out no detail, she continued her tale and went so far as to act certain parts out. By the time she finished, the light had returned to James's eyes, a wondrous grin replacing his grim expression.

"You spin a good tale, Belle. Have you ever considered becoming a storyteller?"

"I tell stories all the time."

His soft, husky laugh made her stomach flutter. "And you do so well. I only meant, in my homeland, that we have people whose sole occupation is to concoct stories for the amusement of others. Then they produce them into plays on stage so all can enjoy them."

"You mean, you *pay* to hear a story?"

"We do."

"But why? Anyone can share a story."

"But only the truly gifted possess the creative endowment to tell them with such enthusiasm and imagination."

James was a fan of big words, she'd noticed, and it endeared him to her even more. A lifetime of exposure to her countrymen in Cairn Ocland had made the rolling cadence of his speech different and intriguing.

She would have listened to him read the ship's travel logs or the meticulous cargo manifest Nigel kept.

But her favorite activity that involved James and his voice was listening to him read poetry at night. He hadn't done that since discovering she understood him. Blast. Had the poetry reading been too personal a thing to continue now that he considered her a woman—a miniature woman no larger than his thumb, but a woman, just the same?

"Would you like another hot bath?" James asked suddenly, the offer intruding on her thoughts.

"Yes, please."

His warm smile raised goosebumps over her skin again. Now that he knew her to be no different than any other woman, he'd taken to pouring a hot kettle of water into the bath of her dollhouse each night, an improvement over the room temperature washes she'd endured for weeks.

Once James poured her bath, he retreated into the private loo where the pounding noise of water against metal and porcelain tile seeped into his personal cabin.

And every night, she always imagined what it would be like to join him.

Chapter 10

A FTER CLOSE TO a week of travel from Ankirith, and an even greater voyage before that, Tink wanted nothing more than to inhale the aroma of green life and fertile soil.

While helping Patrick with the furnace that supplied hot water to the communal shower, Eliza's bath, and James's private room, she heard the words, "Land ho!" belted from the crow's nest. The announcement stirred up the crew and changed the somber atmosphere that had blanketed the ship ever since Croc's attack.

She'd learned since then that a few good pirates had died during the last great attack, James's hand the least of the casualties.

"Go on," Patrick said.

"Go on where?"

The mechanic grinned at her, eyes bright. As bright as they could be with one still healing from an angry healer's right hook. Shades of a blue and green bruise surrounded it. "You go and skive off, Madam Belle. I know you must want to see the green more than anyone, since you're always talking about your pretty homeland."

Aside from the single time he'd fooled her into cleaning all the guns, she and Patrick had formed a tinker's camaraderie, endeared to one another by a common love for inventions and laboring with their hands. He was what the Eislanders called a prodigy, gifted since a young age when it came to dreaming up designs for ships and all manner of devices.

As Tink zipped away from the furnace and ascended from the belly of the ship, the joyous celebration of the pirates grew louder. She reached the main deck to find it bustling with action. James stood at the helm in his dazzling scarlet coat, his dark mane of lustrous hair moving with the wind. For a while, she stood hypnotized by the sight of him, the power he commanded, and the confidence he exuded behind the wheel.

When Tink joined him, he greeted her with an affectionate touch of his thumb against the narrow strip of spine between her wings. She helped herself to the pirate captain's shoulder and made herself at home, accustomed to sitting cross-legged beneath the silky curtain of his dark hair. She loved when he wore it down, framing his face in an abundant tumble of black waves. He'd bathed that morning, too, and the rich scent of his soap surrounded her, spicy, like rum invading her senses.

Without speaking, she breathed him in and soaked in the warmth he emitted.

"Good morning, Belle. We'll be reaching the shore soon," James said.

An emerald hued island came into view on the horizon, with a tall mountain at its heart. The closer they came to it, the more apparent it became to Tink that they weren't approaching one island, but several landforms clustered together, each one topped with swaying trees.

"It's beautiful," she breathed.

"It certainly is."

Mesmerized, she enjoyed the view in silence until they pulled into the bay. Men cheered as the anchor dropped and some burst into song, singing of women and drinks and lazy days under the sun.

"Do you go over first?" she asked.

"Not this time. I give that honor to those with family here. Callum, Little Wolf, and a few others will take the first boat over. Then I'll cross with the second."

A whoop of laughter preceded a double splash, drawing Tink's attention to two men swimming toward the shore. James chuckled and leaned both arms on the rail while observing the race between the two mages.

"I guess there will be room for me on the first boat after all."

"What are they doing?" Tink asked.

"Swimming for it, and I can't say that I blame them. Little Wolf has been eager to see his wife before their child arrives. He and Callum sometimes make a wager on who gets there first."

Surrounded by a joyous atmosphere and the high spirits of the crew, Tink waited on James's shoulder while the pirates lowered the longboat to the water. A volunteer ferried the first round of visitors to the island. Although Tink had missed the conclusion of the race, she located Callum and Little Wolf among the crowd gathered on the beach. As the latter knelt and kissed his wife's round belly, a woman streaked across the sand and leapt into Callum's arms. A little girl no older than Elspeth dashed after her.

"James! It's James!" a young boy's voice cried.

Over a dozen children converged on the pirate captain the moment he stepped ashore from the longboat. Bewildered, Tink remained on his shoulder as the kids threw themselves at him, each one fighting to the front for their turn at a hug. James only laughed and did his best to make sure everyone received his affection.

"Look at you, Georgette, you've grown half a foot since I saw you last," James said to a pretty girl with black ringlets.

"And me?" asked another girl.

"As graceful as a swan, Amira," James replied.

"What about me?" A dark-skinned boy with abundant, sand-hued curls said, standing up proudly and puffing his chest out. He and Amira must have been twins, as both shared the same button nose and sapphire eyes.

"I daresay you're a good foot taller, Viran," James said as he clapped the boy on the shoulder. "All of you have grown. Now, tell me, have you all been good for Tiger Lily?"

"Yes, sir," they all replied in chorus.

"Excellent. I'm pleased to hear it. And your lessons?"

"I learned to ride a horse," Georgette cried out.

"I learned my letters," a small blonde girl said.

"They taught me how to shoot a bow," one of the older boys told James.

One by one, each child shared their recent triumphs while James listened with infinite patience and praised them all. It was a side to him Tink had only seen in quiet moments with Tootles.

"Wow," the oldest of the boys said, staring at Tink. He leaned forward on his tiptoes to look at her then scratched his head of flaxen white hair. "What's that?"

"Hi, I'm Tinker Bell."

"Her name is Belle, and she's a fai—" James began, only for an enthusiastic chorus of greetings to ring out from each child.

"Hello, Tinker Bell!" the boy replied. "I'm Peter."

"Can we just call you Tink?" Viran asked.

"No, stupid. Her name is Belle. I bet you 'tinker' is just like Captain James's title," Amira disagreed.

James blinked at them. "You understand her?"

"Weren't you listening to Joaidane? Children always understand sprites," Tink told him matter-of-factly. "But adults often forget how to listen and have to learn how to do it all over again."

As Peter hadn't stepped back yet from examining her, Tink leaned forward and kissed him on the tip of the nose. His freckled face lit red, and he bounced back, as light on his feet as a leaf on the wind.

"Ah, that explains quite a bit." The gentle smile remained on James's face. "I hope all of you remember to be kind to Madam Belle while she's a visitor to the island. She's never traveled here before, so be on your best behavior."

"We will!" the chorus cried.

"All right, that's enough for now. I promise I shall spend some time with all of you, but for right now, I need to check in with Tiger Lily. Oh, and Peter?"

"Yes?" the boy perked up. His eyes were the fairest gray Tink had ever seen.

"I have another boy on the ship who I'd like you to meet, but he's rather shy. Do you think you could go back to the Jolly Roger with Smee and talk to him?"

"Of course!"

"Thank you." James ruffled Peter's hair before the group dispersed.

"Who were all those children?" Tink asked after the last

tot left.

"I call them the Lost Boys, although we've received a few Lost Girls over the past year or two. They're orphaned children taken from the Ridaeron Dynasty, Samahara, and sometimes Liang. We haven't yet discovered if the Liangese are intentionally selling their children, but we've seen more of them lately."

"They sell *us*," Tink said bitterly.

"I don't believe they realize your lot possess equal intelligence, love. Weeks passed before I registered your tinkling as more than mere bell chimes."

Despite his rational explanation, she still wanted to throttle a poacher or two for her brief stint in captivity. When she thought of the other sprites who had been taken captive, sometimes stolen for more nefarious acts of alchemy, she shuddered.

There had to be something Anastasia and Alistair could do. Something to discourage the Liangese from abducting the fair folk and submitting them to unknown tortures. She'd been one of the lucky ones, a pet in a gilded cage.

Her mind wandered back to home again. What did Conall think of her long absence? She'd promised to return within a week or two. Would he be combing the forest seeking her by now, following the scent of her through the brush wherever she made contact with the trees? If he did, she hoped he caught the two crooks who'd abducted her and tore them into little poaching pieces.

No. Her smell would be long gone from the woodlands. Even the best trackers couldn't follow a trail gone cold for over three months, and the altruistic part of Tink who adored her friend the most, hoped he was at home cuddling his family.

Giving little Kendric kisses. Rubbing Sorcha's feet. That's what Conall should have been doing.

"What are you smiling about?" James asked.

"You can see me smiling?"

"You're always yellow when you're happy. And now you're pink. I haven't yet figured out what that means, but the yellow is certainly happiness. Brighter and more beautiful than the rarest canary. As radiant as the sun."

Her cheeks became hot as James waxed poetic about her colors. She dipped her head and let her hair fall into her face.

"I do believe pink is embarrassment, isn't it?"

"No."

"What is it?"

Tink didn't dare to say it out loud. After all, how could a sprite ever tell a human she'd fallen in love with him?

Neverland had no need for kings and queens. Instead, they had only a single chieftain among them, named Tiger Lily, and she was as fierce a warrior as any man, able to wield a sword, javelin, or bow with deadly accuracy.

James took care never to cross her, as her people were fair and just to the few pirates they gave shelter. Most importantly, he'd come to see the people of the Wai Alei islands as *good* people deserving his protection as much as he needed theirs.

Neverland had no official capital, each settlement and village equal to the next. The members of the tribe migrated as necessary, living among the hundred or so islands dotted throughout the center of the Viridian Sea.

"Now, Tiger Lily leads all of Neverland, so take care to be nice to her," James cautioned Belle.

"Am I ever not nice?"

He glanced at his shoulder and raised his brow.

Belle crossed both arms against her tiny chest and glared back. "It's always deserved if I'm not."

"Right."

A few wooden homes dotted the southern shore of the tropical paradise, closer to the pastures of sweet cane maintained by the locals. During their last visit, the Jolly Roger had stocked up on sugar and traded for new chickens among the locals who had some to spare. Cook would no doubt arrange for more livestock this time, as the fresh chicken had been a hit among the crew, even if the filthy animals made the belly of the ship squalid and required more care each day.

"Why are all the buildings on poles?" Belle asked.

"The locals harvest mushrooms that favor the damp soil beneath the houses, plus it also protects them from flooding."

"That makes sense."

Her no nonsense acceptance brought a smile to his face. Continuing up the gentle incline, he headed past the largest building and up the stairs to a humble home with colorful flowers on a vine twined around the railing beams.

"This doesn't look like a leader's house," Belle mused while peering out at the paradise beyond the rail.

"Oh? And what do they look like?"

"Er… castles? Our king and queen live in a castle. Conall has the topmost room in the den."

"The king in my home country has a castle, as well," he

agreed. "But out here, things are done differently. That big building there is a gathering hall for all who dwell among the island. Tiger Lily doesn't consider herself better than the people who look up to her for guidance."

When James rapped on the frame of the door, Belle leaned forward expectantly until it opened to frame a young woman not yet in her thirties. Tiger Lily's high, defined cheekbones framed a face softened by her small, upturned nose and bow-shaped lips. Her long brown hair was tied back in a plait twined through with orange flowers matched by her bright eyes.

"Welcome back to the island, James. You're long overdue." Her gaze searched his face before she stepped forward to embrace him. When she stepped back, her attention fell to Belle. "She's lovely. A new pet?"

From the corner of his eye, he saw Belle's lavender light burn brighter red than a lit cigar. "No," he rushed to say. "This is Belle, and she's my friend, and a friend to the Jolly Roger, as well."

"My apologies, Belle." Tiger Lily dipped her head. "Any friend of James and his ship is welcome here."

Belle settled on his shoulder once more, glow fading. "Thank you."

"She gives her thanks," he translated.

"You understand her chiming?"

"I didn't at first, but over our time spent together, I've come to understand her clear as day. The children, however, are all able to understand the sprite language."

"You arrived just as I planned to come meet you on the shore. I take it there are new arrivals?"

"Not as many. Only three children this time," James

assured her.

"Good. You'll have to tell me about how you both met along the way."

The stairs gleamed golden-red beneath James's booted feet as they descended to the ground again, always brightest at sunset when everything appeared to be lit by flames. Beyond them a stretch of sand sparkled with all the colors of ground opal, each grain a different color from the last. Smee had already brought most of the refugees to shore, where they'd meet Tiger Lily and go through her ritual to determine if they were fit and willing to dwell in the isles.

Since James had learned the tribe's native tongue years ago, conversation flowed easily between them as he relayed the story of sacking the Golden Goose and rescuing their newest friends. The occasional frown betrayed Tiger Lily's thoughts related to the Liangese smugglers.

Upon the conclusion of the story, sorrowful eyes turned to Belle. "I am sorry for the pain you have endured at their hand," the chieftain said in a solemn voice. "Should you wish to remain here among my people, you are welcome."

"I would if I didn't have to return home."

"She can't," James said. "We've already promised to help her return to Cairn Ocland."

"I am not familiar with the name."

"I'm not surprised. The coastline is nonexistent for the most part, made up of tall cliffs."

"Ah, the home of the giant sea hawks. We have stories of them."

"Sea hawks." Belle snorted. "They're not sea hawks. They're *griffins*. Shifters. How could she mistake them for stupid, mean birds?"

Her derision startled him, and he gave her a quick hard look before clearing his throat and turning back to Tiger Lily. "Belle says they're called griffins. Her kingdom seems to be full of magical creatures who can shift from beast to man."

"Fascinating."

"I think so, as well," he agreed.

"If there is no coast, how do you plan to get her home?"

"I'm not certain yet, to be honest. We'll find a way."

"If anyone can, it is you, James." Tiger Lily set her hand on his arm and smiled. On his shoulder, Belle made a grunt of a sound, and then she flew off ahead of them, her wings trailing green sparkles behind her.

"She's a colorful little thing," Tiger Lily said.

"They seem to change with her emotions, though I haven't quite figured them all out yet." But he was certain green wasn't a pleasant one, and he wondered at Belle's sudden rudeness.

"Have you seen Peter yet?" she asked, keeping up their conversation.

"I sent him to the ship. One of the children we rescued is rather shy. I didn't want him to be overwhelmed, so I asked Peter if he'd bring him over."

"Good. Peter has been a great help with all the children, if a little wild."

"Not any trouble, I hope."

"No. He's different from the other boys and girls, a spirit that longs to roam free, but tempered by a good heart and caring soul. I will see your lost boy when Peter returns with him, but for now, let's tend to the rest."

For several years now, James had delivered slaves and

refugees to Wai Alei, usually bringing helpless women and young children, while taking men without families to the coast of Ankirith to be judged by Joaidane. As a djinn half-breed, the mage had a good sense for truth, and he could determine the true criminals from the innocent, the predators from the meek.

The Ridaeron Dynasty occasionally emptied their prisons to meet the demand for slaves, in light of James terrorizing their merchant ships. For every dozen men and women rescued from the slave barges, at least one had the potential to be a murderer or rapist in disguise.

Tiger Lily had her own way of cutting the wheat from the chaff and determining who had enjoyed a nefarious life. While Joaidane detected truth from lies, she'd commune with inhabitants from the other world. Before the night ended, Tiger Lily always knew who would be allowed to remain among the islanders. She'd once told James the spirits of the dead often trailed behind their murderers like a death shroud and that echoes of pain made discordant notes in the souls of predators who thrived on inflicting misery upon others.

Whenever Tiger Lily made an outcast of someone, James ordered them placed in the ship's brig until they could deliver them to Ankirith—or, better yet, their homeland. Depending on the crime and what Tiger Lily reported to them, the criminal sometimes became fish food at the bottom of the sea, instead. After all, any man who would force himself upon a woman deserved nothing less.

"Greetings to each of you," Tiger Lily said as she approached. Her command of the Ridaeron language had improved over the years since James had brought the first refugees to her. "I am Tiger Lily, chieftain of Wai Alei, and I welcome you if the spirits are willing this eve."

Of the initial seventy-two rescued from the Golden Goose, five hadn't survived their injuries. A dozen had been strong, strapping, and single men willing to test their luck in Ankirith, the rest children or families sold together for the Eisland market.

A few families had stayed behind in Samahara, eager to join the farming community near Ankirith, while the other half came to the islands with the Jolly Roger.

One by one, Tiger Lily spoke with them at length as the setting sun set fire to the sky, streaking it with pink, gold, and scarlet. Night fell before she completed her ritual of communing with the spirit world, and, as always, she had tears in her eyes by the time she finished. Belle, who had remained with Eliza the whole time, was the last to be addressed, and he couldn't help but miss her company on his shoulder, as well asher laughter and insightful comments. He glanced over in her direction and saw the green glow still surrounding her.

"Each of you have a home here among us if you choose to remain."

Tiger Lily's decree brought James's attention back to the task at hand. It wasn't often he had to lock someone up during their stay, but he always worried about it, afraid he'd inadvertently bring a killer to the peaceful paradise.

"They're all safe?" James asked gently.

"Yes, though I sense there are two wild souls who would prefer to remain among your crew."

"The option is up to all of you, of course," James said to the men and women rescued from the Golden Goose. "Life is good here, but it means hard work at times and sharing with the community. Or, if you'd rather, I can deliver you to your homelands, or another kingdom if you wish, but I cannot promise how long such deliveries will take."

"What about sailing with you, sir?" a man asked.

"Jacoby, isn't it?"

"Yes, sir," the man replied. "I was a sailor in Ridaeron, before they attacked my village and took us as slaves to sell. They claimed we were traitors to the crown and hadn't paid taxes, but we had. We were loyal to our kingdom. The sea is what I know and love."

"Then I'll have Nigel speak at length with you. If he believes you can be a valuable addition to the crew, I won't turn you down."

"Thank you, sir," Jacoby said.

"But for now, I invite you to come rest and eat," Tiger Lily said. "You all deserve a respite after the harsh ordeal you've endured. Please, follow me. We have beds and food for you all."

James remained on the beach while Tiger Lily led the others away, until only he, Eliza, Nigel, and Belle were left.

"Any initial thoughts on our volunteer?" he asked Nigel.

"I've a good feeling on that one. He kept his head during the attack. Helped secure things below deck and calmed the other refugees."

"Good. Still, find out more about him and make sure he understands the risks he'll be taking if he sails with us."

"Will do. See you at supper." Nigel waved and headed off after the others.

"I can't wait to eat. I smelled the roasting pig before we

even reached the shore," Eliza said. Her stomach rumbled in agreement with the anticipatory look on her face. "Coming?"

"In a moment. Belle, would you stay back and speak with me?"

Eliza shot him a look that seemed to silently say "fix up your mess" before she headed along the path to the town beside one of the island women. Belle hovered in the air, a glowing speck of green against the darkening sky.

"Belle, have I upset you?"

"No."

"I've never known you to lie before," he continued in a quiet voice. "Please, tell me what offense I've given so I can attempt to make amends."

"You're going to be late for dinner, and then you won't be able to sit next to your precious Tiger Lily."

Realization struck him harder than a thunderbolt, forcing James to study her anew. She'd become a living emerald floating in the evening sky. She hovered with her arms crossed over her chest and her gaze averted.

"Belle, I believe you already know my thoughts regarding Tiger Lily. I see her as no more than a friend. A woman to be admired and respected, yes, but she doesn't have my heart."

"She likes you," Tink sulked.

"Perhaps, but she and I are friends. Don't you like your friends?" When he offered his hook, she settled on the curved metal, but kept her back turned to him.

"She *likes* likes you."

He smiled and ran his finger down her back between her drooped wings. "But I don't return those feelings. You don't have to worry about her stealing my attention away from you."

Soft green bled into vibrant pink. "You promise?"

"I swear it on my life. My attention will always be yours."

Belle fluttered up to his face. As she hugged her miniature body to his cheek, it dawned on him what the color meant. Not embarrassment, but affection. He'd been a fool not to see it sooner.

Closing his eyes, he soaked in the warmth of her embrace and the delicate kiss she laid on his cheek, wishing for all the world that things could be different.

How could he admit that his heart belonged to the one woman he could never be with?

Chapter 11

THE CREW OF the Jolly Roger enjoyed two days of relaxation before they set to the task of unloading the ship. The canons were the toughest challenge, having to be unloaded and ferried to the shore one at a time on the island barges, until Tink offered to make them lighter with her fairy dust. It filled her with a profound sense of belonging and satisfaction to aid them.

Despite Tink's desire to return to Cairn Ocland, relief flooded her when she overheard James's decision to careen the ship on the shores of Neverland for no less than a week during repairs. Working together, the crew and the islanders hauled the enormous pirate vessel onto the beach. Once the low tide swept out, the ship remained stranded on the damp sand, her hull infested with barnacles and all variety of sea life.

"You'll help, won't you?" Patrick asked.

"Of course!"

With her aid, the projected week for scraping away barnacles and replacing damaged wood became four days. Fearing James would whisk them away earlier, she slowed her work to a crawl until the amused captain caught on and assured her they would remain beyond their task's completion.

He'd promised the crew two weeks, after all, and wasn't so cruel to order them away ahead of schedule.

During the nights, they enjoyed the hospitality of Tiger

Lily's home. She strung an additional hammock for James and created a fairy-sized bed within a shell lined with soft feathers and a small square of silk. She wasn't so bad after all, Tink decided. Of course, it was easier to be nice to the woman now that she knew James wasn't interested.

A small inkling of guilt slipped into Tink's conscience. Who was she to deny James a chance at happiness with another woman? As much as she cared for him, loved him, she understood in her heart that she could never be *with* him. And that fact made her heart break, because, more than anything, she wanted to be that woman.

"Will you come join us for the celebration tonight?" Tiger Lily asked, jarring Tink from her musings.

"What celebration?"

While Tiger Lily couldn't understand her speech, the woman still had a knack for guessing what she said.

"Once they get the Jolly Roger back in the water, and at least two of the canons onboard, they always enjoy a bonfire and dancing on the beach," the town leader said. "Then they finish loading it over the remaining days. We've had pigs roasting in their pits since dawn."

Tink licked her lips, and her belly growled in hungry anticipation, causing Tiger Lily to giggle.

"I'll take that as a yes. Perhaps you'd be willing to help me string flowers with the children?"

They spent the afternoon stringing garlands in the meeting house. The fragrant blossoms perfumed the large space with heady scents, and the children laughed and threw petals at one another. Thrilled to see Tootles among the little ones, Tink settled in place at his side. By the time the sun began to set, they'd made hundreds of necklaces. Everyone took up as many as they could carry and dashed outside toward the beach, only stopping to pass out the garlands to the people they passed along the way.

Tink had made one especially for James, choosing creamy white gardenias paired with blue flowers that reminded her of his eyes and a few smaller pink blossoms tucked in with the dark greenery. She weaved through the growing crowd in search of him, ducking past Eliza and one of the islander women then circling around Little Wolf and his heavily pregnant wife.

As the party drums began, she found her pirate on the beach staring out at his ship in the bay. The wind ruffled through his black hair, blowing it back from his face while the setting sun cast a golden light on his proud features. He truly was the most handsome of all men, so she paused to study him, wanting to forever hold his image in her mind and heart.

At that moment, whether by coincidence or an uncanny sense of her arrival, James turned to face her. The intensity of his gaze slammed her pulse into a galloping pace, making it thump wildly against her ribs. Words caught in her throat, she closed the distance between them and settled the flower necklace over his head.

"Did you make this?"

"Yes," she answered, ducking her head so that her hair drifted into her face. "Tootles helped me with others, but I did this one alone."

"I'm afraid I haven't a touch delicate enough to string flowers, but I did come upon this yesterday." James opened his palm to reveal a single tiny pink pearl strung on a silken thread. Tink drifted down and put it on, her throat thick and her eyes wet with tears.

"I'll treasure it forever."

"I hope it will always remind you of me."

Why did it feel like they were saying goodbye? Tink swiped at her cheeks and fluttered up to kiss his cheek. Behind them, the dramatic drumbeat crescendoed before the flutes joined in and the native voices raised in triumphant song. Islanders and pirates joined each other in dance.

"Shall we?" James asked with a smile.

"Yes!"

With Tink riding his shoulder, James took a place in the chain between Peter and Eliza, and they danced around the bonfire in circles, going back and forth, until even Tink was dizzy. The general merriment and laughter were as welcoming as her family in Cairn Ocland, and she thought she could happily live out her days on Neverland if the option to go home became an impossible dream.

If it meant she could stay with James.

"I wish I could really dance with you," she said after they moved away to eat.

"We did dance," James pointed out.

"No, I mean, holding hands. Face to face. Like my glass sculpture."

His teasing smile softened into something tender and wishful. "I would enjoy that."

They sat apart from the others, James on the sand with his back against a slender palm tree and she on his knee. Moonlight sparkled on the water.

"James?"

"Yes?"

"I…" The words stuck in her throat, and she glanced away, picking at the remains of her meal.

"What is it, love?"

"Is it bad that I sometimes wish I could stay? That you couldn't get me home?"

"No," he answered softly. "It's not bad. I wish the same sometimes, but I know you'd be sad if you didn't get back to your family, and I would hate myself for denying you that happiness."

"But I'm happy here, too. With you."

His throat bobbed, and, for a short time, James said nothing. Instead, he stroked her hair with one finger and closed his eyes. "I promised to get you home, Belle, and I'll keep that promise. After that… I suppose we'll see what hand fate deals us."

Fate. Tink only wished there was a way she could have both things her heart wanted, but she feared fate would force her to choose one over the other, and she dreaded that day with all her soul.

Soft voices roused Tink from slumber. She didn't recall when she'd dozed off at the party, only that she had been on James's shoulder and now she was tucked into her little bed. Curious, she remained lying down and strained to listen to the voices beyond the curtain separating the room.

"But the sea witch can grant me my heart's desire," an unfamiliar voice said.

"True, but at a cost," Tiger Lily replied in her placid tones. "Think this through carefully, White Doe. She may grant your wish, but not in the way you hope, or at a price you will later regret."

"I… I know, but I have considered this for a long time, and I am ready to seek her aid."

Tiger Lily sighed. "Then travel the eastern beach northward until you've circled around the base of the mountain, past the point where the pink sands have faded to white. Once you reach where the sands blush pink once more, you'll have reached her home."

"*Thank* you, Tiger Lily."

"Don't thank me yet. I fear for what she may ask of you. Wait for the low tide and enter the cavern you find there. I pray the spirits give you guidance. Do not give of yourself blindly, dear one, and consider her offer well. Remember that she must have your permission to take her price."

"I will."

Tink cracked upon one eye and peeked, but no one noticed she'd awakened. She considered everything she'd heard and wondered if it was true. James had told her the sea witch protected the islands, which surely meant she was powerful and good.

But if the witch was good, why had Tiger Lily warned White Doe to beware?

Chapter 12

A DAY PASSED BEFORE Tink worked up the courage to venture to the northern coast and seek out the sea witch's lair. The few people she'd spoken to about the mysterious sorceress had warned her she was not to be trifled with, and that she always demanded a cost for her magic.

Even Anastasia says magic isn't free, so that's only fair for her to ask a price, Tink thought as she followed the directions up the beach.

Eventually the opal sand bleached white, a dull and lifeless ivory for a long stretch before a hint of blush peach appeared again at the northern face of the Aliki Mountain. The beach thinned and the sea lapped against the rocky shore, crashing against the stone outcroppings and throwing salty spray into the air.

Exactly as Tiger Lily described, Tink made out a cavernous entrance open to the sea.

"Hello?"

She drifted inside, keeping well above the water stirring and foaming around the sharp rocks below. Droplets falling from the ceiling forced her to zig and zag to keep dry.

"Hello?" she called again.

A low and raspy voice snaked around the rocks, appearing to come from all directions at once. "Come in, sweet. Come in."

Around a bend, the tunnel widened into a larger hollow. There, the water cast an eerie blue glow with no discernible light source. A stone ridge led deeper into the cave, where crabs scuttled across the wet floor to a lone figure standing alongside a raised basin carved from the rock.

Dark hair hung around the witch's shoulders in lank strands that reminded Tink of slimy seaweed. Her pale peach skin had a prunish, damp appearance. She wore rags woven from old plant matter and had bone ornaments in her black hair. In place of legs, she had a single long tail winding over the rocks and coiling beneath, though it resembled a dead earthworm more than anything.

Tink hesitated. She darted behind a hanging rock and began to rethink her impulsive decision.

"Don't be shy. Come out and see me. It's been so long since a visitor has come to visit me and now the fates have brought two of you within a day of each other. Come to me, dear child."

"I can do this," Tink whispered. Abandoning her hiding spot, she crossed the room and landed on the basin's edge. "Hello. Are you the sea witch?"

From afar, the woman had appeared huge and intimidating enough to gobble a sprite in a single bite. Closer quarters made it apparent her lower body made up the bulk of her size. Tink's pulse raced.

"I am, and I know what it is you want, little one."

"Y-you do?"

"I could make you as large as a human, my dear. And you would be able to do all of those things you dream of. To dance along the beach with the sisters of Tiger Lily's tribe. To climb the trees with your hands instead of flitting through the branches. You'd dine alongside the pirates who adore you so well, sitting in a chair instead of perched on the edge of a plate. Wouldn't you enjoy that?"

"Really?" Tink clasped both of her hands together.

"Truly. You'd be able to do all of these things if I worked my magic over you. I ask for only one thing in return."

"Anything!" Tink cried. Her heart pounded in her chest, its ecstatic rhythm flushing her body with heat.

"Your wings."

She froze, her elation doused by a cold surge of fear. "My *wings?*"

"Yes. It is no trifling thing you ask me to do. Your wings are a tender component to many… useful potions, and were you to give those to me, I could make all your dreams come true. Besides, what good are they to you if you would prefer to be human?"

"But… if you remove them, then it's permanent."

The sea witch leaned forward, widening grin revealing her mouth of wicked shark teeth. "Indeed. Isn't that what you want? Wouldn't you prefer to remain a human forever, to never find yourself caged and threatened again?"

"I… I don't know. I thought maybe it could only be for a few days, so I could see what it was like."

"And go back to being small? Why deny yourself a new human life?"

Tink bit her lower lip and hung back. She'd never taken into consideration that she'd be losing her wings if she wanted to become human.

"Think of all you could do," the witch cajoled. "You could hold hands with your man."

"I never said there was a man."

The witch clucked her tongue. "My sweet, there is *always* a man involved in requests like this."

"I don't know..."

"It's a small price to pay for what you want. You won't need them, anyway."

The harder the witch tried to convince her, the greater Tink's terror grew. To give her wings meant she'd never have fairy dust again. She'd never work magic, never fly, never help others with her tinkering. "No. You can't have my wings. I won't give them to you. I need them."

"Think carefully on this, little sprite. You are lucky you came to me when you did. Should one more night pass, I won't be able to cast the spell at all for another year. This is your last chance to become a human forever."

"I..." Tink flitted her wings and glanced over a shoulder. Her wings made her who she was, and as much as she longed to walk alongside James on the beach, hand in hand, as true lovers could, she knew in her heart she'd regret her choice. "I just can't!"

Tink shot from the grotto and into the night air with tears streaming down her cheeks. In all her life, she'd never come so close to acquiring what she wanted and had to let it go.

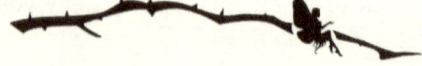

Two days had passed since Belle disappeared to explore the island alone, but she spoke few words to James since her return. Sometimes he thought he heard her sobbing. At other times, soft hints of blue and green shone from the rear bedroom of her dollhouse.

After a failed attempt to coax her out with a piece of cheese, he sought Eliza's aid. "Something's wrong with Belle," he said to her. "She's retreated to her dollhouse, and when I try to speak with her, she refuses to emerge. Not even to eat with me at dinner."

"What did you do to her?" Eliza asked.

James blinked. "I did nothing."

"Perhaps she is homesick. Give her time, James."

"Perhaps," he said, unconvinced. "Just the same, would you speak with her?"

"If she's mad at you, she'll hardly speak to me while you're here."

"She isn't mad. Trust me. She'd be bright as an ember. She's… she's very sad, and there's nothing I can do to help her," he admitted in defeat. "Just speak with her, and I'll leave."

It went against everything in his heart to go, but he was at a loss for what to do. What mattered most was that someone could talk to Belle, even if that someone wasn't him. After squeezing Eliza's hand, he left the cabin and stepped into the balmy, tropical air.

Outside his room, life seemed so normal. Days among the islanders had rejuvenated the crew, providing the pleasant downtime they'd been denied by having to set sail early from Ankirith. Of the few men who remained aboard the ship, a handful had collected on the deck for drinking games with overflowing cups of ale with small glasses of dark, island rum plunked into the bottom of the mugs.

"Join us for a drink, Cap'n?" a pirate called out.

"Or a game!" called another.

"We've 'bout got the stores refreshed."

"No thanks, Brody."

Many bewildered stares followed him to the rail, and a single hushed whisper reached his ears. "What've they done to the captain? He never turns down a drink."

And they were right. He should have joined them, but Belle's misery soured his taste for alcohol and celebration. All he wanted, all he longed for, was to soothe the weeping woman in his room.

"I'm off for a swim and a walk." Maybe the exertion would help clear his mind and set his worries aside, at least for a time. James kicked off his boots and pulled off his shirt, then set his cutlass and pistol on the pile. It wasn't a far swim, and the waters in the bay had calmed to a crystalline, glittering plane beneath the sun.

"We'll keep an ear out for when you come back," Brody called.

James dived off the side into the cool waters. Without surfacing, he kicked and stroked, putting distance between himself and the Jolly Roger before the need for air forced him upward. It only took a few minutes of swimming before his feet found sand beneath them and he slogged his way through the surf to the wet sand. His pants clung to his legs, heavy with water, but he knew it would only be a matter of time before the sun dried them. Slicking his hair back from his face, he wandered up the beach and considered whether or not he wanted to go into the settlement, but ultimately veered away from the path. With so many heavy thoughts on his mind, he wanted to be alone.

Belle's sorrow mirrored the turmoil he held in his own

heart. With the days of leisure rapidly coming toward an end, he dreaded the day they would reach Cairn Ocland and begin the trip to her home. No matter what he told her or himself, he wasn't ready to watch her leave.

The only options ahead of him held no appeal. He could leave the Jolly Roger and stay with Belle, but it would mean giving up a life he loved and abandoning the people who relied on him.

But if he remained with the Jolly Roger, he'd lose Belle. It didn't matter her small stature, he cared for her all the same. Her smiles brightened his days and had renewed the dimming fire within him. When he thought of Rapunzel, he no longer experienced the heartache and remorse, only a quiet regret that he'd never been able to say goodbye and a hope that her life was a good one.

"Hey, wait for me!"

James paused midstep and twisted around to see Peter racing toward him. The boy skidded to a halt and grinned up at him, eyes bright with merriment and cheeks flushed red from exertion.

"Joining me for a walk?" James asked.

"If you don't mind," Peter replied as he fell into step beside him. "I was hoping to see you again, but you've been so busy."

"Loading everything back onto the ship is quite the chore," James said with a quiet laugh. "Why? What did you need to see me about?"

"Well…" Peter wrung his hands together and took a few deep breaths, as though building up his courage. "You're leaving again soon, right?"

"In a few days, yes. I've promised to get Belle home. She's

been away for far too long, and her family is certainly worried about her."

"Was she lost?"

"In a way. Like you, she was captured and put on a ship to be sold."

Peter frowned. "That's awful. But at least you saved her."

"We did, yes. By the way, how's Tootles? I haven't been over to Callum's yet." The mage and his wife had decided to adopt Tootles into their family.

"He seems happy. Quiet as a mouse, though."

The description fit, but hearing the boy was adjusting took a load off his heart. "I'll be sure to stop by and check up on him. I'm also glad you'll be here to help him out after we leave."

"Oh, well, um…"

James's brows drew together. "Is something the matter?"

"I want to join your crew," Peter said in a rush.

James stopped short. In hindsight, the request shouldn't have surprised him, but all the same he studied the boy with concern. "Peter, our life isn't like the fanciful stories you like to tell."

"I know. It's a lot of hard work, and it can be dangerous, but I want to be like you. I want to go out there and help other lost boys and girls get away from the monsters."

"What about the boys and girls here? They all look up to you."

"Nah, they don't need me," Peter said, ducking his head to hide his blush. "Not really. They all have families now, and they all love Tiger Lily."

"What about the family you stay with?" James asked.

"I live in the tree house."

"Peter—"

"I'm not bad, I promise," the boy blurted. "I'm just restless, that's all. I want to be out there with you on the Jolly Roger. I love the ship, James. Please? I'm only asking for one chance."

It was on the tip of his tongue to deny him, but then James remembered how he'd been at that age. Young. Eager. Hungry for adventure. Someone had taken a chance on him, so who was he to deny Peter that same chance?

"Pack what you need and tell your family. You can bunk with Smee if he's not against the idea."

A huge smile spread across the boy's face, and he threw his arms around James's waist, hugging him tight. "Thank you! I promise you won't be disappointed."

"I'm sure I won't, but I want you to think on this in the meantime." James looked down at the boy and met his gaze. "There's no turning back once we've set sail. If you decide a few days in that you hate it, you'll be stuck onboard until we return here to Neverland."

"I know, and I promise I won't start to fuss."

"Like I said, think on it over the next couple days. If you're still resolved on joining us for the long voyage to Cairn Ocland, I'll be glad to have you."

"You're the best, James. I mean… aye, aye, Captain Hook."

Like a flash, Peter was off again, racing up the path to the town center. James watched him and chuckled, already feeling lighter in his heart. He only hoped Belle would soon experience the same.

VIVIENNE SAVAGE

Tink strained to eavesdrop on the two humans, but Eliza and James spoke in low voices too soft for even her hearing. It wasn't until the door shut with a distinctive thump that she dared to draw back the curtains Cook had sewn for her. Instead of finding James, she peered at Eliza's concerned face. The mage had taken a seat on the floor with her arms folded on the trunk where the cage sat.

"Where's James?" Tink asked. She rubbed her slick cheeks with one wrist. Had he finally recognized her infatuation and sent Eliza to set her straight? Her cheeks burned hot.

"Gone for a walk."

"Oh."

"He says you haven't been eating."

"I'm not hungry."

"Sure you don't have room for your favorite fruit?" Eliza reached down to the satchel clipped to her belt and removed a single star-shaped berry. It glistened in the candlelight, ripe and swollen with sweet juice.

Tink's belly rumbled. "I'm not hungry," she lied again.

"Oh?" Eliza tossed the berry into her own mouth, and then the wicked woman removed an identical fruit from the same bag. "Dancing Willow plucked these herself for me, and I thought I'd share them with you, but if you're not hungry…"

Hunger pains cramped Tink's stomach, but her willpower endured. If she could turn down cheese, she could down turn anything. "Don't want any."

"Oh, okay," Eliza said. Her subtle smile remained as she rifled through the sack and found another in a shade of purple, the largest yet. As it rose toward the pirate's mouth, Tink flailed both hands and darted forward to take it. Eliza smirked. "I didn't think you would resist for long."

Tink settled on the edge of the trunk with the berry and bit into it. Juice dribbled down her chin despite her effort to appear ladylike and refined. Wasn't that how James liked them? Refined and poised like Tiger Lily? Or even Eliza? All the women Tink had met since joining the Jolly Roger appeared to be graceful, whether they were mages, warriors, or the natives of Wai Alei.

"Now then, will you tell me what's wrong? What troubles you, sweetling?"

Tink plucked the towel hung by the tiny dinner table and dipped it into the small barrel of fresh water to wash her sticky face. "I tried to become big, but… I couldn't."

Eliza's eyes widened. "Whyever would you want that? And how did you try?"

"Doesn't matter," Tink mumbled. She kicked at a dustball and stared at the floor. "I'm always gonna be tiny, and that's all he's going to see. His tiny little pet."

"He? Do you mean James?" Eliza sucked in a sharp breath then leaned down, lowering her voice to a gentle whisper. "Belle, do you like James?"

She continued to stare stubbornly at her feet.

"You do."

"What's it matter to you?" Tink snapped. A red glow sparked down her wings, and she hated it, wishing her emotions weren't always on display. For the first time in her life, she wished with all her tiny soul to be something she wasn't for more than a passing, impulsive thought. The desire stayed with her and burned through her soul. "I can't be big, so I'm not a threat."

VIVIENNE SAVAGE

"Whoa now. Threat?" Eliza held up both hands, palms out. "What are you talking about?"

"I can't steal him away from you." Pressure built in her chest and hot tears gathered in her eyes while she waited for Eliza to begin laughing at her.

"Tinker Bell, James is his own man. You wouldn't be stealing him from anybody."

"But aren't you...?" Tink sniffled and rubbed her cheeks. "I know you spend time with Dancing Willow, but when you came in... I thought... I worried you and James were..."

"James and I were what? Oh no, darling. No, no, no," Eliza said in a rush. A minor shudder went through her, accompanied by an exaggerated gag. "He's nothing more than a brother to me. We grew up together, you know."

"He mentioned that. He said you were close."

"And we are, but not that close. Not ever." She offered out her hand and, once Tink hopped on her palm, raised the sprite to her eye level. "Have you told him?"

"What's the use? I'm tiny. He's big. The sea witch's price was too high." But now she was beginning to have doubts. Wouldn't being with James make up for not having her wings? Not that it mattered. If what the witch said was true, she'd have to wait a full year for the chance to make the deal again.

Eliza studied her in silence for several moments. Tink paced across her palm, waiting for a lecture or the inevitable laughter. Neither one came. Instead, Eliza smiled.

"You know, there is more magic in this world than the sea witch," the healer said.

"I know. Our queen is a sorceress, but even she can't make me big, I'm sure."

"Have you ever asked her?"

"Well… no." Tink frowned. "I've never wanted to be until now. I've never *needed* to be. But what does it matter? She's so far away."

"Powerful your queen may be, but again, she isn't the only source of magic in this world. In fact, there's a shaman not far from Tiger Lily's village. Ghost Hawk lives alone by choice and ventures into the town when it comes time to trade. The locals buy medicines and potions from him, and his price is never as steep as the sea witch. And if it is, it's because it must be, not because he wants to prosper."

Tink's sour mood perked up. "Do you think he can help?"

"It doesn't hurt to ask. So, what do you say? Will you come out now and stop hiding away in there? James has been distraught."

"Distraught?" Tink echoed.

"Surely you've noticed. He's been worried sick that you were ill, or even mad at him."

"Oh no!" She fluttered up from Eliza's hand, flashing between red and blue. "I don't want him to think I'm mad at him."

"Well, since he's away, why don't you go and see the shaman? Then you'll be able to come back and talk to James knowing you tried. No more hiding out and crying in your room. Deal?"

"Deal."

Chapter 13

BETWEEN INSTRUCTIONS FROM Eliza and some of the locals, Tink managed to find her way to the western marsh where the shaman had made his home. The house stood on stilts between two large willow trees, contrasting the homes in the main village by its dull exterior. Rocks jutting up from the water provided the only dry passage for anyone on foot, making Tink glad she could fly over the shallow water flooding the area.

"Hello?"

Instead of a door, thick hides hung over the entrance. Tink buzzed around and searched for a way inside, but she didn't find any windows or chinks small enough for her to pass through.

"Hello," she called out again. "Is anyone home?"

"I had a feeling you might wander down my way." The deep, gravelly voice came from behind and below her.

Tink spun around. A thin figure with close-shorn gray hair emerged from the thick ferns a few feet away. He carried a pouch filled to the brim with mushrooms and plants slung over his shoulder.

"You understand me?"

The old man smiled, teeth bright within his dark face. "I understand you just fine. I've heard the townsfolk buzzing about the little glowing woman who arrived on Hook's ship.

My dreams told me you'd come my way, and here you are."

"Really? You dreamed of me?"

His warm laugh put her at ease. "Sometimes the spirits see fit to tell me a thing or two. I see better in my dreams than in my old age."

Drifting closer placed her at face level with him and revealed his cloudy, blind eyes. "I'm Tinker Bell."

"Pleasure to meet you. You may call me Ghost Hawk, or simply Hawk if you like."

Once Hawk moved past her, he ascended the steep ramp leading to the mouth of the hut. One gnarled hand held the wobbling rail while the other protected the overflowing contents of his bag.

"I can carry that up for you if you'd like," she offered.

"Can you now? A small thing like you."

"I might be small, but sprites are strong."

"Then I'll accept your kind offer."

The bag was heavier than it appeared, and a peek inside revealed a thick layer of dirt and gnarled plant roots. A quick sprinkle of fairy dust from her beating wings lightened the burden and allowed Tink to carry it to the makeshift door. The old man followed her to the top of the ramp.

"Please come inside," he invited, sweeping back the heavy hides. "The bag goes on the table, if you would be so kind."

Inside it was dark, and Tink provided the only light until Hawk clapped his hands, and a dozen candles lit at once. Their flickering luminescence revealed a tidy room filled with clay flasks on shelves, strange and frightening masks on the walls, books, maps, bowls filled with shells, and other odds and ends. Tink drifted over to one mask that reminded her of Conall's wolven shape.

"Like my totems?"

"What do they do?" she asked.

"Do? Not much except hang there and scare my visitors." His wide smile made his eyes crinkle at the corners. "But they allow me to focus and commune with the dream spirits."

"Are they your gods?"

"In a sense, perhaps. Now, tell me, what has brought you to me?"

Tink abandoned the mask and fluttered over to the shaman. "I want to be big."

"Big like what? A bird? Or perhaps as big as a tree?" he asked.

"No, big like a human. I want to live like them and see what it's like."

"Ah, I see." He dipped his chin. "I have a feeling I'm not the first one you asked for this. What did Caecilia ask for, hmm?"

"Who?"

"The sea witch."

"Oh… I didn't know she had a name."

"She had a whole other life, but that's a story for another time, I think. So? What price did she give you?"

"She wanted to cut off my wings. You… you won't ask to cut them off, too, will you?"

"I have no need for sprite wings, so they're safe from me."

"Good." She blew out a relieved breath and ventured closer.

"As a human, however, you'd be without them until the spell wears off."

"So, you can do it? You can make me big?"

"I can give you what you ask for, but only for a short while.

It will not be permanent, for such magic would have too dear a price to you."

"That's okay! I only want to see what it's like for a little while so I can do more things with James."

Hawk chuckled and followed her with his hazy gaze. "I see. I can grant you three days and three nights, but there will be a price."

Only three days? Her spirits drooped and she lowered to a perch on the table. Were three days long enough to learn what it truly was to be human? To spend time with James the way she wanted to?

"What's the cost?" she asked.

Ghost Hawk's smile faded, leaving a solemn expression on his wizened face. "For all magic, there is always something to be given in exchange. To make you human, even for so short a time as three days, will cost you some of the time you have remaining in this world. One year of your short life for each day. This is by no choosing of my own, but what fate has designed for miracles of this nature, to give you, such a small sprite, the body of a mortal woman."

Three days meant three years. Tink had never pondered her lifespan before. Until James, no one had ever given her any reason to question her mortality. Sprites lived fleeting, brief lives filled with happiness and play. She'd already seen double-digit summers when Conall saved her from a trap years ago. How long had she been with him since then?

How old am I? How long will I be here? she wondered.

As they were so little, even a short time seemed a great while to the peaceful woodkin.

"Three years could be all I have," she whispered.

Ghost Hawk offered his hand and she climbed up onto his palm, allowing him to lift her up to his eye level. His opaque, unseeing eyes stared straight through her. "Very close I'd say, but of course, the choice is yours."

"What would you do?" she asked him.

"Are you happy as you are now?"

"Yes."

"Do you love yourself?"

"I do."

"Then why do you want to do this? Why become a mortal woman?"

"I…" She thought of all the experiences she'd longed to do. She wanted to hold little Kendric in her arms. She wanted to sit at the dinner table among her friends and hold their hands. To ride a horse. To swing a weapon. To spin the impressive wheel at the helm of the ship and leap joyously into James's arms.

She wanted him to lift her from the floor and spin her around the quarterdeck with her crushed to his chest, not because she weighed less than an ounce, but because she was a mortal woman of his own size.

Closing her eyes, Tink imagined so many wonders humans took for granted.

"I want to experience life as a human."

"The Wai Alei have a saying we teach our children. 'Live each day as if it may be the last.' There is truth in these words, little one. No one knows with certainty when their end will come, but it is up to us to enjoy each day knowing when it arrives, we will have no regrets."

Tink nodded. "Do you have any regrets?" He was old, certainly he'd lived a long enough time to accomplish everything he could possibly dream of doing.

"Only one."

While tempted to ask, something in his sad voice and forlorn features dissuaded Tink. "I want to do it. Not only for James, but for me. I want to experience things before I'm gone." She wanted to return to her homeland with amazing stories of climbing the mast, firing the cannons, and dancing across the deck beneath the full moon. And, most of all, she didn't want to live the rest of her short life regretting a missed opportunity.

"As you wish."

Ghost Hawk set her aside on the table and moved to his counter, sorting through an array of jars and pots. Tink lingered behind him, out of the way, too curious not to watch but half afraid of what she'd see him mix up. Hawk crushed herbs and pearls together in his mortar, adding unlabeled oils and strange roots she had never seen before. With each step, the shaman chanted in a language she realized she didn't understand, which was a first.

"Now it's up to you to add the final ingredients," he said, beckoning her over. "Come. Come."

"What do I need to add? I don't know how to offer up my age."

He offered her a thorn, the tip of it as sharp and narrow as her lost dagger. "Three drops of your blood, no more, no less, and a sprinkle of your dust will do."

Tink drew a crimson droplet from her finger and made sure it dripped into the mixture, followed by two more. The magical concoction puffed out hazy pink smoke.

"Now the dust, little one, and hold your intentions in your heart."

  VIVIENNE SAVAGE

Please make me big. Make me human, she wished as she held her hands to her heart and fluttered over the potion. Fine golden motes of dust sprinkled down and disappeared into the mixture, turning it from murky brown with pink steam to a pearly hue laced with gold.

Hawk gave it a final stir then scooped it all into a tiny glass vial as big as she was tall. It had shrunk and cooked down to a fraction of its original volume, filling less than half the vessel.

"Now what?"

"Take this back to your ship and drink it all down. Every little bit."

"Will it taste bad?"

"Potions are rarely sweet, little one. It might upset you some, but you must drink it all. If you do not drink it tonight, the potion will lose its potency, but your years will still have been given."

"Thank you, Ghost Hawk."

"Go, and be happy."

Chapter 14

Tink took the potion back to the ship as instructed and gobbled the vial down once she was within the privacy of James's room. The amount bloated her belly and left her curled in a fetal position on the floor. Nothing had changed except for the addition of a sour stomach on top of her anxious nerves. The drink hadn't been pleasant, as warned, and she thought she might be sick.

One moment she was darting for a little bowl to vomit in and the next, instead of flying, she was running. On feet. Two big and awkward feet, stumbling over a bunch in the floor rug and pitching her naked body to the floor. The little bits of her favorite flora dress floated down to the floor as mere scraps, although the leaves and grass had been wilting anyway and long overdue for a replacement from the new feather wardrobe she'd made.

The shaman hadn't mentioned that bit, although she should have realized the magical concoction wouldn't affect her clothing.

Nausea gone in an instant, Tink stared at herself in disbelief. Everything looked so much smaller, and the carpet under her feet had become soft and squishy, ticking her toes instead of swallowing her in the fibers.

"Oh no!" she realized, a hand flying to her throat. The fragile strand securing her pearl had popped, too, but the little pink pearl wasn't in sight. Fretting for her pretty trinket, she searched the floor on her hands and knees.

James's voice carried through the closed doorway. Panicked, Tink jumped to her feet and spun in circles while seeking clothes, unable to find anything but James's tidy wardrobe closet filled with breeches and tunics. The door opened.

"Honestly, Peter, do you never grow tired of climbing into the crow's nest?" James asked, though he was shouting for his voice to carry up to the young man.

"Noooooo," Tink silently screamed, no sound leaving her. He wasn't supposed to return yet, but he also hadn't stepped into the room or looked inside. He stood at the threshold, talking over his shoulder.

With nowhere else to hide, she leapt into the bed and burrowed beneath the covers, pulling them up and over her head.

The door thumped shut, and James's steps traveled from it to the trunk where he'd placed her dollhouse. "Damn. She's not back yet. Where could she..." After a moment of silence, and a low groan, his steps drew nearer to the bed. "I've told you before, I'm not interested."

Not interested? Oh goodness. He must have seen her, but when had he ever expressed his disinterest before?

He must have thought her to be one of the other ladies on the island who had become fixated on him, although they had seemed too numerous for Tink to count. Planning to flee the bed and dart away, until she remembered her missing wings, she continued to cower, with only the sheets against her bare skin, and nothing between them. "My wings!"

The shaman had warned her, but it hadn't clicked, and James had come in so soon after her transformation, the reality hadn't set in yet. She bolted upright, only the thin blanket held against her chest between them, her hair a tumbled mess around her pointed face.

The first mate of another pirate captain who frequented the islands had made it abundantly clear that she wanted to be in James's bed a year ago. So clear, she'd waltzed onto the deck of his ship, into his cabin, and actually crawled into his bed. Not a man on the Jolly Roger's crew had stopped her.

And why should they have any reason to suspect their captain would be disinterested?

Now that the Scarlet Brigade was moored nearby, she had done the exact same thing again.

"If I've said it once, I've said it a thousand bloody times, Patricia, stay out of my cabin and off my—"

The woman sprang up, defying his expectations of red curls and ruby lips. Belle gazed at him, instead, her face surrounded by disheveled golden waves of waist-length hair tumbling over his sheets and a body far too large to make any sense. If she could grow, she'd have told him, wouldn't she? Staring at her while willing his voice to cooperate with his brain, he realized when he saw her bare toes on the rug that she wore nothing but the steel gray linen.

"Uh," he said, normally so articulate, now struck dumb.

"My wings are gone. He said they'd go away, but I didn't realize how strange it would be," she blurted, making no sense to him whatsoever, because all of the blood necessary for nourishing his brain had promptly flooded to intimate southern regions.

"Um," James replied again, bewildered. "You're..." The sweeping gesture of his hand toward her woman-sized body failed to communicate his concerns.

"Big?" she finished for him.

"Yes. That."

Belle smiled in a bashful, adorable manner and patted the bed beside her. "Lie with me. Then I can tell you everything."

The invitation, as innocently as it was offered, brought his mind to the wrong places. He took a step closer to her while wiping his damp palm against his left thigh.

"Erm..." Something about the suggestive nature of her words after finding the woman of his dreams naked in his bed broke him, like a child's toy. A wrinkle furrowed his brow. Below his belt, he throbbed with an intense and sudden surge of arousal. "I don't think... *How* did you?" He ripped his gaze from her modest bosom to her face. She had freckles. "You're big."

"Is it okay? Do you like it?" Her smile dimmed. "Maybe you want to sit on the chaise instead?" She twisted, misjudging her meager covering, which gave him a glimpse of her slim, pale body. She was a flawless canvas of ivory, hair more golden than any blonde he had ever seen, eyes as bright and deep as emeralds. But there were no wings. No glow.

"No—I mean yes, yes it's okay." But why, was the better question? Why had she changed herself, and how had she done it? If she'd been able to change her size all along, why had she waited so long and until now? He approached her slowly but didn't move into the vacant spot beside her. "Why were you in my bed, Belle?" he asked gently. He tugged the sheet to cover the long length of bare thigh and exposed hip.

"Oh, well, when I changed, my clothes didn't. So…" Her lips pressed together, and a flush swept into her face, but it wasn't the same as the red glow he'd become accustomed to when she was angry. Belle stood, and the sheet fell away. "I'll go then, if you're unhappy."

"Go? And where the hell do you plan to go, naked as the day you were born?" Were fae even born naked? He knew nothing of them but what his sprite had told him, as there were none in Eisland, their magical creatures only ice elementals and stone nymphs in the mountains. And the latter were terrifying, horrible, and wicked she-beasts who dragged men into cavern walls to devour them. Nothing like her, with her radiance and innocent smiles.

Catching the edge of the sheet with his hook, he drew it back up and attempted to cover her again.

"Am I ugly?" she blurted. "I must be an ugly human."

"What? No. Far from it, and there are men aboard this vessel who haven't had a woman in months. While I'd like to think the best of them all, I'd prefer not to have to shoot anyone and toss his corpse into the sea for disrespecting you." That was a half-truth, since most of those men had a woman of their own or had visited the island's brothel by now. If James was honest with himself, he wasn't prepared to share her beauty with the world.

"Oh." She sat down again and allowed him to cover her.

Unprepared for the conversation required by their situation, he gingerly sat beside her. His hand fell to her thigh.

"Now, let's start over again so you can please tell how you came to be this way."

"I wanted to do things with you," she mumbled, looking down at her feet rather than up at his face. "The shaman said it would only last for three days."

"You did this for me?" His chest became as tight as the constrictive trousers, and he shifted, grateful her eyes hadn't dropped to his lap.

"Yes," she whispered. "For us both."

He missed her wings. It felt a petty, ridiculous thing to want back, but it was such an integral part of her that she seemed almost different. The lack of pointed ears changed her entire face, though her curves were as sumptuous and delightful. Only bigger. He'd have to sacrifice his bed to her, of course, as was the gentlemanly thing to do. "I'll fetch clothes for you from Eliza. You're about her size now. Would you like that?"

"I suppose so." She wriggled her toes into the soft carpet and giggled. Shyness melted away and she looked up with a big grin. "Does this mean I can wear a dress? Something pretty so we can take a walk together on the beach."

"You can wear whatever you like, Belle. Perhaps we can even acquire a few pretty dresses from town." Bartering a wardrobe for her wouldn't be difficult, as they were always weaving beautiful silks and dyeing them for the young women. He imagined her in them, and the relentless, merciless throb worsened. "I should find you something to wear in the meantime." Having the restraint to resist her didn't mean he wanted to continue punishing himself.

"You're not happy, though." Her brows scrunched together. "I wanted… I thought you liked me. So I went to the sea witch, but she wanted to chop off my wings." She shuddered, her whole body trembling, while his own stomach dropped and a chill crawled up his spine. "But then the shaman said he could help me, and all it cost was my time and help. He said I'd get my wings back when I go small again, but for now I could enjoy being big."

"I *am* happy, Belle." Albeit horrified when she mentioned Caecilia. He was always happy whenever his sprite was near, and he'd begun to dread the return trip to Cairn Ocland because he didn't know how he could survive her not sleeping in his quarters at night. He'd miss her singing in the morning, her cheerful twinkling whenever he shared a new wedge of cheese from the pantry, and he'd... He struggled with his emotions.

Belle raised his left hand from her thigh and pressed their palms together, the same way she'd done a million times when her entire body was smaller than his pinky. With a larger hand, she laced their fingers together. "Your hand has rough spots," she said in wonder.

"Indeed," he murmured. She still smelled like his Belle, despite her larger size, feminine and sweet, with a hint of floral fragrance.

"Mine don't. Is that bad?"

"Not at all. Mine are rough from a lifetime of working on boats." Despite himself, James raised her knuckles to his lips and delivered a gentle kiss. "You're very beautiful like this, but I'd never want for you to lose your wings," he finally told her before fixing his gaze on her face. "And I also don't want you to go near the sea witch again."

"Oh, I won't." She leaned close and lowered her voice, face serious. "She's scary." She gave a solemn little nod and inched closer, until their thighs touched. "Do you really mean it?"

"That you're beautiful? Have I ever lied to you?"

"No, you haven't."

A disconnect occurred between his brain and aching arousal, urging him until he ended their handhold and curved an arm around her waist. Lifting her onto his lap was easy, both of her slim thighs together, the sheet still bunched around her front. He touched his nose against her hair and breathed her in, hating himself for being weak.

She settled in against him and laid her cheek on his shoulder. "James?"

"Yes?"

She turned her head, breath feathering across his neck, one hand settling on his chest. "Do you think you'd ever want me to stay like this?"

"Stay like this?" Once more she had reduced him to a state of babbling and repeating her like a fool. He groaned when she wiggled against him, seeming too innocent to realize what she'd done—what she was still doing to him—and for that reason, he tried to still his fingers without pawing her up and down.

"Big, I mean. Like you."

"You're meant to be a sprite, Belle. The better question to ask is whether you'd be happy to stay like this? Would you be happy to sacrifice days on the wind, flying from flower to flower?" He took one of her small hands and traced her palm. "Would you miss your magic?"

Belle wiggled again, albeit gently, and any theories he had related to her innocence shattered. His fae knew exactly what she'd done, because she did it again, urging a low groan from him.

"I would miss flying," she admitted. "But when I'm small, I can't do this." She kissed his collarbone. "Or hold your hand. Or share a proper meal." She leaned back so she could look in his face. "I only have a short time like this. A short time left with you."

She truly had done it for him. "We've shared many proper meals." In addition to Patrick's gift, Little Wolf had carved her the prettiest little dining plates and teacups from bone, and each day, she ate opposite James at his private table in his quarters with her choice of tableware. But he knew what she meant. Ideas danced through his mind of walking barefoot alongside her over the warm sand and holding her in his arms. And then he thought of her longing for Cairn Ocland, missing her friends, and resenting him for the loss of her wings.

"If you did this to have three days with me, three days is what you shall have." He ached to kiss her, so he did, slow and tender at first when he claimed her lips, knowing he would be the first while also selfishly wishing he could be the last.

She made a quiet little sound, surprise and pleasure mixed together with eagerness. James coaxed her lips apart, and she followed his lead. Her fingers gripped his shirt and fumbled with the laces until the silk parted and his skin was beneath her touch.

He wanted to touch her everywhere, savor the taste of her skin, and strip away the thin sheet that concealed everything he'd fantasized about touching in human proportions. With a low groan, he drew his mouth away from hers, breathless from the effort. "But I will dine with you and walk you across the beach first. Before anything else. You deserve so much more, but I will give you that."

Setting her aside required superhuman effort, willpower he'd never needed for any other act. He rose from the bed and cleared his throat, leaving his back to her. "I'll fetch a proper dress for you from Eliza."

He didn't run from the room, but it seemed a close thing. The moment he had the door closed behind him, he pressed his back to the wood and drew in several deep breaths.

Patience, James, he counseled himself.

Few men stirred on the deck, most enjoying time off in the town, but a few lingered over a game of cards. An enormous bowl of liquid sat in the center of the table, receiving donations from each man's drinking cup at the start of every round. By now, it would be filled with a mixture of beer, whiskey, rum, and gods knew what else. James grimaced. He'd played the game many times before as a young man. He'd even thought drinking the pot was the prize. As an older man, he knew better.

"Is Eliza onboard?"

"Aye, Cap'n. Saw her heading to her room with a bottle of wine about an hour ago."

"Thank you." He headed down to the quarters assigned to his officers and rapped on Eliza's door.

"Eliza, I need a moment of your time." When she failed to answer, he banged on the wooden panel, practically knocking down the cabin door in his effort to rouse her from sleep. "Eliza!" he bellowed.

He was normally a man capable of controlling his mood and emotions, but Belle in a human-sized body had left him uncharacteristically flustered. All the times he'd wished her to be a larger being, he'd never considered it could actually happen.

"Godsdammit, what?" Eliza jerked open the door, shamelessly nude from the waist up, save an unbelted silk robe revealing the narrow swath of bare skin between her breasts. She put her hands to her hips and glared at him. Behind her, a local woman lay on the narrow bed amidst the rumpled sheets. Dancing Willow was always among the first to welcome them whenever their ship arrived. Now he knew why.

Of course, everyone aboard the ship had a lover but him at this rate. Even Smee had met a lovely widow in Ankirith who he plied with gifts whenever they reached port.

James grunted. "I need to borrow a dress, and then I'll be out of your way."

"A dress? Do I look like I keep dresses lying around?"

He fixed her with a stern glare. "I know you do," he replied. "You never threw any of your things away after we left Eisland, and I recall a handful of dresses for social affairs. As for why…" He released a long-held sigh. It wouldn't remain secret for long, and there was nothing to gain by hiding it. "Belle has… grown enough to require proper attire."

"Aha! So she did it after all. Excellent."

"Wait, you *knew* about this?"

Eliza smiled smugly and crossed her arms over her chest. "Maybe. A dress for Tinker Bell, you say…"

"She can have mine," Dancing Willow offered.

"Thank you. You have my appreciation."

Both women bustled about half-dressed, much to James's chagrin. He stepped inside to close the door and immediately turned his back out of modesty's sake. Eliza was a beautiful woman, curvy and toned, but he had never looked at her with any more fondness than that of a sister.

"Here you go. Let her try these." They plied him with a pile of clothes, a mixture of native islander wear and sophisticated Eislander fashion.

"I'll return them all in good condition, I assure you."

"Be kind with her, James," Eliza warned. "And bring her by when you're no longer occupied with other activities." Both girls giggled.

"I didn't plan to be anything but kind to her." They gave him an armful of women's clothing, but he couldn't open the door to leave, his hook sliding uselessly over the knob. He grunted and shuffled the pile to free his hand. "Thank you, ladies, and now I'll be out of your way." Whether he occupied Belle with other activities had yet to be decided. Was it appropriate— more importantly, was it fair to her?

Chapter 15

Tink wasn't sure whether to be amused or annoyed by the flustered pirate. With his bedsheet wrapped around her in a makeshift gown, she explored the rest of the cabin.

Everything had transformed, no longer an intimidating landscape of dangerous objects and shadows. She admired the saber collection on the wall, a glossy assortment of swords in varying sizes and styles from a dozen different countries. She only knew that because James had told her about each and every weapon.

From above, she studied the model ships on the table, some of which had been painstakingly pieced together inside bottles when James had both hands. He'd given up the hobby after losing his right.

Refusing to leave fingerprints all over the glass, she bounded over to her gilded home and admired it from her new viewpoint. Pretty as it was, it was still a cage. She leaned down and drew in a deep inhalation of the flowers, only to sneeze when the pollen went up her nose. She leapt back and swiped at her face before skipping off to explore the next thing. She peered through the tinted glass windows, spun James's globe, and picked up all the things that had been too big and heavy for her before without fairy dust.

James returned with a load of clothing, opening and shutting the door with his left hand while he clutched a pile of garments against his chest with his right arm.

Tink squealed and rushed over to help, relieving him of the burden. "All of that is for me?" she asked as he guided her to the bed.

"Well, you can see what you like, and then we'll get you your own from town. Eliza and her, um, friend kindly offered these on loan." He plucked a dress from the pile and held it up to her chest, his hook within one of the delicate straps. Her cheeks warmed when the back of his left hand skimmed her bare shoulder.

"You mean the girl she sleeps with?"

"How would you know about that?"

"People don't notice small things. I saw lots around the ship, not that I was spying," she added in a rush. "I mean, she just comes and goes on the ship a lot since we arrived."

His brows raised first, a dubious expression on his face.

"I like to watch people when I'm not with you or fixing things for Patrick."

"Ah, well. That's understandable. There's a lot to be learned by watching others."

Once James finished spreading the clothes over the bed, arranging garments together as they were intended to be worn, Tink stepped up alongside him and studied the borrowed wardrobe.

"Which do you like?"

"This is about what you like, Belle. Try them on. I'll be just outside the door."

"You don't have to leave your own room," she blurted out, "unless I make you uncomfortable."

"Far from it, but a gentleman never ogles his lady friends,

especially while they're preparing for an outing." Giving her no chance to argue the point, James left the room and shut the door behind him.

The first dress reminded her of bed curtains, and the thick, green material itched against her arms. Worse, the collar choked her, tight and high around her slender neck.

"Ugh. No." Tink wrinkled her nose, shucked the garment off, and set it to the side. The next dress reminded her of one of Sorcha's fancy gowns, although she wore them infrequently and only to fancy get-togethers among the clans. The canary yellow fabric and dozens of ruffles appealed to her taste, but the skirt was too short in the front. She was fairly certain it was meant to fall to her ankles. As beautiful as Eliza's dresses were, they didn't suit Tink.

She turned her attention to the next two dresses and shimmied into the pink and white sheath. It had no straps, was lighter and simpler than the other two garments, and had accents in aquamarine that matched the pristine waters off the coast. Tiny beads made from coral had been stitched into delicate lacework.

"I'm ready," she called out.

James stepped inside and froze in the doorway. He looked her up and down, his gaze lingering first on her bare feet then moving up the rest of her. In another step, he had the door kicked shut behind him and his hand curled around her nape.

When he kissed her again, all she wanted was to remove the dress and cast it aside. Her heart fluttered when he leaned back to gaze at her, his blue eyes lidded with unconcealed desire.

"Shall we take our walk now?"

"Y-yes," she stammered.

"Excellent."

He tucked her arm in his and opened the door, allowing her to step through first before he pulled it shut behind him. The full moon hung high in the sky, casting silver light over the deck, the only illumination besides a lantern hanging from a hook on the main mast. Three men sat around a table under the lantern with cards in their hands, a pot of booze in the center, and silver bits in a pile on the table around it. When one glanced over and blinked, the others twisted around to see what he was gawking at.

"They're all staring," she whispered.

"They've only ever seen you as a buzzing ball of light."

The pirates jumped to their feet and offered cordial greetings. One even bowed. Tink smiled shyly and tightened her grip on James's arm.

"Belle and I will be going for a walk. Keep an eye on the Jolly Roger for me, would you?"

"Aye, aye, Cap'n."

"Bye, Harras, Osrim, and Frederick," Tink said as they passed.

Thankfully, shedding her tiny body hadn't altered her agility too much. She climbed down into the longboat with minimal help from James. He rowed them ashore to the small dock then swept her into his arms before she could step onto the rough planks. Tink squealed and clutched his shoulders, fingers curling into the fabric of his shirt. James chuckled and carried her across the treacherous walkway. He didn't set her down until they reached the beach, where the golden sand retained the day's heat.

"It sort of tickles." Tink burrowed her toes into the sand and spun about. The dress swished around her knees, and the breeze tousled her hair. She skipped forward a few feet, pausing an inch beyond the water washing up on the shore. James stepped up behind her and took her hand in his.

"Since you only have three days, did you want me to keep the Jolly Roger here at the island?"

Tink shook her head. "No. I can't learn to sail if we're in port."

"Sail?" The warmth of his laughter tickled across her hand when he brought it to his lips. "Is that what you want to do with your three days as a human?"

"One thing at least. You can show me how to steer the ship, unfurl the sails, and catch fish. I'm a good learner. I really am."

"If that's what you want, who am I to deny you? But what of tonight?"

"Well..." She dragged her toes through the wet sand and let the water wash over her feet. "I see couples dancing sometimes. In the town square. Then they go eat and shop."

"It's a little late for shopping."

Her brow wrinkled. "But they all go into a building with beaded curtains in the windows."

James made a strange sound that sounded like a laugh crossed with a choke. Tink crossed her arms and waited for him to regain his composure.

"Forgive me," he said. "That's not, ah, a place for shopping. At least, not in the sense you understand."

"What do they all go in there for, then?"

His gaze darted away, and a warm flush crept into his cheeks. "It's a brothel, Belle."

Her brows drew inward. "I don't understand that word. What's a brothel?"

"A house of ill repute, as some would call it in my former kingdom."

"Ohhh. They're ill? Is it like a healer's clinic? Oh, I want to go! If there are nice people like Eliza, I want to meet them."

"People pay for sex," he said in a rush, catching her by the hand and pulling her back before she took more than two steps.

She jerked to a stop and blinked, then stared at him for a long moment without understanding. Why did people pay for something that was meant to be between lovers?

"We don't have places like that in Cairn Ocland. Most shifters mate for life, so they don't get intimate like that before bonding." Clearing her throat didn't diminish the heat rushing to her face. Had it not been for those smoldering kisses in his cabin, she'd wonder if James would ever consider being intimate with her.

"The shapeshifters of your kingdom must be quite fortunate to find their better halves so easily."

"It isn't always easy," Tink protested. "Conall had to track down an evil skinwalker with his mate to earn her love, and he helped her destroy a wicked faerie."

His brows shot up, and his eyes widened. "Oh?"

"Yes, and our king was cursed for years by a fairy until his mate showed up and battled an invading kingdom. She broke the spell on him."

"Your people sound fierce. And drowning in fairies."

"Not really. I only know of two. A good one and a bad one, but Maeval is dead for real this time."

"Well, I'm glad to hear that."

James pulled her in close, taking her right hand in his left before placing his hook flat against her back. Then he began to move and guide her to take small steps to the left then the right.

"What are we doing?" she asked.

"Dancing."

"But there's no music."

"Would you like some?"

"I thought you needed music to dance," she said.

"Ah, but you can always hear music in your heart and mind, if you want to."

"But what if we're listening to different tunes?"

James laughed and dipped his head, claiming a kiss that was too brief for Tink's liking. Then he began to sing, and her irritation vanished. Bringing her closer, James sang in a rich baritone against her ear, their bodies pressed together as they moved across the sand beneath the moonlight.

"I never knew you could sing," she said some time later as they walked hand in hand down the beach.

"I don't do so often."

"Why not? You have a lovely voice."

James came to a stop and turned to face her. Their heights were almost even, only a couple scant inches separating them. Eliza only came to his shoulder, and it was with sudden glee that Tink realized she was taller than the woman.

"I only sing when I'm truly happy, I suppose." He cupped her cheek in his hand and stroked his thumb across her lips. "I feel like I'm dreaming."

"But you're not. I'm here. I'm a woman now."

"You were always a woman, Belle."

"A *big* woman, then. A *human* woman. And… I want to experience all that I can in the time I have. With you."

She watched his face as she spoke, her heart racing so fast she wondered if it would burst in her chest. Would he feel the same?

"This has to be a dream," he whispered again. "Yet here you are before me, and I haven't the slightest clue what to do. Three days seems so little."

"Then we'll make the best of them," she said.

"That we will."

He offered her his arm, and they made their way back to the boat. As much as she didn't want their evening to end, she looked forward to having him alone again in his room, away from prying eyes.

"How do you row?" she asked once they'd pushed out from the shore.

"Come here, and I'll show you."

Careful not to tip the boat, Tink moved around and took a seat in front of him, her back to his chest. "Is it hard to row with your hook?"

"Not hard exactly, but it took some practice. We screwed in these small loops on the oars, you see? So I can hook through one. Now place your hands like mine and I'll show you how it's done."

Under his instruction, she rowed them around the bay in circles for a time, in no rush to leave the warm embrace of his arms. She cherished every touch and every laugh they shared, but eventually her arms grew tired from the effort and James took the oars once more and rowed them back to the ship.

Once they climbed the rope ladder to the deck, they retired to his cabin.

"My arms hurt," she whined. Far too much to resume the search for her pearl, which she'd wanted to do right away without admitting to James she had lost it.

"It takes time to build up the muscle. Without your magic, you'll find moving heavy things takes quite a bit more effort."

Tink flopped down on the bed and stretched out, enjoying the soft comfort of his mattress and blankets. It was no wonder he slept so soundly each night.

"I'll leave you to sleep and see you in the morning," James said, taking a step toward the door.

"Please don't go." She reached out a hand for him.

"You need to rest."

"So do you," Tink countered. "See? I barely fill up your bed. There's room for you, too."

"It wouldn't be appropriate for the men to know I'm sleeping in here with you."

"Why not? You always sleep in here with me."

"I—" He stopped short and then chuckled, running his hand up and down the back of his neck. "I suppose you're right. However, it would be more prudent of me to take a hammock below."

"James, please. It's your bed and… and I like sleeping with you." She loved listening to his even, deep breaths and seeing the peaceful look on his face.

"As you wish," he said in a soft voice. Then he crossed to the door and turned the lock, ensuring no one would barge in upon them. "I didn't think to ask the ladies for nightclothes for you."

"That's all right. I can wear this."

James nodded, silent and pensive, crossing the room toward his desk while he began to fiddle with his hook.

"Here, let me help." She bounced up from the bed and crossed the distance between them. Night after night, she had watched him remove his hook prior to bed. The limb had been severed above the wrist, a neat and rounded stump just below a muscular forearm. She traced her fingers down the cool metal before giving the device a twist. At least she tried to.

James smiled. "You have to press that little button there, remember?"

"Oh. Right." As a sprite, she'd watched this part of his undressing ritual multiple times during their weeks at sea, but standing alongside him in a human body added a new layer of intimacy. Heat surged to her face again, so hot she feared her body was compensating for her lack of magic by glowing in another way.

She located the small depression and pushed as she twisted. The whole device came off smoothly, detaching from a metal cuff that had been fused to his arm by some unknown magic. It looked different now that she was big. James stood perfectly still while she explored his arm and ran her fingers over the band.

"Does it hurt?"

James's stoic features softened. "No. Not really. There are phantom twinges at times, but I've learned to live with them."

"The hook is so light." She hefted it in her hand a few times, startled by the unexpected discovery. She'd always imagined it being heavy.

"Specially crafted in Samahara by their finest artisans.

Nigel had it commissioned for me, actually. I think it started off as a joke, but I rather like it."

"You always have a weapon," she murmured.

"Indeed. It took a while to learn how to use it in a fight, but it's saved my life more times than I can count."

While she put the hook away in its case, James kicked off his boots. And nothing else. Tink put her hands on her hips and studied him.

"James, why do you always sleep in all of your clothes?"

"Not all of them."

Her gaze dropped to his stocking feet and swept over his breeches, sash, gun belt, and shirt. "You took off your boots. That's it."

"Technically, that means I'm not in all of my clothes."

"Smartass," she muttered.

"Tsk, tsk, such language."

"You've said worse," she countered. "And you didn't answer my question."

"As the captain of the ship, it's my duty to be prepared for anything. It wouldn't do to be caught in my britches during an attack and, despite what you've seen, we are constantly at threat by the Eisland and Ridaeron navies."

"Fair enough, but we're in port now. In the one place you've said neither of those groups can ever breach."

"I did say that, didn't I?"

When Tink reached for his pistol, James grabbed her by the wrist. Her gaze darted to his face, hoping her eyes were as imploring as she wanted them to be. "Tonight, please?"

"Belle…"

"You don't need this tonight." Her wrist slid from his grip

as easily as she drew the pistol from the tight leather band over his sash. She set it on the adjacent night table beside the bed and unbuckled him.

"Every night you undress behind the screen near your water closet. I want to see."

"Surely you've seen a man naked before."

Living among shifters and other sprites, who were prone to moments of spontaneous desire to skinny-dip in springs and puddles, meant she wasn't a stranger to unclothed bodies. "All the time, because most of the wolves are big sillies who don't know how to keep clothes on, but it's not the same. I want to see *you*."

"All right," he agreed in a quiet breath.

While her heart pounded a staccato beat, drumming inside her chest, she loosened the scarlet sash circling his waist. His shirt fell open, revealing hard abs and a smooth chest. With each exquisite inch she unveiled, James's perfection took her breath away. Seeing countless naked shifters throughout her lifetime hadn't prepared her for the sight, as none of those men had been hers to appreciate and caress to her heart's content.

"You don't have hair everywhere," she said, tracing her fingers across the muscled contours.

His husky chuckle made her stomach tighten and a flutter clench between her thighs. "Is that a bad thing?"

"No. It's different." She'd never met a shifter without a generous dusting of chest hair. Months ago, during a visit, she'd teased Ramsay that she couldn't tell the difference between his human and bear forms, for both were covered in golden brown fur.

Not once, in all her time among them, had she ever felt

anything remotely sexual for the shifters. She'd seen them as brothers, her kin, and beloved friends.

Was it the deep contrast between James and her dear friends that intrigued her the most, or was it something more?

It had to be more.

Fascinated with the carved dips and angles, as well as the muscular planes, she pushed his shirt back from his shoulders and let it pool on the floor. Her palms smoothed over his bare chest while James rested his hand on her hip.

"I want to see the rest."

James inclined his head. "As you wish."

A pair of laces stood between Tink and her goal. She tugged both loose. Once his breeches pooled around his ankles, desire made her mouth as dry as the Samaharan desert. She couldn't focus on anything above his waist, awestruck by the sheer masculine beauty of him.

"You're gorgeous," Tink whispered when she could finally meet his gaze again, attention skimming over his chiseled torso. His golden, tanned skin was offset by the dark treasure trail beginning below his navel.

"Gorgeous?" His low chuckle sent a stutter to her pulse.

"Yes." She couldn't fathom a more appropriate word.

She trailed her fingers down over his hips, then inward, until her knuckles skimmed his stiffened erection. James's fingers pressed into her soft skin, but he said nothing while she began her intimate exploration.

How was it possible, she wondered, for him to be both hard and soft all at once? Dark curls tickled her fingertips when she reached the base. Then she ran her fingers over the smooth skin and traced the ridges of its crown. His sharp breath prompted her to jerk her hand away. "I'm sorry!"

"For what?"

"I hurt you."

"Far from it." His gentle fingers interlaced with her slim digits. "I love your touch, but I won't be responsible for what happens if you continue that."

She shivered. Goosebumps arose over her skin, raising the hairs on her arms. "You don't have to be…"

"I would prefer to be a gentleman this night, and nothing you say will persuade me otherwise, Belle. No matter how much it tempts me." He kissed her, a tender and brief touch before parting contact altogether. James retreated to the small tile- and porcelain-lined box in his private privy, and then the sprinkling tap of water pelting the floor became the only noise in the room.

Now or never, Tink thought. She dropped the pretty sheath around her ankles and stepped toward the small door.

When she stepped inside, it was to the delicious view of James's muscled backside. His rear may as well have been carved from stone, the lean line of his back and sculpted shoulders as enticing as his front. Steam swept over her—she'd have to peek at their water source's inner workings one day when she returned to her normal size—and the aroma of spicy soap invaded her senses.

"This space is tiny."

He spun around to face her and slicked his hair back from his face. "What are you—"

"Joining you," she said, figuring it was obvious. She squeezed in alongside him and squeaked at the hot temperature. James liked his water near boiling.

"Sorry," he apologized, fumbling to reach the knobs.

"No, it's fine. Surprised me is all." She maneuvered around until the water sluiced over her cold body. Once wet, she adjusted to the temperature without any trouble. In truth, it was nothing compared to the heat of James's wet, naked body pressed to hers.

"This is rather—"

"Inappropriate?" she offered with a smile. "You like that word a *lot*."

"I was going to say delightful, but your word will suffice, as well."

Her smile dimmed. "Three days, James. I only get three days like this, and I want to enjoy them. Propriety be damned."

Indecision flickered across his face, as though he were waging an internal battle. Tink opened her mouth to say more, only to be silenced by a demanding kiss. Rather than sweet and chaste, he introduced her to her first true taste of passion, plundering her mouth with his lips and tongue. She moaned softly and surrendered beneath the onslaught, looping her arms around his neck.

Each kiss grew hungrier than the last, and sensation zipped along her body. His wandering, soapy left hand trailed over her ribs and teased her right breast, his coarse thumb circling the tensed nipple. Then his head dipped down to claim the same tight bud between his lips. She threw her head back and pleaded to the starry night beyond the porthole window for him to continue, but James didn't linger. His mouth explored higher until his lips reached her ear.

"Gods, you're tempting."

"Is that bad?"

  VIVIENNE SAVAGE

His teeth scraped across her earlobe. "You deserve more than me tossing you into bed, Belle. I'd like to give you a proper courtship."

"But—"

"I know you have only three days. So, grant me this and let me make those three days count. I promise, by your final night, every moment we've waited will be worth it." His nose skimmed down her bare throat. Then his lips sealed over the point of her wildly beating pulse. She trembled, body captured between the unyielding wall and his muscular physique.

"I need… I feel like I'm on fire," she whispered. The heat blazed through her, spreading from her core to every slender extremity.

"Then let me quench the flames."

His left hand slipped between her legs. With one touch, he turned her molten with desire. Tink writhed against the wall as the talented play of his fingers found her most sensitive spots. She rose to her tiptoes, and he followed with another thrust of his agile digits. The two fingers that had teased, buried inside her.

"James!"

His lips sought her mouth again and resumed the passionate kiss between them. Her entire body became sensitized and responsive to him, a flick of his thumb all it took to snap the tightening band of tension and reduce her to a quivering mess. Her knees no longer cooperated, and pleasure spread throughout her body in euphoric waves, turning her mind heady with bliss.

If not for James's body pressed so close, Tink was certain she would collapse in a limp, boneless pile to the wet floor. She struggled to draw in a proper breath, eyes closed and heart racing while James delivered tender kisses to her brow and cheeks.

"Have I rendered you speechless?" he asked in a low voice filled with mirth.

"I—that…" Words were impossible, so she gave up the attempt, much to his amusement. He kissed her again.

"That was a mere glimpse of what I promise to show you, Belle. But not tonight."

The knobs squeaked to her right, and the water shut off. James scooped her into his arms and carefully carried her from the shower to the bed. She didn't even care that she was wet. After what he'd done, the cooler air felt good against her flushed skin.

After laying her down, he disappeared, only to return with a towel. Then he dried her body and hair with the utmost care.

"Are you all right?" he asked.

"Uh-huh." She managed to crack open one eye, gaze focusing on his smiling face. "What?"

"I've never managed to render a woman mute before, and you look absolutely beautiful like this."

"Like what?"

"Euphoric," he replied. "You look as if I've made you the happiest woman in the world."

"I am happy," she agreed, reaching for him.

James tossed the towel aside and crawled beneath the sheets with her, pulling the blanket up to cover them both. Tink rolled over and snuggled against his side. If James's plan had been to exhaust her from pursuing her original intent, he'd succeeded. She wanted nothing more than to cuddle close and sleep.

"Is what you did a normal part of human sex?" she asked.

"For many, yes. There are many ways to share pleasure, Belle. Even to grant it to yourself."

His words provoked her curiosity, though, for once, she was hesitant to voice her questions. She didn't want to please herself.

"Do your kind make love?" James asked, interrupting her thoughts.

Tink shook her head. "Sometimes. We have the parts, but the desire isn't usually there. And if it is… we don't have babies. Sprites never have babies."

"Then how are sprites born? You came from somewhere. You didn't merely blink into existence."

"Oh, but we do. We're tied to the lives of the little ones in Cairn Ocland, and whenever a new baby laughs for the first time, a new sprite is born. Only the big fae get to have babies."

"I see. And what are big fae?"

"Fairy godmothers. Queen Anastasia's grandmother is a big fae, but a nice one. Not evil like Maeval was. She's beautiful and tall and radiant. I'm… an honorary fairy godmother, but I'm not the real thing."

James smoothed the drying strands of hair back from her face before his gentle kisses touched her brow. "I'm sure to your little godson, you will be. Now sleep, my Belle. Tomorrow, there are many wonders to teach you."

How could he possibly expect her to sleep for even a wink while his hard body pressed against her beneath the bedcovers?

Tink's hand crept beneath the sheets. Before she reached her prize, James caught her by the wrist and pressed her small hand against his chest, instead.

Fiddlesticks. So much for that plan.

Chapter 16

BELLE DIDN'T REALIZE how much of a temptation she posed. Exercising his willpower, he managed to leave her snuggled in bed. He tossed on clothes, adorned himself with the usual wardrobe befitting pirate life, and tucked his pistol into his belt. All the while he prepared for the day, his golden Belle lay motionless.

Unable to bear disturbing her, he vacated the cabin and made his way to the galley to find Cook preparing the breakfast platter he normally took in his room.

She blinked at him, eyes owlish behind her horn-rimmed spectacles. "Why aren't you in bed?"

"Should I be?"

"Well, we all assumed…"

Blast it all to oblivion. He'd been worried about this, and fixed Cook with a stern glare. "I know I'm not the purest man in the world, but I'm not a cad. You should know me better."

Cook met his censure with a hard look of her own. The older woman never withered under his gaze. "No one thinks you are, sonny, so settle down. But you and Belle are so close, and I've seen the way you look at her."

"She's a beautiful woman."

"*Before* she grew to your size."

James scowled, but he couldn't say a word to the contrary. "It's complicated."

"I'll say. I was certain I'd see neither hide nor hair of you both for three days. Nigel, Callum, and Eliza had already decided to divide your duties among them and set sail within the hour."

"Honestly, Savina, I'm not about to keep her locked up just to sate my sexual appetites."

Cook laughed and dished him up three fried eggs alongside crispy shredded yams with onion. "No one would blame you if you did, that's all I'm saying. Still, I'm glad to hear it. What's next then?"

"We get underway as planned. Belle wants to learn to sail."

"I suggest you find her some pants then, else no work will be getting done."

"Eliza's things are too short for her."

"Hmph. I'll see what I can do. Now git. Begone from my kitchen."

"As always, a pleasure talking with you, Cook."

Hoping the aroma of breakfast and melted cheese over eggs would awaken Belle from her slumber, he placed a tray on the table in his quarters. Afterward, he sought Nigel on the lower deck.

"Well, well, well. I didn't expect you to be up and moving this early."

"Why's that?" James asked, giving his friend the benefit of the doubt.

"Figured your face would still be buried between your Belle's thighs, is all."

James grunted. "You crass bastard."

"We all know how you feel about her, mate. Honestly. I merely wonder why, if she's got the magic to become a human woman, she's waited so long."

"She doesn't. This is temporary."

"Well then, as your best friend, I order you back to your cabin to get between those thighs."

"Nigel, mention her thighs again and friendship won't save you from this bullet."

"What? Thighs or no thighs, the woman of your dreams is in your cabin while you waste time on the deck, preparing to perform duties Smee and I can accomplish without you."

"Does everyone expect me to stay in my cabin shagging?"

"Pretty much. Callum and I had a wager on when you'd show your face. I lost." Nigel's frown placed deep furrows between his brows. "He said you'd be back to business as normal, and I thought you'd enjoy a little downtime with your lady love."

"We've had over a week of downtime while the ship underwent repairs, and even longer to allow the lads time with their families. Sorry to disappoint you, mate, but the little lady herself has asked for us to teach her how to sail. I aim to fulfill her wishes. *All* of them, not merely the ones she makes in bed."

Nigel's grin widened. "So you have been—" James reached for his pistol. "Been enjoying extracurricular activities, that is."

"What goes on between Belle and me is between us. Kindly ensure it remains that way."

"By your foul mood, I have my answer, but fine." His friend raised both palms to him in surrender. "It amazes me that your honor has remained wholly intact after years of piracy. Were you not the same man who claimed to leave no brothel unexplored?"

"That's different."

"Have you not had a lover in every port?"

"Quite different."

"I do recall you were once so drunk you swung around a light post in Ankirith and shouted, 'Dickings for everyone' until Joaidane ushered you away into the tower to sleep it off."

Heat surged over James's face. "I'd never had their desert fire rum before."

"What about that merchant woman whose ship we saved from sea poachers two years back. You two were rather chummy."

"Are you done?"

"Ah, James, you can't blame me for wondering. You swore there'd be no one for you again, not since you left Rapunzel in Eisland."

"Rapunzel and I were very young. I'm a far different man now, and I'm sure she's a different woman."

"Agreed. You've become an even greater man than the scared youngster she once knew. It's a shame Rapunzel and Joren haven't made a stand against the king's barbarism. Regardless, that old life is behind you, and Belle is here now."

"For a short while," he said in a quiet voice.

"Then I have another question for you. If this is temporary, if she's merely to be a woman for a few days, what will you do once she's small again? Once she returns to her people?"

His shoulders sagged beneath the crushing weight of reality. In three short days, the ideal and perfect woman would be no larger than his thumb again. "I don't know. I... considered asking her to remain as a member of the crew." But what he'd truly wanted to do in that moment, when he'd first entered the cabin to find her wrapped within his bed sheets, was lower to one knee and ask her to be his wife.

"She misses the little tyke and her friends. You know that."

"I do, and we're headed for Cairn Ocland as soon as we set off, as I promised."

"That returns us to my previous question. What will you do?"

James gazed at the island shoreline without an answer. The truth was, he had no idea, torn between desire and duty. Sensing his inner turmoil, Nigel pressed no further and left him alone to his thoughts.

Tink did not like pants, but James had insisted when she emerged from his private cabin in the dress she'd borrowed from Eliza's lover. When the wind kicked the hemline around her thighs, he dashed over and rushed her into his cabin again.

Then the big silly hadn't allowed her to leave, although they were quite similar in height. From what she could discern by comparing him to the crew, James stood among the tallest of them. Magic had made Tink his feminine equal, mere inches shy of the captain's impressive stature. He claimed her dresses to be inappropriate for sailing, each of them far too short.

Cook's timely arrival with altered castoffs from Eliza's wardrobe abruptly ended her isolation in the cabin. The older woman provided her with everything she needed to travel among the crew without causing unnecessary distraction or injuring herself.

At first, Tink had thought it unfair that James should require her to wear additional clothing, until he brought up her reaction when admiring his nude body. What reaction? As far as Tink recalled, she'd gone fuzzy and empty-headed the moment she removed his breeches.

"Thank you for making my point, Belle," James had murmured, making her want to swat the smug expression from him.

Hours later, she looked the part of a pirate, clothed in golden brown breeches stitched with additional fabric and a fitted leather vest over a white tunic. Callum had found a pair of Little Wolf's outgrown boots from three seasons ago before he'd hit his most recent growth spurt.

"How do the boots feel?" James asked.

"Odd. I've never had to wear shoes before."

"Trust me, you'll appreciate them after climbing rigging or running up and down the ladderwells. Your feet will be safe from splinters."

"Now that I'm dressed, what first?" She bounced on her toes, and her gaze darted to the door, eager as a wolf cub. James laughed at her enthusiasm and opened the door with a gallant bow, gesturing her through.

"We've left Neverland already," she cried, dismayed.

"You didn't miss much," he assured her. "We are at the mercy of the tides when it comes to certain ports, so it was either leave while the tide was high or wait around hours more, perhaps even another day."

The distant shoreline resembled a thin strip of pearl curving around thick clouds of dark green flora. With one hand raised to shield her eyes from the sun, she watched the beautiful island grow smaller on the horizon.

Had she possessed the foresight to realize how much

she'd miss the island, she would have asked for more time to explore, but one glimpse at James soothed her disappointment. Fate had placed her exactly where she needed to be, on a sea adventure alongside her pirate.

"What should I do first?" she asked. "Tell me everything about the role of a sailor. Does someone have a harder job than anyone else? Who's the most important?"

"One thing at a time." He took her hand and kissed her knuckles. "Every man on this ship has a duty to perform, and every man is equally important in the ship's operations. Without Cook, we couldn't eat—well, we'd eat, but rather miserably, I wager, and that's poor for morale when the pickings aren't generous in our raids. On top of repairing our arms, Patrick is a master shipwright, and I've seen no one better at the craft. Although Fatima is new, she's among the first to board another ship, and her enthusiasm inspires the others. I couldn't do this without Nigel or Callum. They're next in the chain of command, followed by Eliza, who mends our wounds and keeps us alive when we've been injured."

"What about Little Wolf? He didn't come with us."

"Without Little Wolf, we'll manage, but it won't be as easy. We've navigated these waters for years without him on board, faced down the Eisland Navy, outmaneuvered battleships from the Ridaeron Dynasty, and we're still here to tell the tales."

"When will you tell me all the tales?"

James chuckled. "You'll have to give me the chance first."

The day passed in a flurry of action. James took her around and introduced her to every aspect of the ship, while the crew went out of their way to make her welcome. Patrick taught her how to work the windlass for the anchor, and Peter showed her how to climb the ratlines to the top of the mast.

Up on the highest point of the ship, Tink almost felt as if she were flying. The wind whipped through her hair, and the rocking motion of the ship seemed exaggerated, as if the mast were a living entity swaying back and forth to throw her off.

"Most people think it's a punishment to be sent up to the crow's nest," Peter said. He clung to the ropes like a monkey.

"How come?"

"Because it sways so much. Most of them get sick."

"But not you?" she asked.

"Nah, I like it. Sometimes I pretend I'm flying. Is this what it feels like?"

She turned her face into the wind and closed her eyes. "A little, yes. As close as you can get, I suppose."

"I wish I could fly," Peter said with longing. "But as long as I can sail, that's fine, too. It's better than where I was."

Tink opened her eyes and peered down at the deck far below. James waited close to the mast, keeping a sharp eye on the pair of them, but he didn't call them down. In no rush to leave, she looked back at Peter and studied his freckled face.

"Will you tell me about it?"

The boy glanced away for a brief moment before looking back at her, his smile gone and his eyes sad. "I'm a Ridaeron, but I came from a poor family. My folks… Well, my father was a mean one, especially when he drank. He said it was 'cause we look nothing alike. And my mother…" He blinked a few times, failing to diminish the tears shimmering against his lashes. "She wasn't much better. It was her debts at the races that got me sold."

"I'm sorry," she whispered.

"At first I thought maybe it would be good. No more belt on my bottom and at least one for sure meal a day. It wasn't so bad until they piled us on the ship so thick you could barely breathe. Captain Hook saved me from that. Saved all of us."

"The other children all stayed in Neverland."

Peter's smile returned. "Tootles didn't. He's with Callum in his room. Wanted to come along with him, too, so the captain said it's all right."

"And the others?" Tink asked.

"Tiger Lily will find everyone homes. Real homes with nice folk. If she can't, or if they want to be on their own, they stay in the town and learn trades. Play."

"So why didn't you stay?" she asked.

"Because of this." He leaned out with one foot twisted in the lines and one hand gripping tight, the other stretched out into the air. A euphoric smile spread across his face, making Tink smile in return. She secured herself in the same manner and leaned out beside him, then giggled.

"You're right. It does feel like flying."

Later, once they'd climbed down, Nigel and James led her to the gun deck.

"You wanted to shoot the cannons, right?" Nigel asked.

Tink whooped and clapped her hands together. "You'll let me shoot the guns?"

"*A* gun," James said, "but only if you load it yourself. If you want to shoot the heavy artillery, you've also got to load them for the complete experience."

Something about their devious expressions raised the hairs on her nape, but she thought nothing of it and followed their instructions to the letter, already versed with cleaning the guns of gulls' nests and other debris. Ramming the charge down the mouth of the device wasn't as difficult as she expected it to be.

"Splendid job, Belle. Go and fetch a ball from the monkey."

Despite the warning in their amused voices, Tink rushed toward the brass plate designed for holding the stacked pyramid of iron cannonballs. Her fingers surrounded cool metal, and then she balked at the weight of it.

"It weighs a hundred pounds!" she cried.

"Twenty-four actually," Nigel said between snorts of laughter.

"Why aren't either of you helping me?"

"As we said, we're here to teach you, not do it for you, love."

And teach they did, maintaining a hands-off approach that provoked her into uttering a few of Conall's favorite words. Her arm muscles strained under the weight of it, and she waddled the entire way to the cannon. How did human men and women survive without fairy dust?

Nigel and James only laughed harder then. "*Now* you're a pirate," James said.

Despite her exhaustion and the sweat beading her brow by the end of it, there was nothing more satisfying than the thunderclap that hurled her cannonball across the sea. The recoil shook the enormous weapon, startling her, but she watched the iron projectile land with a splash.

And that was only the start of her morning. By evening, Cook had prepared an enormous dinner to celebrate Tink's first day as an official member of the crew. Her arms ached and her legs trembled with every step. Sitting down to eat with everyone had been a relief. When she finally couldn't stuff in another bite, she gracefully accepted James's suggestion that

VIVIENNE SAVAGE

she retire for the evening and retreated to the sanctuary of his cabin.

Fear of wasting their water stores drove her from the shower before she was ready to leave. She would have soaked beneath the steaming spray for hours if James hadn't knocked to ask if she needed help.

"My everything hurts," Tink whined as he toweled her dry. For balance, as her legs resisted cooperating with her commands, she rested both hands on his broad shoulders while he crouched before her, dabbing water from her shins.

"You asked to learn what it takes to become a sailor."

"I did," she admitted. But she hadn't expected the grueling day he'd created for her. Narrowing her eyes, she peered down at her pirate, aware of how he took his time. "You did this on purpose."

"Did what?" he asked, voice innocent.

"You created all of that work so I'd be too tired for sex."

"Would I do such a devious thing to you, my golden bell?"

Yes, she thought, pursing her lips and eyeing him.

"Did you ask to learn how to work on the Jolly Roger?" he asked.

"Well, yes."

"Did you want to see how hard the men work each day?"

"I did, but—"

"So then, by your agreement, we did everything *you* asked."

She huffed and stomped her foot, but James only laughed.

"What? What's so funny?"

"You did that once before, and I thought it the most adorable thing. I'm glad to see it remains so."

"I'm not supposed to be adorable," she grumbled.

He rose and wrapped the towel around her body, always impressing her with the deft maneuvers of his hook in lieu of his right hand. "You're gorgeous, but the act itself is adorable." Then he kissed her throat and found a sensitive spot that made her squirm. "Get in bed."

"I'm not sleepy."

"You told me you're exhausted."

Tink scowled up at him. "I said everything hurts."

"My mistake. What shall we do, then? A game of chess? I could read more from my book."

Tink turned her gaze to the windows where the golden light from the setting sun had already begun to dim. "Can we go out and look at the stars?" Eliza had suggested it just prior to dinner.

"Of course we can. Get dressed while I freshen up, and we'll go out for as long as you like."

James exited his quarters to find a deserted deck, empty save for one lone pirate making his way by with a mop. The wood gleamed beneath a fresh coat of aromatic oil, filling the sea-scented air with spice and heat from Samahara.

"Where is everyone?" Belle whispered.

"I don't know. I'd like to know the same."

Tom, the youngest member of the crew aside from Peter, picked up speed but failed to duck down the stairs and into the hold before James could address him.

"Where is everyone, Tom?"

"Ah, games have been moved to the quarters tonight,

Cap'n. Deck's all yours. Eliza said you wanted it."

James had said no such thing, positive he hadn't inferred it either. A glance behind him revealed Eliza at the helm. She mimed tipping a hat to him.

The blasted woman must have arranged for him and Belle to enjoy a private moment under the stars, and despite his irritation with her for failing to include him in the plan, his affection for her only grew. Eliza was a good friend.

James slid his arm around Belle's waist and guided her to the rail. "I suppose we have the deck to ourselves to stargaze to your heart's content."

"They all look so different out here." Belle raised one hand up to the sky, finger pointed outward, and traced the different constellations. "It's almost like you can touch them."

"You should see the nights when the ocean is completely still. It looks as though we're sailing amidst the stars." After moving behind her, James placed his hand on the rail to her left, his hook propped on it to the other side. It gleamed beneath the moonlight, reflecting the tranquil silver glow.

"I'd love to see that."

Belle leaned against his chest and tilted her head back, humming a quiet, melodic tune. He'd heard her singing before many times inside her little garden dollhouse, but he'd never asked about the words.

Soaking in her warmth, James wrapped both arms around her midsection and drew her flush with his body. The addictive floral fragrance he associated with her fairy dust wafted from her hair, present even when she was a human. Or was it his imagination and wishful thinking?

"Are you enjoying the night?" he asked in a quiet voice.

She shivered. "Yes."

"Cold?"

Belle shook her head.

Two streaks shot across the night sky, disappearing beyond the horizon. Belle gasped and leaned forward.

"Shooting stars," James said. "Have you never seen that before?"

"I have. In Cairn Ocland, the stars are said to be our gods watching over us. When one shoots across the sky, it's their way of sending us help. Or a gift."

"I've never heard of such a thing. You mean that figuratively, yes?"

Belle twisted in his embrace to face him. She tilted her face upward, moonlight reflected in her green eyes. "No, it's real. The sword they used to kill Maeval came from the stars themselves, sent when Sorcha asked for help. Don't you believe in the gods?"

Unable to resist touching her, James tucked a golden strand behind her ear and considered his response. "Our gods in Eisland are nothing like yours. They're beyond reach, and they certainly don't interact with us to provide miracles."

"That's so lonely."

"I've never thought so. It's taught me to rely on myself. My own decisions and actions."

Her nose scrunched and lips turned down at the corner. If she'd been in her natural state, there would be a cobalt glow surrounding her, kissed by a hint of purple. How long had it taken him to differentiate her moods? To learn each color and the subtle variances in color to read her emotions?

"I don't know," she finally said. "Conall makes his own

decisions. Well, he did before Sorcha. Now they make them together. He's not weak because he believes in the gods and needed their help once."

"I envy him, then." He kissed her brow then laid his cheek on her head. "I wonder whose prayers they're answering."

Belle said nothing and only held him tighter. She squeezed her arms around him then turned her head, bringing her lips to his.

Any other women he'd kissed may as well have been a lifetime ago, banished from his memory. There was only Belle, fondness for her overriding all else. And he couldn't get enough of her. No matter how much he tried, each sweet kiss led to another until he wished he had both hands to fully explore her body the way it deserved.

He had to wonder at his own honor sometimes, struggling to maintain his sensibilities when all he wanted to do was carry her to his cabin and never come out again. The memory of her cries in the shower haunted him, the sweet way her body tensed and responded to his touch a siren's song he no longer wanted to resist.

He tore his mouth away before lust overtook him completely and pressed his cheek to her brow, waiting for his racing heart to slow. Suddenly parched, he loathed his lack of foresight to bring drinks up to the deck. He glanced to the side and saw a tray on a folding table with a decanter of wine and two long-stem glasses.

Eliza. A subtle, magical shimmer still shone around its edges, the telltale sign of her using spells to summon and place objects. She could move and relocate small, inanimate things with a casual gesture of her hand.

"Shall we have a drink?" he asked.

"Yes, please."

More than wine awaited them on the table. Cook had taken the time to bake her famed petit fours. The tiny, iced delights were arranged on a silver plate with chocolate truffles and fresh berries from Neverland.

"This wine has bubbles." Belle held up the glass he passed to her and watched the small beads stream up to the surface.

"A special vintage from my family's vineyard."

"Yours?"

Her startled look reminded him of how much they had left to share about their lives—so many conversations to have and memories to relive. In a way, he was glad Little Wolf's absence would require them to rely on the natural wind, extending the duration of their voyage to her homeland. It gave him that much more time with her, as selfish as it was of him.

"Yes. We had half a case onboard when we left Eisland, and I've hoarded them over the years. At the time, my family was the only one who made the style. Now, there's no telling."

"I've never seen a vineyard. We don't make wine in Creag Morden, but Clan Ardal brews the best mead."

"I've never had much taste for the stuff."

"Then you've had bad mead," she told him in a serious voice.

"Perhaps so." He chuckled and sipped from his glass.

In true Belle fashion, she delighted over the way the bubbles tickled her tongue, then hopped from one subject to the next without any seeming connection.

"Eliza called you a manwhore once. What's that?"

A little wine went down wrong. James coughed until his

eyes watered. "She told you what?"

"Not to me, but I overheard it when she was speaking with Dancing Willow."

James grunted. "It's difficult to explain."

"Try me. I'm not dumb, James."

"I know you aren't." He blew out a heavy breath and averted his gaze. "There was a time before I met you when I slept with many women. I'd bed anyone with two legs. Sometimes even one," he said in a quiet voice. "And I'm not particularly proud of that man."

"And the brothels?"

He hated that she'd ever learned about them but gave a little nod. "Aye, I've visited my fair share of them as well. In Samahara mostly, and sometimes Liang, but never in Neverland. The island is…" It was different, too pure for his worst behavior. He'd always controlled himself while there, even if there were some island women who practiced the sensual arts.

"Is that why you're reluctant to be with me and wanted to court me?"

"I suppose so," he said after a heavy breath. "Such rakish behavior is encouraged among the Eisland elite, for men and women both. Successful young nobles have the freedom to do what they want, and our cities hold several gambling dens where pleasures of the flesh are always available. However, I don't want to treat you like any other conquest I've had in some other land and tossed aside once it was time to ship out or move on. I want…" What the hell did he want? He tried to grasp it, but the slippery concept eluded him until he gazed into Belle's green eyes.

Something about her had wound around his heart and wouldn't let go. It wasn't that he was afraid of using her—he was afraid of *losing* her. Somehow in the months of their voyage together, she'd come to mean more than any woman of his past. She was the only woman he wanted in his future.

If he wanted to uphold his promise, he'd have to return her to Cairn Ocland and say goodbye in less than a month.

How had a sprite become his ideal woman?

"Well?" she prompted in the same gentle voice.

"I want you to stay aboard the Jolly Roger. With me." And with the stars as his witness, he wished she could.

James made the one offer she could never accept. How could she possibly choose to remain on the Jolly Roger when her family waited for her back home?

He watched her with imploring blue eyes, waiting for her to respond. "Belle?"

"Um."

"You won't stay."

"I didn't say that…"

"But you didn't say you would, either," he pointed out. A weak, fleeting smile came over his face. "It's all right. I understand. You have a life in Cairn Ocland, and you're eager to return to it."

"I miss the baby," Tink said. "I'm supposed to protect him."

"And you can't do that from a ship. I understand."

Despite his composed response, Tink's shoulders drooped with guilt. Was she any better than the James Hook of the past, eager to enjoy his body before flying away to her old life?

"I have a letter to write Joaidane. He supplied me vital news about the upcoming travel routes planned by Ridaeron, and I should send him my gratitude."

"James—"

He kissed her brow and smoothed her wind-tousled blonde strands away from her face. "Come to bed when you're ready, love."

After his descending steps faded and the door to his private cabin closed behind him, Tink sank down to sit at the makeshift table. She tipped back the remainder of her wine and gazed glumly at the tranquil water reflecting the starlit night.

I wish… I wish I could be with James always.

When nothing happened, Tink refilled her glass. She sipped a while longer, lost in her thoughts until the thud of footfalls against wood drew her attention to the hatchway. Eliza came down the steps from the quarterdeck and frowned.

"Drinking alone? Where's James? And why haven't you eaten any of those cakes?"

"He has a letter to write."

"Ah, I see. Enjoying the fresh air a while longer?"

Tink nodded.

"I can't blame you," Eliza said. "The smell of rum has been infused into the wood in that damned cabin of his. It would help if he opened the windows."

"What are you doing out here?"

"Keeping the Jolly Roger on course is my duty tonight. The bunch of us, we alternate, you see. It should be James, but as your time with him is limited, I claimed the wheel."

Belle and the Pirate 250

"That was nice of you. We didn't even notice you."

"There isn't much I wouldn't do for him." Eliza crossed the last little bit of distance between them and laid a hand on her shoulder. "You're looking troubled."

"I am."

"It's just us girls up here. Want to talk about it?"

"Don't you have to steer the ship?"

"It's fine. The wheel is lashed since we're on a straight course for a bit. So? Will you tell me why you look so glum?"

Tink, clasped her hands on her lap and shrugged, gaze trained on her slippered feet.

"What's the pompous lout done now?" Eliza demanded. "Honestly, Belle, if he's hurt you somehow, I'll set him straight myself."

"No, it's nothing like that," she said in a rush, looking up. "It's… He wants me to stay on the Jolly Roger."

Eliza's fair brows lifted. "Does he now? Well then, what's the problem?"

"I'll be small again soon." She rose from the seat and moved to the rail, shoulders slumped. "I want to stay, but I'm Kendric's godmother. My family is so far away."

"I know how it is to miss your family. When we left Eisland, I left behind friends and cousins. Even a man who might have one day become my husband."

Tink turned, putting her back to the rail, and looked at Eliza in surprise. "You did?"

"We all have someone back home we can't see anymore without risking our safety, but I wouldn't change my decision if it was offered to me. Sometimes we have to go where life leads us, even if it's away from those we love, because you never know when it will bring you to others you'll love as much or even more."

"I never thought of it that way... But..." Tink wrung her hands together. "I don't know how long I'll be around."

"What do you mean?"

"Sprites live very short lives. I... I never counted mine in human years before, but we age differently. We're born as adults, not children. And... I have only a year or two left. I'm old, Eliza."

"You're scared of leaving him."

"What will he do if I tell him the truth?"

"The only thing he can do, my friend. James will love you deeply for what little time you have. But you don't need me to tell you this, Belle. He'll tell you it on his own if you share your concerns with him."

Tink nodded and wiped her face. "Being human is exhausting."

"It can be at times." She offered a sympathetic smile. "Tell you what. Since I'm stuck up here for another two hours at least, why don't you go enjoy the tub in my cabin?"

"Oh, I don't know... I already washed and that's your room."

"And I'm offering it to you for a bit. Mull things over, relax in the water, then go and talk with James. Take the plate with you. Trust me, a bath with wine and sweets is the best cure for a burdened heart."

"Thanks, Eliza."

"Anytime. And, Tink, no matter what you decide, all your friends here on the Jolly Roger will support you."

As she wound her way down through the ship to the

officers' quarters, Tink's heart wasn't eased. If anything, Eliza's kindness and easy friendship complicated the decision. The Jolly Roger had become like a home to her, and the crew her family.

How could she possibly abandon one family for another? James had said they weren't due to return westward to Cairn Ocland's shores and had ships to raid in the east, but they would travel hundreds of miles out of their way to deliver her safely home.

Tears sprang to her eyes anew when she entered Eliza's private bedchambers. She shut the door behind her and made her way into the back of the room where a pretty porcelain, four-claw tub sat behind a screen made of wood and thin paper. Painted butterflies and flowers covered the delicate material. A small table nearby provided the perfect spot to set the tray of sweets and the wine.

Tink started the water and sat on the rim while it began to fill. James had boasted about the Jolly Roger's plumbing, claiming his ship had been the first to outfit more than the captain's cabin with hot water and pipes. Even the shared berthing deck had a small shower for the crew.

While she waited, she reached across to the table to sample the petit fours. The thin layers of cake, sweet fruit, and icing truly were a delight. She'd never tasted anything so airy and delicious. Greedy for more, she popped another two into her mouth and closed her eyes as she experienced dessert heaven.

"Tink!"

Startled by the cry, Tink tumbled off the ledge of the tub and hit the deck, coughing and sputtering her mouthful of cake. She rubbed her stinging backside and looked around in confusion, certain the voice calling her name had been Sorcha.

"Hello?"

"Tink, over here."

Sorcha's voice echoed from a nearby oval mirror hung on the wall. Instead of Tink's reflection, two of her favorite people peered back at her.

"Queen Anastasia? Sorcha! What took you so long?" Tink cried. She'd been waiting forever for them to contact her with the queen's crystal ball. For two-way communication, Anastasia required the recipient of her messages to have a reflective surface at hand.

"Thank the stars," Sorcha sobbed. Her shoulders shook as she sniffled and wiped her face with one wrist. She clutched Kendric to her bosom with the other arm. "We thought you were dead. We were certain you—wait a moment. Where are your wings? You're *large*."

"Only for one more night. A nice shaman helped me, but only after a sea witch asked to cut off my wings forever. I wanted to know what it was like to be big for a little while."

The two women wore matching expressions of horror. Anastasia recovered first. "Tinker Bell, what's happened? You've been gone for *months* now. Conall enlisted Ramsay and Victoria's aid. Even Alistair and Teagan have gone out into the southern woods seeking you."

Sorcha leaned closer to her. "We were so worried something had happened to you when they found evidence of poachers from Liang inhabiting the lowlands."

"Poachers did happen to me," Tink said grimly. "But I'm free now."

"Where are you? Conall had enough and set out on foot

over a month ago. Queen Anastasia searched all of Cairn Ocland and even Liang for you."

Tink bit her lower lip. "I'm not in Cairn Ocland anymore. I'm on a ship in the Viridian Sea."

Sorcha's eyes widened. "The Viridian Sea?"

"The poachers sold me to Ridaeron merchants, and then a pirate ship sacked them." When both women turned white as sheets, Tink hastily continued, "But the pirates are my friends and they're very nice people!"

"Tink, pirates are dangerous," Anastasia told her. "Creag Morden has a small naval fleet, and they've run afoul of pirates before. They steal whatever they can."

"Not James," Tink declared, defending the man with a fierceness that surprised even herself. "He saves people. He rescues children bound for the slave markets and sees them to safety and freedom. He's a very good man."

"James…" Anastasia stared at her. "James, as in James *Hook?*"

"You've heard of him?" Her smile brightened. Of course they'd heard of him. How could they not, when he helped so many people?

"Tink, he's a murderer!" the queen admonished her. "You must escape at once—no, wait, where are you? Have you any idea of your location? I can send Alistair to fly to you at once."

Horrified by the accusation, Tink reeled backward and stared at Anastasia. "That's a lie! I've never seen James murder anyone—well, he did shoot a sea hawk, but it was trying to eat me," she reasoned, finding absolute logic in the single killing. "The Lost Boys love him, and Tiger Lily says he's a good leader."

Queen Anastasia's eyes appeared positively stormy, arcane

light shimmering within her green irises. "I've pinpointed your location and found you. I will send my husband at once to fetch you and dispatch with this criminal. It's for the best, and for the safety of all who travel the seas."

"No!" Tink cried. "What about what's best for *me*? I love him, and I want to stay with him. Whatever you've heard about James isn't true."

"King Harold of Eisland himself told the tale to my father. I heard every word regarding this man's atrocities," Anastasia began. "He—"

"It's lies told by an awful king who deals in slavery. Eisland is full of monsters. If you take James away, I'll… I'll hate you forever!"

Sorcha gasped. "Tink."

"I'll hate all of you, and I'll never forgive you." And then she burst into tears, unable to stop the torrent of moisture flooding down her cheeks. She wanted to love them for caring enough to rescue her, and loathe them equally for daring to utter a word against James's sterling reputation. As a sprite, she'd never experienced more than one emotion at a time, but as a human, they became too complicated to control. "He's a good man. He *helps* people."

Stunned, the two women said nothing, speechless throughout Tink's insuppressible sobs.

"Ana, could it be possible that there could be any truth at all to whatever this man has told her?"

"I… My father and King Harold are good friends. Victoria's mother is his niece. I can't imagine such lies lasting for long without a shred of truth to them."

"Victoria's mother isn't the most likeable of people," Sorcha reminded her. "She was banished back to Eisland, remember?"

"I'd always assumed her to be one of a small minority… For many years, James Hook has been a boogeyman of sorts, plundering all merchant ships in the Viridian Sea."

"He left because they wanted him to ship slaves," Tink said between sobs. "He r-rescues ch-children. I've seen it myself."

Ana's lips thinned. "During our last trip, I did see an unusual number of young people in their vineyards. I was told they were all paid, though, or working off debts."

"They wouldn't likely put children out there with visiting dignitaries nearby, now would they?" Sorcha said.

The queen's expression turned grim. "I will speak to my father at once and investigate the matter. As far as I'm aware, slavery is outlawed in all civilized kingdoms save the Ridaeron Dynasty. And they're not part of our Compact."

Tink sniffled and swiped at her wet cheeks. "I want to stay here. James will bring me home when he can. He promised, and I believe him."

When Anastasia opened her mouth to speak again, Sorcha laid a hand against the queen's shoulder and leaned forward. "We miss you, Tink," she said. "Very much. Conall will be relieved to know harm hasn't befallen you."

"I'm sorry you all were worried. I avoided one trap but fell into another. If it wasn't for James, who knows where I'd be. He said the ship I was on was headed for Ridaeron."

Anastasia pursed her lips then dipped her head in deference to Sorcha. "When he brings you home, we'll have to thank him. In the meantime, I'll investigate the matter of slaves in Eisland personally. I consider it an affront to everything my father has worked for if Eisland has broken the Compact behind his back."

"James is safe?"

Anastasia nodded. "I wouldn't break my word to you. I can't imagine an evil man gaining your trust easily. Sprites are often excellent judges of character."

"We'll leave you to the rest of your bath, Tink, I…" Sorcha sniffled again and rubbed her cheek. "You look very beautiful big, even if it is different to see you without wings."

Beautiful? Sorcha thought she was beautiful?

Still drying her face, she nodded and murmured a shy, "Thank you" before the two women bid her to have a good evening and the queen ended the spell.

Left exhausted by her crying fit, Tink crawled into the bathtub and sank to her chin in the hot water. She tilted her head back against the rim and closed her eyes, wondering how many others out in the world believed the lies about James and his crew. For one terrible moment, she wondered if Anastasia's fears had any foundation. Could James be fooling her?

"No."

She dismissed the thought almost as soon as it had formed, guilt swamping her and flooding her with cold despite the water. As the sole audience of his deepest thoughts and worries, no one knew the soul of Captain James Hook better than Tink. Eisland had lied.

Aside from the occasional soak with Sorcha and dip in a freshwater spring, Tink had never enjoyed an actual bath prior to James pouring her a bowl for the dollhouse. She lingered with her wine and sweets until her fingertips wrinkled and the plate was empty, then crawled from the bath. She emptied the tub using the elaborate pipe system, dried, and shrugged into her dress.

When she entered the cabin, James was sitting at his desk. He'd already uncapped his usual bottle of rum, from which he often drank at night prior to bed, and slumped forward with his brow against his left palm. He didn't move when she shut the door.

"Is your letter finished? Would you like me to seal it and take it to Ylis?"

"Please. Tell her it's for Joaidane."

Tink found pleasure in doing the simpler things for him. James may have adapted to life with one hand, but nothing rewarded her as much as his smiles of gratitude. "Eliza lent me her bath," she said while folding the letter and tucking it into the leather cylinder used for Callum's messenger bird.

"I thought you smelled of her orange blossoms."

Before an awkward mood could settle between them, she hurried from the cabin and to Ylis's roost. A small holster had been secured to the eagle's feathered leg with a metal band.

When Tink returned, James still hadn't moved from the seat. Sensing something was amiss, she joined him at the desk and slipped into his lap, burying her face against his throat and simply breathing in the scent of rum and spice. They remained that way for a long while, his arms around her, one hand smoothing up and down between her shoulder blades.

She lived for the quiet moments, and wondered if they'd ever be the same once she was small again.

"Have you changed your mind?" he asked, voice calm and nonjudgmental. "It's all right if you have."

"No. I still want you."

"But…?"

"I don't know what to do yet. But I do know, for now, that I want to stay with you. I told the queen not to send her dragon to get me."

"The queen? As in Queen Anastasia of Cairn Ocland? That queen?"

"Uh-huh."

"How in the world did you speak with her when we're in the middle of the Viridian Sea?"

"Oh, um… Queen Anastasia has this crystal ball, you see, and she finally found me in it. I talked to her in a mirror."

"At this point, nothing about you should surprise me," James muttered. "But are you saying you had a chance to go home? It'll be weeks before we reach the Cairn Ocland shore, love, especially now that we're lacking Little Wolf's guidance."

Tink raised her face to gaze into his blue eyes. "The queen wanted to fly here to rescue me and lock you away. I told her if she did, I'd never forgive her. She said you're an enemy to her home kingdom, too."

A quiet, bitter smile came to his face. It didn't reach his eyes. "I imagine they've told all sorts of malicious stories about me to Creag Morden. They'd have to, I suppose, to explain why such a well-decorated officer made off with their newest ship at the time."

"But… they're lying. They can't do that. It's not right."

James drew her close and kissed her brow before laying his cheek atop her head. "It's not, but there's little I can do about it beyond what I'm doing now. Let them call me a monster and a murderer. What matters is, I know the truth, as does my crew and those we rescue." His arms tightened around her. "As do you. No one else's opinion matters to me."

"When I told her what you're really like, Queen Anastasia was furious. Not at you. She's going to look into their claims."

His small chuckle warmed her heart. "If only I could bear witness to that conversation. I can't imagine King Harold withstanding the scrutiny of a sorceress and a dragon for long. Perhaps one day the people of Eisland will have the honorable leader they deserve."

"I hope so." She wrapped her arms around his waist and never wanted to let go. "For now, I just... I want to be with you and to enjoy whatever time we have. The rest I still need to figure out."

"Fair enough."

James scooped her up into his arms and stood, then carried her over to the bed. Even though he drew back, his warmth remained with her.

"Aren't you coming to bed?"

"Not just yet. I have a few things to check on before I retire, but I thought I'd sit here with you first."

Tink gazed into his handsome face and read exhaustion in his features. His smiles became more strained over time, weariness etched in the lines creasing his brow. "Then do your things and come to bed with me."

"All right," he agreed amicably.

While he did whatever duties were required of a pirate captain, Tink curled up with the book they'd been reading prior to her transformation. She stroked her fingers down the page and wished she could be as brave as the two women the story followed. That she could run away and be with the one she loved while fighting injustice.

She simply didn't know if she had the courage to leave

everything else behind.

Chapter 17

ANOTHER DAY HAD passed with Tink alongside James as an honorary lieutenant. He'd taught her to handle the wheel and given her amateur lessons at reading a sea chart, though she doubted she'd retain most of what he said. They even fished together from the rail on the main deck once she became proficient in baiting her own hook, and the two challenged one another to pull in the largest catch.

"I haven't fished in years," James admitted. "I usually leave the task to the men who enjoy it."

"You don't enjoy it?" Tink asked. Conall loved fishing, but she'd never participated due to her small size, always a quiet observer beside him.

"Oh no, I do," he backtracked. "But when one has many enjoyable activities and limited time, one must choose their preference."

"And you prefer reading."

"When I'm not navigating at the wheel—"

"Or causing hell below deck because someone's skivin' off at his duties," Harras called out, to much laughter from the others with their poles.

"You're hogging Lieutenant Belle, Cap'n," Tom fussed good naturedly. "How can any of us show her the ropes if you keep her to yourself?"

James smiled. "By all means, if you have something to

show her."

"I do," the young man boasted, puffing out his chest to appear larger. James grinned even more. "Around this time of the year, the other guys like to work the trawl nets through the water to catch the migratin' Coral Fins, but I get even better with this." He opened his grimy hand to reveal a handful of sausage bits against a dirt-smeared, greasy palm.

"Sausage?" James asked.

"Fins love 'em," Tom said. As though to prove his words true, his line pulled taut. Within moments he had a fat Coral Fin pulled up on the deck. The large fish's pink and orange scales glittered in the sunlight.

"It's huge," Tink said.

"Cook fries them up. One fish can feed two or three men, depending on how hungry we are," Harras told her. "Now you need to catch about ten more, Tommy lad."

Calls came up from the men at the nets. Tom and Harras rushed down to help their fellow crewmates.

"What are they using nets for if they catch the fish with poles?"

"Jellies," James replied. "Cook grinds them into the breakfast mash."

She stared at him. "I've eaten that."

"You have."

"You let me eat jellyfish?"

"You seemed to enjoy it."

"But...but..."

His handsome grin widened, his blue eyes sparkling with mirth. "You—"

A pained yell split the air. James twisted around, then

he dropped his pole and rushed toward the cry, heavy boots thumping against the wooden deck. Tink managed to catch his pole before it was lost to the sea and set both down before she followed him. A crowd had gathered around a large net, although the fish and jellies trapped within and spread across the planks were completely ignored.

It took some pushing for Tink to make her way close enough to see what was happening. Tom lay on the deck, his limbs flailing while two men tried to get a hold on him. James had forced his way to the front of the throng of people and moved to assist.

"Ah, hells! He's been stung by a dartfish!" Frederick cried.

"Why weren't you wearing your drakeskin gloves, lad?" Osric asked.

"What's happening? What's wrong?" Belle asked.

"Dartfish sting!" Frederick bellowed, applying enough bass to his voice that the entire ship seemed to tremble. "We've got a dartfish sting!"

"Dartfish are poisonous," Peter whispered in her ear. He'd appeared out of nowhere during the commotion. "I've never seen one before, but I've heard the others talking about them. Even lost a sailor last year. They had a man overboard, and when they fished him out he was covered in stings. Only takes one to die."

Tink furrowed her brow. "How do they know it only takes one to die if he was stung dozens of times?"

"My father died of a sting to the foot," Harras said.

"Make way, make way!" Eliza cried as she rushed through the hatchway. The crowd split apart as their healer moved to the front. Tom's finger had turned an awful shade of purple and swollen to twice its size. The blood vessels beneath the skin appeared livid and angry, a fine, spiderweb network of violet spreading from the affected digit toward the back of his hand. She wrapped a tight band around his muscular forearm, tying it until it bit into the skin.

Another second passed, the discoloration reached the back of his hand, ascending toward the rest of his limb. Eliza drew her cutlass and slammed the blade down across the young sailor's wrist.

Tom screamed until he was hoarse. The larger men flanking him, James included, all held him in place while Eliza did her work. As fascinated as she was distraught by the spectacle, Tink watched her cup a palm engulfed in radiant, magical essence against the severed stump. It was like the purest, most pristine white light Tink had ever seen. Even Queen Anastasia didn't exhibit such strength when it came to healing.

Eyes rolling back in his head, Tom passed out. Whether it was from the pain or the sheer relief of having that pain taken away, Tink had no idea. James knelt by the man's head, keeping it steady. Eliza continued to work, knitting together the severed veins, muscle, and skin. When she finished, Tom had a stump quite similar in appearance to James's, though it was pink and shiny.

"Was the best I could do in a pinch under short notice," Eliza murmured. "Dartfish toxin is a certain death once it reaches the bloodstream. Had it been anything else… It wasn't worth the risk had it gone higher. I'm sorry, kid." She tousled his dark hair and sighed. "Take him off to the infirmary to rest in one of the cots. I'll keep an eye on him."

"Aye, lieutenant," Osrim said.

Osrim and Frederick lifted Tom from the deck and carried him to the hatchway. James spoke a moment with Eliza in a low voice Tink couldn't make out, then he and the healer parted company.

When James returned to Tink's side, he took her hand in his and squeezed. "Well. That was certainly a profound lesson in ship life for you."

"Does that happen often?" she asked softly. A tremor ran through her pirate's hand, so she smoothed her fingers across his knuckles.

He shook his head. "Often? No. I'm sorry you had to witness that."

Eliza remained at the rail with the severed hand cradled to her chest, head bowed as she murmured unheard words. Without glancing up, she tossed the bloated thing into the water.

"What is she doing?" Tink whispered.

"A prayer to the god of the sea and a sacrifice. She does it whenever there's an injury at sea," he replied, breath a tickle against her ear. "It may be her job to keep us alive, but she hates whenever it's necessary to use her gift."

Her brows raised again. "You never say much about your gods."

"I'm not as devout as Eliza and her mother. Cook is always lighting candles to our health and makes the occasional sacrifice through the galley porthole. It's a prayer and a wish that whatever blood the god of the sea has already received from us, will be enough to sate his appetites until we're safely ashore again."

"What will happen to Tom?"

"So long as none of the poison remains, he'll recover in time."

"But his hand…"

"I'll see to it he gets a replacement if he wants one. At least I'll be able to teach him how to use it." He kissed her brow. "Did you want to fish more?"

"No, I think I'm ready for a break."

"A book then?"

"Only if you read it aloud," she replied.

James smiled, amusement replacing the sorrow in his eyes. "I will, gladly so, but my clothes will be staying *on*."

"Until tonight," she reminded him. Her last night as human and their last chance to be together in any intimate, physical sense.

His voice and smile softened and he reached out, caressing her cheek. "Until tonight."

James stood at the railing and watched the golden light fade from the sky. Streaks of deep purple and dusky pink colored the thin clouds and the first stars twinkled overhead. He thought back to Belle's belief that the stars were the gods and smiled, wondering what they saw as they looked down on the Jolly Roger.

If they truly were gods, surely they must have been laughing at him. He'd been given the perfect woman, who even now waited in his room for him to join her, but only for this last night. Tomorrow his sprite would become little again.

"How is that fair?" he asked in a quiet voice, dropping his

chin to his chest.

Was it punishment for all the years he'd enjoyed a cavalier sex life without attachment or love? A cruel twist of fate had at last introduced him to a woman capable of thawing his frozen heart, but he'd never experience physical pleasure with her beyond a single night.

Part of him had hoped Belle would change her mind and withdraw her interest in exploring human intimacy, shrouding their potential encounter in mystery.

But she hadn't. Instead, she'd shielded him from a queen and a dragon, displaying loyalty he'd only come to expect from his closest friends.

"I don't deserve her," James murmured against the cool breeze. He closed his eyes and breathed it in. Bell would be expecting him soon. Less than a half hour ago, she'd retired to their cabin after making him promise to give her time to prepare.

To commemorate Belle's final day as a human, Nigel had stepped aside and abandoned his post in favor of Belle assuming his duties. She'd been temporarily elevated to the rank of quartermaster, tasked with fulfilling the role.

And she'd loved it. Her smiles had brightened the entire sea whenever a pirate ran to her for advice. Then, at the conclusion of their magical day together, James dreaded the sunset. A third and final night with his human-sized Belle had come too soon.

A wet slap struck the hull of the ship, jerking his attention back to his surroundings. The long, slimy length of a serpentine body curled over the edge of the railing, and rheumy eyes gazed back at him. Caecilia, the sea witch, held the cargo netting of the ship.

"My, my, my, driven to talk to yourself now, are you?"

James stumbled back a step. "Aren't you a little far from home, witch?"

Her lips spread into a wide smile, revealing each of her sharp teeth. "How cruel of you to speak to me this way when we were once such good friends in the past."

"Which is exactly where our friendship should remain."

The witch's lips pursed into a pout. She lifted herself up and perched on the wooden ledge, her serpentine body shimmering until human legs replaced her scaled tail. "Whatever have I done to offend you, James?"

"You tried to cut Belle's wings off, for one."

"Bah, a mere triviality. What human needs wings?"

"Ghost Hawk was able to do it without maiming her."

"Of course he was, and yet it's merely a temporary solution to a long-term problem, isn't it? Now that she's tasted his poison once, it'll never work again."

His hand fisted at his side. "What are you doing here?"

"I came to save you from a broken heart, dear one. You may hold me in poor regard, but I've always protected your best interests."

He scoffed. "You care only for yourself."

Her spine straightened and her bare shoulders tensed. Damp hair stuck to the edge of her jaw, clinging like pieces of seaweed against her toned upper torso and slender arms. She wore nothing, as was common among the merpeople who inhabited the seas, but she lacked the sensual appeal of her comely counterparts. "Then why do I guard these islands from the very people who hunt you? Why save them from the slavers' net if I care only for myself?"

James averted his gaze and clenched his jaw, unable to answer. The blasted woman had a point, and everyone owed her their gratitude. There'd been a time long ago when the slavers of the Ridaeron Dynasty had made Wai Alei natives their stock on the flesh trade. "Everyone appreciates your protection, Caecilia, there's no doubt of that."

"Everyone but you."

"I've always respected your care for Neverland. It's your methods I don't tend to agree with." James wanted to wince the moment the words left his mouth.

"Did you disagree when I capsized the King Peter's Folly?" she hissed. A hint of mottled color spread over her shoulders and crept up her neck as her milky eyes narrowed into furious slits. "Should I have allowed them to fire on the Jolly Roger?"

Chastened, James dipped his head. "Apologies. I know the good deed you did for us then."

The witch quieted. Spindly pale fingers reached out to touch the narrow strip of bare skin exposed by his shirt. "There are better things to discuss than Wai Alei. You'll never have happiness with her, James. You know that, I know that, and your bug knows that. What good will she ever be to you once she's a little firefly again?"

He removed her hand. "That doesn't matter to me."

"She'll return to her friends in Cairn Ocland and abandon you. Don't you realize that? Souls like ours belong to the sea, and *I* will always be here for you."

Unable to bite back the snarl rising in his throat, James growled as he thrust his hook at her. "Is that why you sent the crocodile after me? Because you care enough to always be there? I may respect the good deeds you've done while protecting my crew and the islanders, but I won't allow you to manipulate me."

Her face fell. "He misunderstood my commands. I never meant for him to cause you harm. Never," she murmured. "I could return your hand."

"No one can return the hand *your* pet took from me, and I've already seen the best mages and healers the Viridian Sea has to offer."

Her features darkened for a split second before a predatory smile spread across her damp gray face. "I can do what they failed to do. All you have to do is stay with me. Promise to remain here as mine, and I'll protect your ship as I've always protected these islands. You dedicate your life to saving children, and I dedicate mine to defending Neverland. Don't you see that this means we were meant to be together?"

"Never. My heart may have belonged to the sea once, but now it belongs to Belle, no matter her size."

Caecilia snorted. "Do you think she can satisfy you? You'll be ready to move on from her as soon as you grow thirsty for physical satisfaction, James. Like all men."

"I'm not like other men."

Her gaze ran over his body from head to toe, then up again. "No, you most certainly are not."

"Begone, witch. I've paid my price for your help in the past. You have no hold over me now, nor will you ever again."

The tranquil breeze became a turbulent wind. It ripped across the deck and tossed James's hair in his face, stirring the sails above him. Her murky eyes narrowed. "You'll never have a life with your glowing gnat. I've seen her future. Mark my words, you *will* live to regret this. A year from now, when her little light twinkles out, you'll wish you had taken my offer."

Caecilia dove over the side of the ship and returned to the water, sending up a salty splash against the hull. Long after she was gone, the cold lingered in James's bones.

Something about her words hadn't struck him as a mere threat against Belle's life. It had been a warning filled with truth.

Tink paced the bedroom a dozen times while awaiting James's arrival. He'd promised on the third night there'd be no more excuses or delays. Despite her anticipation, she couldn't fault the legitimate reason for refusing to bed her right away.

According to her pirate, Eislanders courted their beloved for weeks and sometimes even months before moving forward. Given the circumstances, he'd settled for three days and treated her to two amazing evenings.

A chill traveled over her body and raised anxious goosebumps beneath her robe. It was the prettiest thing she'd ever owned. Too bad she'd never be able to wear it again. She snuggled within the silk and breathed in the scent from the natural dyes used to paint it, and then she closed her eyes.

Hers. Even if she could never wear it again, she'd never let it go. Much like James.

If she had only a year or two left in the world, she'd have to do her best to divide it between her loved ones in Cairn Ocland and sailing the high seas as James's companion.

Decorating the room had given her an outlet for her

  VIVIENNE SAVAGE

nervous energy. Since she and James had already dined on the quarterdeck, she'd taken the liberty of pouring wine. Candles scented with fragrant oils burned around the cabin, giving every adjacent surface a romantic glow. While she had intended to gift them to Conall and Sorcha when she returned home, the night had provided an ideal opportunity to use them.

Outside, the wind howled and the ship heaved. Tink stumbled and grabbed the bedpost to remain upright until the rocking ship began to settle. Before the motioned evened out, the door opened and James stepped through.

"Is everything all right? I heard the wind pick up."

"Everything is fine," he assured her. "A rough patch is all—" He stopped to gaze at the room with an appreciative half smile on his face. "You did all this?"

"Do you like it?"

"It's lovely." James crossed over and ran his fingers through her hair before tucking the strands behind her ear. When he traced the curve with his calloused thumb, a pleasant tickle raced down her spine. "*You're* lovely."

Tink rose on her toes and leaned in, met halfway by James. He claimed her mouth in a gentle kiss while drawing her closer, holding her anchored against him with his hand at her nape. The sash around her waist loosened, pulled free with the utmost care by his hook, and allowed the silken robe to part. Bare skin awaited him beneath.

"I don't know what to do," she confessed on a whisper. For all her previous eagerness and boldness, she found herself suddenly shy. James tipped her face up, his thumb rubbing across her lower lip, and smiled. "I mean, I know what happens, but I don't know how to begin—"

James silenced her with a kiss. "I know enough for us both."

He stepped away long enough to remove his hook and set it in the case beside the bed, but when he reached toward his waist to remove the sash and gunbelt, Tink stopped him with a touch of her hand.

"Please. Let me."

One by one, articles of clothing tumbled to the floor and pooled around their ankles. By the time James lowered Tink to the crushed velvet comforter, her entire body buzzed with excitement. With his weight braced upon his right arm, he introduced her to the reassuring weight of his body and the sensation of bare skin to skin. He stretched over her, long and lean, his bottom shapely beneath her exploring fingers.

There had been no shortage of cuddles since her transition to human that first night, but the promise of advancing their relationship placed Tink on pins and needles. Each nerve ending tingled, and desire ached between her thighs. She wanted him to touch her.

Craving that contact more than anything, she grasped his left hand and guided his fingers where she needed them most. James made an appreciative sound in his throat before exploring her downy, golden mound.

"I knew I wanted you to be mine from the first moment I saw you," he said, voice a husky murmur against her cheek. "You were bathed in this breathtaking, vibrant purple glow and as curious of me as I was of you. At the time, I was selfish enough to dare hope I could keep you as my companion."

He hadn't called her a pet—not as the Liangese had while

discussing their illegal cargo—but a companion and cherished friend. Rapidly blinking away the tears burning in the corners of her eyes, Tink raised one hand to cup his face when he leaned back to gaze upon her.

"My desires haven't changed, Belle. Stay with me here. It matters none to me what size you are. You bring light to my life I haven't seen in so long."

To stay with him, even as a sprite, and leave her old friends in Cairn Ocland… With so little time remaining in her sorrowfully short life, the temptation grew into a terrible, selfish desire.

Was it so selfish to do what she wanted with her remaining time? To love and be loved by someone who saw her as an equal?

Or would she miss her wolven friends, her dear brother Conall, Sorcha, and their little one? Why did he have to make the decision so difficult?

"I want to," she whispered.

His mouth traced a scintillating path from her throat to her breasts. A whisper of his lips circled one nipple then the next, wet by a stroke of his tongue. Then he teased her body with his fingers and held her on the precipice again, proving he only needed the one hand to introduce her to limitless pleasure.

The moment of their joining came on a painless thrust, uniting them in blissful intimacy that sent trembles of ecstasy coursing through Tink's body. Startled, she arched beneath him and raised her hips into the next movement.

How could one body endure so much sensation and so many conflicting emotions, each one warring against the next? Triumph for attaining what she'd wanted, satisfaction because their puzzle-perfect fit surpassed her expectations, and profound sadness that it would be only a single night.

There was no shortage of kisses and whispered promises, the Eisland tongue never sounding prettier than it did in those moments when James swore he would give her the world.

True to his word, she learned the rhythm of their lovemaking, and those awkward, uncertain raises of her hips became a timed dance of give and take. She curved one calf above his rounded bottom and traced her fingers down the back muscles bunching beneath her touch. Tension wound within her, stretched to an impossible limit.

And each time she came within seconds of reaching the peak, her lover ceased all movement then slid free of her to saw the delicious length of his manhood against her slick skin.

"James," she wailed. "I need... I need..." For lack of knowing what to call it, she buried her fingers in his dark hair and sobbed in frustration.

"What do you need?" The seductive whisper skimmed against her ear, and her core tightened, empty and aching for him again.

She wanted the delicious completion he'd given her in the shower, so desperate for it she reached between their bodies and guided him home where he belonged as she arched her hips off the bed. Tink savored the long, sweet moan of her name that fell from his lips.

For a while, they met one another stroke for stroke, giving and receiving mutual pleasure until James stiffened above her and swore under his breath, releasing a low, guttural groan of pleasure. He ground against her, and, in the next thrust, Tink saw the stars. The tension unraveled with a snap, introducing her to golden bliss. Together, they coasted on a turbulent sea of pleasure, each second of climax more intense than the last.

Eventually, the sweetest relief settled over her exhausted limbs, turning her body leaden and useless beneath him. Even James appeared reluctant to move, as he did nothing more than kiss her throat and remain buried inside her.

"My magnificent sprite," he whispered. "I never want to let you go."

And in a perfect world, he wouldn't have to. Instead of answering, Tink laced her fingers through his ebony hair and enjoyed the beautiful warmth he emitted.

After all, a few more hours were all that was promised to her.

James resisted sleep while the sweat dried on their skin. He trailed his fingers through her golden hair and basked in the afterglow, wondering when he'd last felt at peace with absolute contentment in his world.

Never. Not even when he'd first taken command of the Jolly Roger, on what had been the proudest day of his life.

"I want to do it again," Belle murmured, interrupting his thoughts. He'd thought her to be asleep until then.

"*Already?*"

She pounced on him and straddled his hips, leaning forward on both palms. "Yes." Her hair slipped over one shoulder and tickled his chest. "Right now."

"A man needs a moment afterward to recover," he muttered.

"No, you don't. Look."

His body proved hardier than his mind and stiffened at her touch. Groaning, James surrendered to her zealous hunger for him. No matter the activity, Belle proved to be a quick learner.

Afterward, she stretched along his lax, exhausted body, feathering lazy kisses over his pulse. She traced her fingers through his hair and hummed a quiet lullaby. "I don't want to sleep," she murmured. "The sooner I sleep, the sooner..." She blinked a few times, unable to disguise the moisture in her eyes. "I don't want it to end."

"It will never end if we hold it in our hearts. Besides, the morning and day remain for us. Sleep, my love."

She sighed and pressed her face against the warm hollow of his throat. "Okay."

Even if it's only tonight, this single night will be enough, James thought as the gentle motion of the ship lulled him to sleep.

When morning came, they showered together and made love another time with desperate urgency, speaking none save murmurs of affection and pleas for more. They tenderly washed each other afterward in the semi-cramped space, the moment full of laughter and giggles whenever they knocked into one another.

"You took all of the hot water," she accused while toweling her hair dry outside of the box.

"That entire thing was your idea," he quipped before dragging her up against him. He'd already donned his wardrobe while she pranced around the stateroom in nothing. "Would you like help with your dress laces or shall you be a pirate again? This is your day, so the choice remains yours."

"The dress, please."

James helped her into the two-layered dress and tightened the laces, securing it around her ribs and slender waist. It was all white save scarlet blossoms and windblown pink petals over a sea of blue covering the lower half of the outer skirt.

Belle spun in a circle, letting the ankle-length skirts swish around her calves. "I'm ready. But… I… We need to talk. I can't face the day without telling you."

"Yes?"

"I… I have something to confess, and I'm afraid you'll be upset with me if I do."

James cupped her chin and gazed into her eyes. "Unless you plan to set fire to the ship or run away with Nigel, there is nothing you could say to make me upset with you."

"I'm afraid it'll ruin our final day together."

James wrapped his arms around her. "It won't."

"I'm… older than I thought myself to be. I don't think I'll live much more than a year or two."

His heart stopped as she spoke the words he'd already known, confirming a terrible suspicion. "I know, Belle. I've known since yesterday, and… I'll…" His arms tightened around her, and he buried his face in her hair. She smelled so good. "I've decided to pass over command of the ship for the next year once we return you to Cairn Ocland. If you won't remain on the seas with me, then I will go where you go."

"James—"

"I've made up my mind and discussed it with Nigel. If you'll have me, I'll follow you anywhere to cherish every day, every hour, down to the last second your stars bless me with your light."

As her green eyes brimmed over with tears, Belle's voice came as little more than a choked whisper. "Of course I'll have you."

"Thank you."

"But... tell me how you found out. Who told you?"

"The sea witch herself. She visited last night after you retired to our cabin. I know she meant to cause me pain, but she's only strengthened my resolve. I won't leave you when you need me. Not because you'll grow little, not because our time is limited. I won't run away from this, even if it scares me."

"James—"

"Because you've shown me what love is about. If the children taught me self-sacrifice, then you've taught me to love—to truly love—and I would rather have that love for one year than to have an entire life without it."

Unable to utter another word, Belle threw her arms around his neck and hugged him tight.

"Now, shall we go fire those cannons one last time?"

Sniffling, she leaned back and wiped her cheeks with one wrist. "Your pistol, too?"

"And my pistol, too," he grudgingly agreed before they stepped from his cabin and into the noon sun.

When sunset approached and Tink's final day as a human reached its conclusion, she retreated to James's cabin to endure the transformation's reversal in privacy. Three days had been too short, but she had reveled in each moment given to her and cherished every unique experience.

VIVIENNE SAVAGE

James shut the door behind her and shrugged from his coat. Silence had fallen between them over the last half hour, and they'd done nothing more than hold hands on the quarterdeck and watch the dwindling hours paint the sky in watercolors.

"I wish we had more time," she whispered.

"I know." James's arms surrounded her from behind, and a tug drew her back to his chest. "I know. So do I. But know this, my feelings won't change because you're small again."

Tink twisted around to face him. "But we won't be able to kiss. To hold hands. To…" She closed her eyes and gestured toward the bed.

James tipped her chin up. "That doesn't matter. Not to me."

The flutters in her stomach matched the racing tempo of her heart. She opened her eyes and tears spilled past her lashes. "I love you," Tink whispered. "I don't think I've ever said it."

"And I love you. Sprite or human woman, that love will never change."

Without another word, she seized James's face between her hands and kissed him, imbuing every ounce of her affection and passion for him into the gesture. She wanted to burn the moment into her memory forever.

The last rays of sunlight slanted in through the windows as they broke apart, marking the moment she'd raised the glass vial to her lips three days prior.

A painless transformation swept over Tink's body, though she was spared agony in the physical sense alone. The enormity of her love for James surpassed her profound sadness, and the fairy glow surrounded her first with surreal, rose-hued light before her appendages shrank and her lover rapidly grew in size. No longer standing before him as his equal, she hovered at eye level, instead.

Sorrow and heartache became a turbulent storm, warring against the whirlwind of emotion surging inside her condensed frame. While tears spilled over her cheeks, an inevitable surge of affection for James smothered the minute pangs of anguish thudding inside her chest.

I love him. I love him with everything I have, and nothing will ever convince me those three days weren't worth it.

James offered his hand. Once she perched on his fingers, he raised her to his lips and kissed her golden head. The same love shone in his blue eyes.

"The way I feel for you will never change, Belle. This merely marks the beginning of another adventure for us. A different one borne of love, not lust."

"Companionship without sex," she whispered.

"And I will happily cherish you until the last day we have with one another. For your mind and your heart. Now, shall I pour you a bath, or will you join me in the shower box on the ledge?"

Tink wiped her face with both hands. "The ledge."

If she couldn't touch her pirate and caress him the way she wanted, she could at the very least enjoy the view.

Chapter 18

CONALL PRESSED HIS nose to the damp soil at the base of the tree and inhaled the scent of wilderness and morning dew. Tink had always told him tenders of the green preferred to rise with the morning sun. The grass still smelled sweet, fragrant with the sprite who had crawled out of her tiny burrow.

And then there was something else, smoky and acrid, a smell he'd never forget because it had been all over the foul trap he'd found Tink inside years ago: Liangese gunpowder.

Positive they were on the right trail, he raised his head and nodded sharply left and right. Four of the wolves in the pack fanned out as directed to scout their surroundings while he proceeded ahead with two more in a tight triangle. A pair of his largest wolves fell behind, the stocky brutes prepared to charge forward and leap into battle if the three charged into an ambush.

The Liangese loved ambushes. Alistair had warned them of that.

Whether or not the poachers even spoke their language had been his concern initially, until he realized there'd be no conversation or apologies from the lawless invaders.

A hint of crushed grass and disturbed flora told them they were on the right path. Another mile took them to the edge of a glade where a gentle stream trickled over rocks. Beside it, a single tent stretched between the trees. While no one was in sight, mesh cages of steel and gold had been piled beside the smoldering campfire. Faint wisps of smoke arose from it.

Some sort of toxin or sleeping agent, Conall thought, *keeps the little ones docile and weak, incapable of using magic to escape their bondage or fool their captors.* The thought of Tink in such a trap infuriated him and turned his vision red with anger. Across the glade, a noise rustled in the brush, and two men emerged from the trees carrying two more tiny cages. They both wore green and brown garments stained with mud and decorated with leaves. Their faces had been painted.

All the better to hide among the sprites and lure them to captivity. Filled with rage, Conall charged them.

His claws tore into the ground before he pushed off the earth and lunged, elongating his furry body into a powerful pounce. He took one by surprise, but the man's companion ripped a vial from his vest and hurled it at the ground.

Snarling a warning to his kin, he spring-boarded off the second man and bounded away. At the same time, three other wolves ran a circle, nose to tail, widening out as they summoned wind magic to create a wind tunnel. The mysterious fumes rose skyward and dispersed.

The shorter of the two poachers danced beyond reach and drew a knife, while the taller, broad-shouldered one drew an enormous saber from his belt. As a dire wolf, Conall stood eye to eye with most men, but the agile Liangese people knew how to outmaneuver shifters with spry acrobatics.

Can't let them hit me. No telling what's on those blasted things.

It could be liquid death itself, a toxin able to kill him with a single nick. With that sobering thought in mind, Conall watched his footing and remained light on all four paws. Then he feinted to provide one of his pack mates a precious opening. The long, curved knife came within an inch of slicing Conall's throat, but the result was worth it.

Bhaltair, one of their massive bruisers, darted across and tore the dagger-wielding poacher's thigh with his teeth. Pain broke his adversary's concentration and gave Conall the upper hand, a chance to disarm him and close his teeth over the wrist of the man's dominant hand. He mangled it without lingering, darting away to initiate a lethal game of tag. When Conall rejoined the circle, Raghnall dashed in and tore out the tendon above the second poacher's heel, hobbling him. The wolf narrowly missed a swing from the blade, blown off course by the force emitted from Conall's howl.

Back and forth the wolves took turns, wearing down their enemy without allowing them the chance to fight back. They staggered in the wind as blood dripped from their fingers and shattered vials littered the rocks at their feet.

One poacher fell to his knees and clutched the grisly remains of his hand to his chest, powerless and stripped of his only defense.

A thunderous crack split the air. Behind them, another man stood in the trees with a smoking weapon in his hand. Raghnall stumbled forward as a bloom of crimson spread across his majestic snowy pelt.

There had been more poachers after all, armed with a weapon Conall had never seen. And then it was the only thing he saw, the only thing that mattered, his perception of it colored by the scarlet haze of his fury. His paws barely touched the ground, and time around him slowed. Raghnall had already collapsed, his breathing labored and difficult as blood seeped beneath him. The poacher had shoved another charge of gunpowder into the mouth of his tool, his movements mechanical and well-practiced, unflinching in the face of potential death.

Conall raced toward him. Gunpowder and smoke filled the air again, and the ball punched him in the shoulder, knocking him off course for less than a second. His pulse thumped. Before the next beat of his heart, Conall landed upon his enemy and took the man's face in his jaws. Fingers pushed with futility against the alpha's thick neck. Then a final scream echoed between his teeth before he clamped down.

Two other wolves appeared at his side the moment he stumbled off the body. Pain radiated up and down his shoulder, and blood dripped to the forest floor.

"He got you with his boomstick," Bhaltair said. "Raghnall, too."

A short distance away, Lachlan knelt beside the motionless mound of ivory fur that had once been his brother. Conall swore under his breath.

"Dig it out with your hunting knife," he said to Bhaltair.

Another wolf emerged from the forest. "What was that thing? You were right about them planning to ambush you, but this one snuck by us. We killed one of them not so far from here returning this way with a much longer weapon."

"I think it's a pistol," Conall growled. "I've heard of them before, but never saw one with my own eyes until now."

"It killed Raghnall," Lachlan groaned into one hand. "Killed my brother with one blow. Where's the fairness in that?

Where's the honor?"

Conall grimaced as Bhaltair wedged the tip of his blade beneath the hard iron ball and pried it loose, sending sparks of agony flying down every nerve ending from Conall's neck to the tips of his fingers. "There is no fairness, lad. None at all. The bleedin' cowards come into our land, taking what they want and using their alchemical trickery. But we'll stop them."

"Damned right we will," Lachlan growled.

They doused the campfire with water from the stream and freed the trapped sprites. The little ones trembled with gratitude, but none of them had crossed paths with Tinker Bell or seen her.

After they buried their packmate beside the tranquil stream, the pack continued west along the riverbank. By evening, they found evidence of another group in the area, though two threw themselves at the mercy of the wolves and surrendered after one of their cohorts fell.

"What do we do with them?" Bhaltair asked, rubbing his chin. They hadn't prepared for prisoners.

"I say we kill them," Lachlan muttered.

Conall shook his head. "It isn't for us to decide now. They may not deserve our kindness, but we should ask our king and queen what they want."

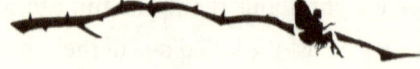

Less than a day had passed since the last update from the search party, but Anastasia remained on pins and needles. She hated staying behind while they headed into dangerous territory.

Alistair and Teagan had already encountered a foe armed with dragon's bane, proving the treacherous worms had prepared for an encounter with him. Fortunately, they hadn't expected *two* dragons, and together the pair had overcome the poison-wielding bandit.

Ever since, she and Sorcha had done their best to keep Elspeth ignorant of their fears while entertaining the younger children. Just as they set the lads down for the evening, a high-pitched whistle, like the harmonic note of a crystal glass, came from the room where she kept her scrying ball. Anastasia rushed into the library with Sorcha on her heels and slipped into the chair. Conall's solemn features gazed at her from the cloudy sphere.

"What's wrong?" Sorcha blurted out. "What happened?"

"We've set several sprites free." Despite the good news, pain tightened the alpha's eyes.

There had to be more to the story. "You lost someone," Ana whispered.

Conall nodded. "Aye. Raghnall is gone. One got the drop on us with a pistol. Shot me, too."

Sorcha sucked in her breath and reeled. Without wasting a second, Ana abandoned the seat and put her friend on it instead. "Are you all right? How bad was it?"

"Not serious," he assured his wife. "I swear to you, I've been careful since. I'm already healing from it."

"Would you tell me the truth if you were seriously hurt?" Sorcha demanded.

"I would. The injury is minor and not why I've summoned you both." He glanced away from the mirror toward another wolf nearby before his blue eyes darted back to them. "We encountered more since then, but two surrendered. What do you want us to do with them?"

"Do with them?" Ana echoed.

"Are we to kill them or keep them prisoner? Lachlan is angry and hurting from his brother's death. He wants them dead, but they've surrendered, and it feels like nothing less than murder to me."

"How bad is it there? Do you suspect there are more?"

"Aye. We've encountered them in groups of four and three today. There are bound to be more. They're bold, and they'll only grow worse if we don't take back the south from them."

Anastasia kneaded her brows with two fingers. "You're right. We've spent so long clearing away all signs of the Scourge and rebuilding, we hadn't realized we lost the south to Liang."

"Tell us what you want us to do, and we'll do it," the wolf said.

"If they surrender, take them captive. They'll be our prisoners and a bargaining chip until we've gained what we want from their emperor."

"And the others?"

"Kill them."

"Aye. Will do. We've already liberated a dozen terrified sprites."

Contacting her husband to share the news introduced Ana to a hint of the old Alistair—the dragon who had razed villages on the border of Cairn Ocland and Dalborough to avenge his fallen parents. Before she could talk reason into him, he flew into a fitful rage and declared he was heading to Liang. Teagan hastily promised she would convince him to return home, and then the communication ended.

Blast.

Sorcha wiped one of her cheeks. "I can't believe Raghnall is gone."

"This has gone on too long. If their emperor won't answer our letters, he certainly won't see Alistair in person."

It would come down to a fight, no doubt, and while Alistair had grown powerful over the years, she doubted he could stand against the force of the Imperial Army. What if he didn't see reason? What if Teagan couldn't talk him down?

"This is hopeless. I... fighting a war in our own homeland against the Scourge was one thing, but these aren't mindless undead and ghouls. Save for building a wall, how do we keep them out?"

Anastasia clenched her jaw. "Perhaps we *should* build a wall. A great, enchanted wall of thorns and brambles too tight for any human to penetrate. It would take me days, but I could do it. I've got Eos's blood in my veins, after all. The greater problem is that it doesn't return our lost ones already taken."

"No, it doesn't. Sweet stars, I feel sick. Why can't everyone just leave us be? First Dalborough with their hate of our gods, and now these... Is there no one who will side with us and help?"

"My father will, but his hands are tied as he's north of us, but there's..." Anastasia jerked her gaze toward the map on the wall. South of Liang, the vast desert nation of Samahara stretched across the parchment as a glorious beige and gold stain. "I know who we can ask."

"Who?"

"I've recently been in contact with another sorcerer. The Grand Enchanter of Ankirith. We've exchanged spell components by bird for a year now." Anastasia bent down and circled her palm above the crystal ball. Within moments, the handsome visage of Joaidane appeared.

"Hello, Joaidane."

"Greetings, Anastasia. To what do I owe this pleasure?"

"I… I need your help."

The welcoming smile faded from his face. "Something dire has happened? What may I do to aid you?"

"A good friend of ours went missing. While searching for her, we've discovered Liang has trespassed across our southern borders and abducted dozens of our citizens. Perhaps even hundreds right under our nose."

"I see. Would you like my assistance in seeking this friend, as well?"

"No. We've already located her. Tinker Bell is—"

"Tinker Bell, you say? I've met her," Joaidane cut in. "A little woman as large as my thumb with golden hair and green eyes. She traveled with a good friend of mine."

"You're friends with Captain James Hook?"

"Proudly so."

Anastasia stole a look at Sorcha. The huntress fixed her with a smug smile and mouthed, "I told you so."

Indeed, she had. Blinded by her father's faith in Eisland's monarchy, she'd thought sweet and innocent Tinker Bell had been deceived by a suave crook. Tink hadn't been the one fooled, however; her father was the one charmed by an evil man.

"He's a good man, then?" Anastasia asked, unable to hide the doubt in her voice.

"My friend, if he were not a good man, I would have struck

him down with lightning and sunk his ship to the bottom of the Viridian Sea. He isn't merely a good man, he is the *best* of them. Do you not realize what Eisland has done?"

"We've heard a little bit from Tinker Bell," Anastasia replied. "And I've spoken with my father about the claims. He says the idea of Eisland dabbling in the slave trade is preposterous at best, a story made up by a deserter who stole the kingdom's best ship. Tell me, Joaidane, what do you know?"

"I've seen the slaves," the sorcerer said, eyes glinting with inner fire. "Broken and dispirited, some damaged and near death. I have seen mothers with bruises from protecting their children and little ones who were ripped from their families. This is the reality of the Ridaeron Dynasty. They sell their people to Eisland to work the vineyards under the guise of indentured servitude."

Aghast, Ana raised a hand to her mouth. Blinking didn't soothe the burning at the corners of her eyes. "Children?"

"Yes, even children. And he has saved them all, allowing them the chance at a new life. A better one. Many refugees from their slave ships come and seek a new life here in Samahara, and we grant it to them. Had I known Belle was a friend of yours, I would have offered to try and send her home myself, but you may rest assured that once he has given his word, James Hook is good for it. He will see her to Cairn Ocland once he is able."

"We've been worried about her."

"For good reason, as I've understood it. He rescued her from the Golden Goose, a Ridaeron treasure galleon that often sails between its homeport, Liang, and Eisland in the transport of goods both legal and less so. As I understand it, James found her caged in a box destined for a Ridaeron nobleman's house."

"Poor Tink."

"Fear not. She was quite free and lively when I saw her. In fact, she fought several mercenaries alongside him. I've rarely seen two souls so in sync."

"*Our* Tink fought mercenaries?"

"She did. Mercenaries hired by the emperor himself. In the past, I've told him to keep his bounty hunters away from my city, but my warning has gone unheeded." Joaidane steepled his fingers. "So, as you can see, I have a bone to pick with Emperor Da'Wio myself."

"I've written several times without any response."

"Then I vow the aid of Samahara during your time of need," the sorcerer replied. "Give me time to contact the emperor, and we shall see what he says regarding your lost citizens."

Anastasia's shoulders dropped, and she tilted her head back with her eyes closed. The tension drained from her spine before she sagged forward on the chair. "Thank you, Joaidane. *Thank you.* Truly. We owe a great debt to—"

"No. You owe nothing to me," he interrupted her. "Your cousin brought my family together again, and for that, I can never repay her, so I shall not try. What I do, I do because it is right, and for no other reason. Please, tell your husband and his aunt to turn back. Don't approach the emerald gates without invitation, but trust that I'll do whatever is necessary to gain them an audience with Da'Wio."

"Thank you. I'll contact them to share the news immediately."

Joaidane inclined his head to her. "You're very welcome. Until we speak again, my friend."

Chapter 19

DAYS HAD PASSED since Belle's transformation back to her small size, and James had done his best to make every moment count. Her change in stature didn't make him love her any less, and he made every effort to prove it despite the unrelenting melancholy smothering her mood.

"In another week or so, we'll see your kingdom," he said as he stood at the rail on the quarterdeck. "I've been giving some thought on how to get you home, since the coast is a wall of cliffs."

"Oh?" Tink sat on his shoulder with her head leaned up against his neck.

"I thought it might be best if we approached through Creag Morden. It would mean days of travel, or perhaps we could find a way to contact your queen."

"But that will put the Jolly Roger in Eisland's waters."

"The only other option is to travel north through Liang. Given their inhospitable nature toward me, it would be a treacherous journey. At sea, we can make a run for it, if needed."

Belle fluttered up and hovered near his face, surrounded in a dim blue glow. "I don't want anyone to get hurt."

"Love, we'll be in no more danger than we face any other day. Everything will be—"

"Sails!" Peter cried out from the crow's nest. "There's a war ship flying Eisland's colors on the horizon."

Belle became an alarmed blip of red and wrung her small hands together. "Does that mean we have to fight them?"

"Nothing to fret over, love," James said, dabbing his brow with a handkerchief. The unusual temperature of the afternoon had made for an unbearable day of sailing. "I prefer to avoid battling their ships if we can help it. We'll be long gone before they reach us."

"Are you sure?"

"Of course I am. I've yet to come across a ship that can match the Jolly Roger in speed."

So why did uneasiness curl in his gut and knot his shoulders with tension? James looked back at the speck on the horizon and stared at the blue sails.

Nigel approached with a gnomish telescope clutched in his hand. "James, I think we have a problem. That ship over yonder? It isn't just any Eislander ship. It's the Queen Anne's Revenge. Have a look."

Once the powerful scope exchanged hands, its lens revealed a magnified image of the vessel King Harold had awarded Teach only days prior to James setting sail from their shores for the last time. Weeks later, he'd encountered the Golden Goose and found himself incapable of remaining under Teach's command another day.

James grunted. While beautiful and enormous, they'd outrun the Queen Anne's Revenge numerous times over the years, leaving only choppy sea foam in their wake whenever the warship attempted to engage them in battle. "This changes nothing. They had the fortune of coming upon the others while they were at a standstill, but we've got the wind in our favor.

Between the cargo we've unloaded at Ankirith and Neverland, we're lighter than ever."

"Not to mention our clean hull," Belle said.

James grinned and passed the telescope back to his lieutenant. "Good thing, I say. They'll never come within range to fire their mystery weapon, but let's have everyone at the ready, shall we? I have no fear of this ship-destroying weapon when they're unable to close in on us."

"A good plan," Nigel agreed. After he moved away to shout new orders to the crew, James gazed at the dark speck in the distance.

Was it coincidence they had been found? Or was something more at play? He was too clever to think they could live like this forever, escaping Eisland time and time again, but he'd be damned if he went down now—not before he kept his promise to Belle.

Before he could return to the wheel, the ship lurched to the side and a tremendous wave rolled over the deck. James stumbled to the side before regaining his balance, every sense on high alert. He canted his head and listened. A subdued ticking reached his ears, but when he spun and glanced at the water, nothing remained but a faint disturbance.

Croc had returned for more. "Load the cannons, men! Arms at the ready."

"We can't aim a cannon at a creature beneath our boat, James," Nigel replied.

"No, but when the beast resurfaces, we can blast him to hell. Callum!"

The mage emerged from the hatch, Tootles a few steps behind him. "Yes, Captain?"

"Do you think that boy of yours can assist us again?"

"We'll see what we can do."

"James, the Revenge—"

"I know," he snapped at Nigel, "but it'll be impossible to escape with Croc nipping our heels."

"It's not only that. Look at our sails. We've lost the wind, but they're approaching faster than ever. Blackbeard may have an aeromancer at his command this time. It's too much of a coincidence."

As the shifting elements turned the tides against them, James closed his eyes and dipped his chin. The wind, time, and now the relentless pet of a spurned woman stood between them and freedom. Caecilia had been blameless before and claimed no responsibility for the crocodile's behavior in the past, but had she sent it as a final act of vengeance? James had dared to deny her in no uncertain terms.

Tinker Bell floated in front of him and wrung her small hands together. "What do we do, James?"

"We fight," he said grimly. "Fetch the gunpowder and supplies. We haven't been defeated yet. I'll be damned if I give in and roll over. Eliza's trained a little alongside Little Wolf to learn the craft. Ask her to join Callum and Tootles. I know wind isn't her specialty, but she's all we have."

Nigel nodded and hurried away to give commands, as Belle darted through the cargo access in search of gunpowder. They'd need plenty of it.

Too many people depended on James to surrender the ship. He glanced toward the crow's nest. Peter had already begun the long trek down, but he and Tootles needed his protection the most.

I won't let them have you boys again.

Regaining his composure, as well as his morale, James sprang to the wheel and took it in his hand. Eliza had already joined Callum and Tootles on the forecastle, and together the three mages joined hands to take control of the rocking vessel each time Croc nudged it from beneath the hull. A swift wind blew from behind them and billowed the quiet sails as the low hum of their magic washed over the ship, raising the hairs on his arms. A low buzz filled his ears.

Little Wolf had handled the wind currents like a natural, but those three needed every ounce of concentration to harness a power they hadn't trained all their lives to use.

We'll make it.

Those words became James's mantra as they navigated the waters on the best course to keep the Queen Anne's Revenge beyond firing range. Judging by the speed of their approach, he had less than fifteen minutes for Croc to make his appearance for a proper thrashing.

Then the gods answered his prayers and Croc rose from the churning waves. Water sluiced over the beast's gargantuan body and the fetid stench of his last meal rolled over the deck. Despite the report of a dozen flintlock pistols launching high-powered, magically enhanced rounds into its body, Croc lunged forward at the closest pirate at the rail and closed his teeth around the man's lower body. Hands beat uselessly against the sides of the beast's massive maw, but nothing could save the man's life. Bloodcurdling screams raised the hairs on James's arms, the agonized shrieks of a man in his final moments. Croc slid into the water anew and took his prize with him.

VIVIENNE SAVAGE

Their attacker reappeared within a minute of dragging the screaming sailor to his death. Wounds inflicted from the wave of pistol shots revealed the pink flesh beneath his tough, mottled green hide, but their show of force failed to deter him. He surged from the water anew. The monster must have perfected his vertical leap in the time since their last battle, as he displayed his acrobatic prowess by soaring from the pink-tinted waves and onto their deck before anyone had a chance to fend him off. Wood creaked beneath his weight, reinforced beams and planks shattered, and his thrashing tail swept one man into the rail with a sickly crack.

Seconds after taking the deck, Croc became a living whirlwind of death and destruction. His tail took six men off their feet, smashing them against the wall and one another before slamming into the mast.

A hairline crack formed in the wood. Croc thrashed again before its awful intent became apparent to James. "He's trying to break the mast!" he shouted in warning to the others before he sprang over the rail and down to the main deck.

Peter was above them, shrieking in terror each time the mast groaned in protest. The gods-awful noise of cracking wood continued, and the boy missed his footing during the descent.

"James, help me!" he cried.

The moment James sprinted toward the mast, Croc spun about toward him and smacked the wooden pole again. It feinted at James and growled low, guarding the newfound leverage it had found. A low chuckle rumbled from its throat, sending rotten fish breath over the deck.

"Ahh... the great Captain Hook. At last, I know what

you fear losing. Does this boy mean so much to you?" Croc rumbled.

Unseen by the beast, or written off as no threat to him, Belle darted toward Peter. Her courageous scarlet glow circled around him several times, trailing fairy dust like glitter.

What is she doing? James wondered, although he didn't dare draw too much attention to her. "He's only a boy. Your grievance is with me, Croc. I'm the one who took your eye. I hurt your mistress. This boy and my crew have done nothing but try to defend themselves."

"They defend you. That is crime enough," Croc hissed.

Before James could lurch forward, the crocodile delivered the final blow to its target. As the main mast snapped in half, lines broke and the pillar toppled into the foremast, tangling sails and rigging. The force of the collision shook Peter loose, and the boy tumbled from the lines, on a direct course for the deck dozens of feet below and Croc's waiting mouth.

Before Peter fell more than a dozen feet, he hung suspended in the air. "Haha!" Belle crowed in triumph. "You won't get this snack, you big bully!"

The soft inner flesh of Croc's mouth lay exposed to them, and, at that moment, James realized what he needed to do. All the time they'd wasted peppering its tough hide with rounds, they'd ignored the most tender and vulnerable part of it. Whipping his sword from the scabbard, he lunged forward and stabbed it in Croc's mouth.

The crocodile roared viciously and snapped after him, missing the mark by mere inches. The click of its teeth echoed in James's eardrums, and foul breath washed over him anew.

Now that he knew its weak spot, how did he communicate

it to the others without alerting their prey? He couldn't.

And if he couldn't share the news with the others, that meant it was up to James, and James alone, to deliver the killing blow. Confidence surged through him as he tightened his grip on the sword hilt. He spun and danced, providing the perfect, infuriating distraction to his opponent while Nigel directed the crew to cut the sails loose before the sheer weight of them capsized the ship.

Belle swooped down again and trailed golden dust over the heads of Patrick and Nigel. Within seconds, both lifted from the deck and floated in the air. One by one, his magical and wondrously courageous sprite made his crew members airborne. Realizing his folly in ignoring her, the ticking crocodile whirled and spun.

James leapt in again and stabbed it behind the left foreleg, capitalizing by attacking its blindside. Croc returned its attention to him with a vengeance, lunging forward and giving chase, snapping and snarling until the pirate dropped the sword in lieu of drawing his pistol. Beseeching the gods and goddesses he'd never cared to acknowledge, he prayed his shot would be true and pulled the trigger as the beast lunged toward him for the kill.

Fueled by the magic of Samahara's most powerful sorcerer, the ball exploded from the muzzle of the pistol surrounded by a halo of fire. It flew on a perfect course, and, the moment it hit unprotected tissue, it split the interior of the monster's mouth and lodged in Croc's brain. Dead at that instant, the bulky corpse slumped to the deck.

It was over. At last, they'd finally done the impossible and slain one of the largest beasts to ever haunt the Viridian Sea.

Chest heaving, James stood above the corpse of his fallen enemy, too petrified to move a muscle. Once his body cooperated, he nudged its nose with his boot. The blast from the flintlock pistol had done something he'd never witnessed before, tearing through Croc's skull and exiting through the rear of its head as if he'd fired a comet instead of a leaden ball.

Joaidane may have promised magic, but James hadn't anticipated a *miracle*. Maybe the gods had been with him, after all.

Tink stared at the fallen crocodile and silently thanked the stars and the ancestors that James had survived the encounter. She'd been struck mute and frozen with terror when she'd spotted him, certain she would never see her beloved pirate again. Yet there he stood, victorious.

Thanks to Tink, they'd lost only a single man during the battle. While there were plenty of broken bones all around for Eliza to set, no other loss of life had occurred. The others had already touched down, but Peter remained airborne and hovering weightless beside her.

"Now what?" Nigel joined them at the slain croc's side, his breaths heavy. "James, without our mast, we can't hope to outrun the Revenge. We'll be limping until they close in on us with their weapon."

Belle crossed her arms and looked toward the fast approaching ship in the distance. During their battle with the crocodile, it had gained on them, and it would only be a matter of minutes before the Revenge caught them.

"What if we destroy the weapon so they can't shoot us?" she asked.

"That would be a splendid idea, love, if we had a way aboard their ship without dying."

"What about me? I could fly over there and destroy it before they ever knew what was happening," she said.

"Absolutely not," James snapped. "I won't allow you to do it. It's too dangerous."

"If they reach you with that weapon, *everyone* will die."

James scrubbed his face with his left hand. Sweat had plastered his dark hair to his brow and his cheeks. "Launch the longboat," he said at last. "I may not have much of a chance at escaping, but most of you can get away. Nigel, take Tootles, Eliza, Callum, and Peter along with anyone else with a family. Fit as many onboard as you can, and the others can swim for it until the worst is over. Croc's presence will have chased away any other predators for miles. Create an invisibility curtain. With three mages working together, it shouldn't be difficult to fortify the protections on the longboat. Belle, you ride on Nigel's shoulder."

"You can't be serious," Nigel said. "I'm not going anywhere."

"You are. I've given my orders."

"You don't order me, James. This isn't the military. I'm your second-in-command, not some bloody subordinate here to follow your every directive. I'm staying here with you to the end."

Heads nodded among the crew. Even Callum crossed his brawny arms against his chest. "I won't go, and I'd like to see you try to make me."

"I won't go, either," Smee said. "Why don't you hear Belle

out?"

"Because it's suicide. She's already weakened from expending so much fairy dust."

"It *is* suicide," Tink agreed quietly. "If I sabotage their weapon, I may not have enough dust to return. But it can be the last thing I do to help you all."

James shook his head. "Then I forbid it."

"Good thing you don't control me."

Tink shot away, narrowly missing James's hand when it swung up to catch her. The Queen Anne's Revenge appeared as little more than a tiny speck in the distance at the edge of the horizon, but she'd already read the accounting from the Twilight Witch regarding the power of its enchanted cannon.

Her captain's cries echoed across the water, following Tink even as tears blurred her vision. Instead of stealing one final look at her lover, she flew like a thunderbolt over crystalline blue waters reflecting the setting sun.

"Belle! Belle, don't do it! Not for us!"

Not for them. Not specifically for the Jolly Roger. She was doing it for *him*. For Peter and Tootles, who had their entire lives ahead of them after enduring a traumatizing childhood. For the kids at Neverland who needed James and looked up to him as a savior. For the slaves he fought to liberate from captivity at the cost of his commission and the life he'd known in Eisland. Because the world needed Captain James Hook and his crew of benevolent pirates as much, if not more, than one little sprite.

Her only regret was that she'd never see Kendric grow into adulthood. Wiping tears from her face, she skimmed down low over the water while praying no one aboard the Queen

Anne's Revenge noticed her dwindling sparkle.

As she came closer, the boisterous voices of the crewmen reached her. They'd grown excited and thrilled at the prospect of finally destroying their quarry.

"Who would have thought we could trust that bloody crocodile to keep his word. There they are, just as promised, like sittin' ducks on a pond."

Tink flushed hot with anger but squeezed herself beneath a cannon until she was able to control the rising fury.

No wonder they'd found the Jolly Roger. After conspiring with James's greatest enemy, they set sail to collect their hobbled prize. Too bad they hadn't taken Tink's presence into account and known there was a little sprite on board.

Tink crawled onto the edge of the wooden rail, too still to emit much of a glow. When no outcries arose from the sailors aboard the ship, she peered over the railing at the deck.

Blackbeard, as the pirates called him, stood above his sailors on the quarterdeck. She recognized him at once, a large man with broad shoulders dressed to Eisland military standard. When James had shown her old images of him wearing the old uniform, she'd been taken by his handsomeness. The blue and silver coat had suited him, and it was then that she'd seen how little the years had changed her darling pirate. The admiral wore a similar uniform with the addition of a silver sash worn over his right shoulder and several gleaming medals upon the left breast of his jacket.

James had called him a well-decorated officer with decades of experience. Tink only saw a monster, and she hurt for the younger James Hook who had lost his beloved hero.

Blackbeard had the audacity to smile while addressing one

of his sailors. "Most likely, the blast will leave survivors in the water afterward to fill the brig. Are we prepared for captives?"

"To your specifications, Admiral Teach. Fishing them out of the water will be a joy, as usual."

Due to the sheer size of the monstrous cannon, it had been bolted to the portside deck instead of occupying a gun port below. It shone like black glass beneath the sun and a corona of magic surrounded it.

If there was anything she remembered from her lessons on the Jolly Roger, it was that a cannon needed a charge to fire. There had to be some kind of charge inside it, something she could remove or a mechanism she could damage. Committed to saving the pirate vessel, she darted into the cannon the moment its tenders turned their back.

I can do this!

The magic prickled against her skin and stung. Nevertheless, she forged on and persisted. Tink wiggled into the infernal machine and examined the inner workings. An enormous, fist-sized fire ruby emanated warm pulses, the light directed by a lens toward the mouth of the cannon.

That must be to focus the magical blast, Tink thought. Touching the glittering ruby blistered her fingertips. Distraught, she let it be and groaned. What could she do? The complicated magic surpassed anything she'd ever created as a tinker.

But she didn't need to understand it. Realization came to her like a thunderbolt. She didn't need to understand how it all worked, she only needed to break it.

While the distracted crew made their preparations, Tink scanned the inner workings then sprinkled what little remained of her fairy dust over cogs and gears. She twisted metal and bent pins, but the ruby continued to glow and the building energy intensified until sweat dripped into her eyes.

I have to knock it loose, she realized. *I have to crack the gem or knock it free entirely.*

Grabbing up one of the pins she'd broken loose, she wedged one end in between the gem and the setting and applied pressure. The metal sizzled and melted against the frame.

"C'mon…" She groaned, pushing all her weight against the makeshift lever. A tiny crack, barely longer than her pinky, split the crimson surface.

"Ready…"

She dropped the metal pin and looked around, frantic for anything else she could use to try and wedge the gem free. Nothing. There was nothing.

"Aim…"

Using the last specks of dust she possessed, Tink screamed and slammed into the setting with all her might, scorching her shoulder. Bits of her dress stuck against the mechanism, along with pieces of her skin seared to the metal. The tiny fissure splintered and spread.

"Fire!"

The last thing Tink saw as the ruby shattered into molten bits was the image of James's face in her mind.

James watched the explosion from the distance. It lit the skies with prismatic colors, releasing a torrent of magical energy. Eventually, water lapped against the boat, shoved by the shockwaves rippling miles across the sea.

His Belle couldn't have survived it. No one could have survived such a feat, not even a magical creature such as she.

The crew of the Jolly Roger stilled, each man on the deck silent. Together, they gazed at the distant horizon at the smoldering remnants of the Queen Anne's Revenge.

"No, no, no," James wept into his hand, voice thick with the building sorrow gripping his throat. "No!" He banged his fist against the rail and screamed in fury.

Nigel touched his shoulder. "James. She died doing what she believed in. What she thought was right."

"She didn't have to die. If you'd all—"

"If we'd allowed you to go down with your ship? Think about this a moment, James," Smee said, the quiet and fatherly man stepping up to the other side of James. "Our Belle is a hero now. Don't dishonor her sacrifice like this."

Dishonor her sacrifice? The words added another layer of realism to what he'd witnessed. His throat clenched again, refusing to allow air to pass into his lungs. He sagged against the railing and let his head fall forward.

Gone so fast. In and out of his life before he'd had a true chance to know her.

"She's truly gone," he whispered. He ought to have had another year with her at the very least. Ought to have been introduced to her family, the wolves and huntress she'd been so eager to show him. Now, he'd have to venture west into the mainland to deliver news of her death.

She deserved that much. He sank down to his knees by the rail and closed his eyes. Nigel crouched beside him and placed a hand on his shoulder.

VIVIENNE SAVAGE

"I know there are no words to ease your pain, James, but take your time to mourn her. Let me help you to your cabin."

"No," James said, hating the hoarse sound of his voice. "No. Smee's right. I can't… I can't dishonor her sacrifice. We've got repairs to make and canvas to raise." He pushed himself to his feet without looking at the horizon, although the stains of magical color gradually leached across the sky, creating rainbow colors in the clouds as the stars emerged.

She would have loved the view.

I only wish she were here to admire it with me. I wish I had more time with her. Oh, I wish so many things at this moment, dear stars, but above all, I wish I could see her smile one more time.

With Peter's help, the Jolly Roger became mobile minutes after sunset. They lit lanterns and completed the remaining repairs while James issued orders from the quarterdeck. He didn't drink. No. He'd save the rum until it was time to retire to bed without his Belle resting on the pillow beside him.

"How long do you suppose the boy will be able to fly?" Eliza asked.

"There's no telling. The adults she sprinkled with dust are already grounded again. Perhaps it's his small size. Or maybe there's something different about him that responds to her magic," James mused.

"It's bloody useful, for certain. Need anything?" Her gentle fingers touched his back.

James shook his head. "I'll keep the night's watch."

"Come eat, James. You need something in your belly."

"It would sour in my stomach."

"James—"

"Eliza, please. I only wish to be left alone for a time."

"All right," she agreed in a soft voice. "But I'm—"

A golden shimmer coalesced above the Jolly Roger, hundreds of starlight sparkles against the hazy evening mist. Low murmurs of confusion grew among the demoralized crew, and none of them dared to move. They merely stared, awestruck by the beauty.

The force radiated warmth, its sunny yellow reminding James of Bell's miniature smiles. He watched it, and, for a moment, his grief subsided.

"What's happening, Captain?" Patrick asked.

"I don't know. I… It's magical, but it doesn't feel malevolent at all."

"I don't sense any danger either," Callum said.

"Nor do I," Eliza agreed. "It's almost like… starlight." As she reached out toward the nebulous light, it spiraled downward toward the deck and became an intense blaze too bright for them to see. Dazzled, James shielded his face with his arm until it subsided enough to blink the afterimage from his vision.

A solitary figure stood at the center of the deck, given space by the crew who had scrambled away from the source of the light explosion. Wavy blonde hair tumbled past ivory shoulders, the strands golden against a pristine dress shimmering in opalescent shades.

"Belle?"

Tears shone in her green eyes. "James."

She met him halfway, bare soles pounding against the wooden deck before she sprang into his arms. He caught her around the waist with one arm and swung her around in a circle.

Nothing about her had changed from the night he held her in his arms. Soft curves molded against his body, slim arms encircled his neck, and the sweet scent of her bathed his senses with joy.

Belle was real and alive and in his arms, not some figment of his imagination.

"You came back to me. *You came back to me.*" He could have repeated it a thousand times, her return nothing less than miraculous. Lacking concern for the onlookers watching from every position on the deck, he tilted Belle's head back and seized her lips. He kissed her without caring for breath or their audience, drinking her in as if he'd been starved.

Her fingers tangled in his hair, matching enthusiasm anchoring him to her. They kissed without interruption, both needy, both clinging to the other until James couldn't discern who held who the tightest.

"How?" he asked at last, once he could bear to take a breath. Had the stars answered his prayers?

"The stars heard your prayers, James. I'm… I'm a real fairy now." She glanced over her shoulder at her luminescent wings. They had no physical form and merely glowed behind her like a network of constellations against the darkening ocean backdrop.

"The stars? How do you know it was them? I don't understand. What does this mean?"

Belle scrunched up her face in concentration, and then she poofed from his arms, her human size shrinking down to her small sprite body. The only thing that had changed were her wings, though they still shifted colors, their color at the moment was pink shot through with gold. After another moment, she became large again, taking her place in his embrace.

"Because they told me, silly! I can change when I want, and… I have all the time we need," she whispered. "I have more than a year or two years, or even three. I'm a *real* fairy. We can be together."

Together. He had never heard a word sweeter than that.

Chapter 20

GIVEN THE ABILITY to change her size at will, Tink spent as much time in her little body as she did the larger one, enjoying the nostalgia of riding upon her pirate's shoulder. But there was also a thrill in being large, as she discovered during countless nights curled against his chest while he reclined in bed or on the settee. During those evenings, she snuggled in his lap while he read aloud to her.

While she could read on her own now, no longer overwhelmed by the size of the massive words, their reading sessions would always be her favorite shared pastime that didn't involve activities beneath the sheets. Of course, she enjoyed those, too, and vowed to never take their intimate time for granted.

"We should be reaching the coast of Cairn Ocland soon," James murmured as they sprawled over the settee, Tink's body stretched over his naked frame. His fingers trailed over her bare back, smoothing away the blonde hair sticking to her skin.

"Home," escaped her as a dreamy exhale. She'd missed the green glades and swaying treetops. She missed flowers and dry land, as well as the scent of meadows and freshwater.

"And I should make an appearance to my crew before they fear you've become a succubus, rather than an elf. Mind moving just a touch?"

"Fairy," she murmured, without any energy to argue the point. "I'm still a fairy, even if my wings aren't always visible." Her wings came and went with concentration when in her large form. She'd have to find Eos, Anastasia's fairy grandmother, to ask the experienced fae for help adjusting to her magical new body.

James traced her ear down to its fine point, both distracting her and sending shivers of delight down her spine. She snuggled into his chest and buried her left hand in his hair, hoping to dissuade him. It didn't work. Eventually, he crawled from beneath her and entered the shower room unaccompanied, otherwise he wouldn't make an appearance before the crew for hours longer if she joined him.

A short while later, as they both dressed and made themselves presentable, she caught James studying her.

"What?"

A quiet smile remained on his face. "Nothing."

"There's something. Watching me without saying anything at all is unnerving. And creepy," she chastised him while donning her favorite blouse and boned bodice, both of which she'd borrowed from Eliza, although the latter had been a tight squeeze only after they'd let the laces out to their limit.

"If you must know, I was thinking of what a fashionable pirate you make, my love."

"And?"

"And that something is missing."

Missing? She'd donned knickers, despite her disdain for them. Bewildered, she searched herself in the adjacent full-length mirror until James approached and lowered to one knee in front of her. He balanced a long, golden-brown box to her upon his left palm.

"This."

"A present?"

"Open it," he told her.

Raising the lid revealed a flintlock pistol nestled amidst a bed of plum velvet.

"A gun?" Of all the pistols she had ever repaired and cleaned during their maintenance schedule, she'd never seen one prettier. An intricate pattern of gold leaves and flowers had been etched into wood polished to a mirror shine.

"Yours. I wish I could claim absolute credit, but…" He gestured with his hook.

Tink trailed her fingers over the weapon. *Her* weapon. Now she'd be like everyone else onboard, able to defend herself without resorting to magic.

"James, it's beautiful. I love it!"

"There's one more thing," James murmured. "Look closer."

Nestled in a small groove, Tink found a slender golden band set with small, cream-hued pearls set to resemble a flower. At the heart of the design was a flawless pink pearl. Her lost pearl. Her eyes misted over with tears before she threw herself down on her knees and hugged him. "You found my pearl!"

"Days ago, in a cranny under the bed."

"But why is it in a ring?"

"Because, in my country, when a man loves a woman very much, he presents a ring to her. And if she wears it," James said as he placed his arm around her back, "she agrees to accept him as her husband."

Tink stared at him with large eyes. "You want… you're

asking me to marry you?"

"I am."

"Yes!"

"You haven't let me ask the question yet."

"But my answer is still yes."

James laughed and hugged her close. Then he set her back and looked into her eyes. "Will you do me the honor, Belle, of becoming my wife and making me the happiest man in this world?"

"Of course, I'll marry you."

As there was nothing she wanted to do more than to kiss her handsome betrothed, Tink wrapped her arms around James and anchored him in place. He didn't argue, nor did he draw away until alarmed cries interrupted their deepening kiss. Breaking apart, she and James both hurried to the door and outside.

A large shadow passed over the ship. Tink had to shade her eyes against the sun as she looked up, but there was no mistaking the majestic feathered creature circling above them in a downward spiral.

"Don't shoot!" Tink cried, running across the deck. She grabbed Nigel's arm and pulled the gun he held aimed upward away from its intended target.

"What are you—"

"The griffins are friends!"

One of the massive shifters alighted on the deck, taking human shape in a flawless transition at the exact moment his claws touched the wood. The ship didn't even rock.

Despite a dozen guns pointing at him, the shifter stood tall, proud, and unalarmed by the gun-wielding pirates. His

  VIVIENNE SAVAGE

loose, golden-red hair blew in the breeze above a cream tunic and the purple and silver tartan of Clan Leomlaire. "I am here for Tinker Bell and Captain James Hook," he announced in clear and crisp Eislandic, startling Tink because she hadn't thought any of the shifters knew the language.

"I'm Hook." James stepped forward. "Might I know who I have the pleasure of addressing?"

"I am Muir, son of Gerta of Clan Leomlaire."

"I'm Tinker Bell," she said, drawing the griffin's attention. He studied her with a critical eye, then his dark brows shot upward.

"You are no sprite, yet I recognize your face."

"A long story," James said before she could launch into a lengthy tale. "Belle and I were going to try making our way to the king's castle by way of Creag Morden."

"There is no need. My brethren and I will take you to Braeloch where there are many eager to see you both."

Tink clapped and squealed with joy, throwing herself into James's arms. "Now we don't have to sail north!"

"So it would seem."

"We can leave as soon as you are ready," Muir said.

"What of my ship? Will she be safe here?"

Muir canted his head, then looked up toward the sky. Far above, three griffins circled. "I will ask Brenach to remain. Your ship will be protected, on my honor."

Before Tink could dismount from Muir's back, Conall surrounded her with his brawny arms and yanked her down against him. Her wolfy brother had tears streaming down his face.

Tears.

From there it was a blur of hugs, kisses, exclamations about her size, and even more embraces as everyone she held closest to her heart welcomed her home. Through it all, James waited to the side, quiet and patient as ever, until Conall noticed the pirate and welcomed him with a backbreaking hug.

"Thank you for looking after my Tink."

When James's questioning blue eyes darted to her in confusion, understanding dawned upon her. "He says thank you for looking after me," she translated.

"Oh! To be honest, it was the other way around more often than not, wasn't it?" After all, Tink had singlehandedly saved the Jolly Roger and rescued his whole crew from a fiery death.

Once they found a common language—Anastasia's native tongue of Mordenian seemed to be known by most in attendance, including Alistair, Sorcha, and Conall—the shifters welcomed James into their home and hearts as only Oclanders could, reaffirming Tink's belief that she had the best family in all the world. Even the king and queen had waited among the throng of visitors. Once the two monarchs greeted her and James, the celebratory welcome home feast began.

Shifters used any excuse they could make for throwing a banquet. The celebrations lasted long into the night, until Tink took her smaller form and curled up in Kendric's bed, leaving James to the mercy of her family

She didn't wake until after noon the following day. After scrubbing her tired face and washing away the taste of too many mugs of mead, she crafted a fresh wardrobe for herself out of starlight magic and flew through the den in search of her beloved. The brief hunt led her to a table overlooking the lake, where James shared tea with the king and queen. They all wore solemn faces, and the sight of their stoic countenances added a skip to her racing heart. Fearing Anastasia meant to go back on her word, she hurried over to join them.

Then she paused to eavesdrop behind a stone pillar, instead.

"Admittedly, when Tinker Bell claimed you weren't a murderer, I had a difficult time believing it," Anastasia said. "But Liang has shown us a new side to them, and King Harold refuses to discuss the matter of slavery at all. Not a denial or an admission. Instead, he avoids the subject."

James shook his head. "He won't confess to it."

"So it would seem, so we've decided to send one of our clan leaders to investigate your claims, Captain Hook. As Cairn Ocland is part of the Compact between Creag Morgen and Eisland, we would be committing a breach of the law to allow you to go free," Anastasia said. "Unless we were to grant you amnesty, of course."

Alistair rubbed his bearded chin. "Amnesty for a pirate. I can't say he didn't operate for a good cause."

"A just cause," Anastasia corrected her husband. "Still… you did rob people, did you not?"

Tink buzzed over and transformed from little to large, standing behind James's chair. "He didn't rob for fun," she defended. "He even let an honest merchant go without taking a single coin."

"It's fine, love," James assured her. He set his hand over hers and drew her around, pulling her down to his lap. "They have a right to question my deeds."

"No one is faulting him, Tink," Ana said.

"As far as pillaging goes, I can't say we didn't enjoy the treasure," James admitted, "but it wasn't the driving motivation behind leaving the navy. If anything, it financed our adventure and granted us a fighting chance. Amnesty would be appreciated."

"Then consider yourself and each member of your crew to be under the protection of Cairn Ocland. From this day forward, you are all citizens of our kingdom, and free to make a fresh start on dry land if you choose," Alistair said.

"That is most appreciated."

Ana studied his face and her features softened with concern. "You don't seem happy."

"Forgive me, as I don't mean to seem ungrateful. However, a part of me is unwilling to give up what my crew and I have spent years working on. Destroying the Queen Anne's Revenge won't end the slave trade. We've only hobbled Eisland, but Ridaeron ships will continue their dastardly work, moving your sprites and slaves between their country and others like Liang."

"I see. Then what would you suggest we do?"

"Stop it!" Tink cried, unable to stand it a moment longer. "Something has to be done. James wasn't enough to change their ways, but you have the power to make them see reason and to force them to stop."

The monarchs grew silent, exchanging quiet glances before Anastasia said in a gentle voice, "We may be powerful, Tink, but there's very little Alistair and I can do from across the sea."

"What if Cairn Ocland had its own navy," Tink suggested.

The dragon's brows rose. "Our own navy?"

She nodded several times. "Yes! Shifters are powerful and strong, but your focus has been on the land. What if you could also travel the seas?"

"Tink, we don't have a bay."

"No, but we have Clan Ardal."

Both monarchs stared at her, as well as James. "Those are the bears, yes?" her pirate asked. "What do they have to do with a bay?"

Alistair sucked in a sharp breath then released it on a laugh. Ana looked at him, brows knit together, before understanding seemed to dawn with her as well.

"Tink, you never fail to amaze or surprise me," Alistair said. "We'll ask Mother and Father Bear and if they can commit their earthshaping skill to sculpting a bay. It won't be any small feat, but if anyone is capable, it'll be their clan."

"Of course, there's the matter of our lack of experience when it comes to sailing," Anastasia said. "We'll need someone to teach our men and women how it's done."

"Yes. Someone with knowledge and skill, as well as a ship. Seeing as how we have none of our own," Alistair agreed.

Tink clapped her hands together and blinked her teary eyes as the king and queen looked to James with matching smiles.

"I would be honored, Your Majesty."

Anastasia grinned. "Then we will hire the greatest shipwrights in Creag Morden to our cause."

"If you'll forgive me, Your Majesty, I know the perfect man for the job to serve as their advisor. While the ships of your native country are true beauties, they're ill-suited for combat and war. They'll never stand up against Ridaeron's forces or the Eisland Navy."

"Patrick," Tink blurted out. The man had a tinker's soul, drawing beautiful designs in his private cabin during his free time, and she'd enjoyed watching him make his miniatures, once she was no longer upset at him for skiving off at his duties and setting her to performing all his repairs.

"Yes," James confirmed. "If he'll accept the post."

"We'll trust you to make adequate recommendations for all roles within our new navy... Admiral," Anastasia said, eyes twinkling with mirth.

James rocked back on his heels and stared at them, jaw working before he voiced a word. "Admiral?"

"Of course. Who better to lead us than James Hook, the fiercest pirate to ever sail the Viridian Sea?"

"I don't know what to say."

"Say you'll accept," the queen said.

"I accept. Thank you."

Giddy with excitement, Tink beamed up at her pirate—he would always be a pirate to her—and tried not to bounce up and down, or worse.

"In the meantime, we'll have to coordinate with the griffins, especially since the mountains are their home and it will take time to build a fleet worthy of opposing Ridaeron's evil," Alistair said.

"I might have a way to get you two, possibly even three, ships now. There are other pirates out there, some as fearsome as the tales say, but others who are simply trying to survive. I believe, if given a chance for a new life and honest pay, they'd join you."

Alistair and Ana exchanged looks. "We'd certainly be agreeable to meeting with these people so we can make our own judgments. Who did you have in mind?" the queen asked.

"Captain Amerys Vandry of the Twilight Witch, for one. She is a skilled sorceress and has sailed the world over multiple times and even visited the distant nations across the ocean. I don't imagine it will be difficult to persuade her to join us if there's good pay and the promise of continued exploration. She's one of three captains allowed in Wai Alei. The Scarlet Brigade and my ship are the other two."

"Tiger Lily only lets people with good hearts in," Tink added.

"If you draft up letters of invitation, we will gladly receive them on our shores, once we have a safe bay for them," Ana said. "I'd also like to see about meeting this Tiger Lily, in time."

"I have a feeling she'd like you very much," James said.

"Of course, we need a bay first, which means we should send for the Ardal leaders as soon as possible," Alistair continued. "We should also send a delegation to Eisland to see if we can salvage any of the friendship between our countries and convince them to give up their slaving ways without bloodshed."

James nodded. "And what of Liang?"

When Alistair rumbled a low growl, Anastasia touched the back of her husband's hand. She smiled. "Grand Enchanter Joaidane has vowed to join our side against Liang. In the meantime, I plan to create a vast barrier between our countries to discourage his poachers from entering Cairn Ocland."

"I wish you the best of luck with both tasks," James said. "Joaidane is a man of his word. As for King Harold… he's is a stubborn man. With Blackbeard dead, I fear his resentment will make him impossible to deal with."

"A good thing we have a perfect negotiator for such difficult and delicate tasks. If anyone can deal with an obstinate ruler, it's a griffin. They have the patience of a dragon without the quick temper."

"You mean Muir?" Tink asked, thinking of the griffin who had brought her home.

"Yes. As a leader among the griffins, he's equal to that of any noble lord and capable of speaking to King Harold on our behalf," Ana replied.

"He'll be great," Tink said. "Everyone in Eisland needs to know the truth about James. Especially his family."

"Then the matter is settled, and Cairn Ocland will take its first steps into a wider world. We have you both to thank for it."

"Is there anything else we can do in the meantime?" Alistair asked.

James smiled. "There's only one more matter we would need to attend to."

Tink turned to her lover. "Oh? What's that?"

"Our wedding."

Epilogue

REFUSING TO EXCLUDE either half of their combined family—the pirates of the Jolly Roger or the shifters of Cairn Ocland—Tink and James delayed the wedding until the bears constructed the new bay. Tink spent much of the month traveling between the den at Mount Braeloch and the Jolly Roger, helping wherever she could with the construction efforts.

During that time, the ship remained anchored a mere mile off the coast of griffin territory. Mystified and awestruck pirates watched the progress each day as bears carved a canyon through a region of the Floraivel Mountains. The earth shapers even widened a large section of beach. With the tons of displaced rock, they created a protective barrier out in the sea, forming a new bay that was deep enough for the Jolly Roger to sail within but hidden from invaders.

Tink worked alongside the carpenters and master artisans who came together to draw the plans for a new port city. Men and women traveled across Cairn Ocland to place their support behind the king and queen's new venture, as did many of her sprite friends.

But, on the day of her wedding, there would be no work. Not for her, and not for anyone else, as the king and queen had declared it to be a day of rest for all involved.

Standing within a gauzy white tent on the beach, Tink

waited for the moment to proceed past her family and friends to the man who would soon become her husband. Since Eisland and Creag Morden shared wedding traditions, Queen Anastasia had organized the event and walked Tink through the intricacies of the ceremony. As her closest family, Conall had offered to lead her down the aisle to James.

She waited in a dress the color of fresh cream, made from yards upon yards of silk that Anastasia had gifted her and Sorcha had sewn into the prettiest dress Tink had ever seen. The fabric at her back dipped low, allowing room for her wings. Her only jewelry was the pearl ring James had given to her.

"Tinker Bay," Conall murmured, his gruff voice interrupting her silent musings.

Tink turned to find her dearest friend studying her from the mouth of the tent, dressed in his best tartan and whitest shirt, blinking but failing to disperse the tears in his blue eyes.

"It feels odd to have it named after me."

"You deserve it, Tink. This was your brilliant idea. I couldn't be prouder of you."

Although tears stung her eyes, too, Tink dried his scruffy cheeks with the bell sleeve of her dress. "Don't be sad," she whispered to him.

"Who says I'm sad?"

"I'll be close this way. You in Braeloch and me here in Port Harmony."

"Or out on the Jolly Roger being a pirate."

"You can come be a pirate, too," she teased, earning a quiet chuckle and a warm smile from her friend.

"It will take some getting used to, is all," he said, then

VIVIENNE SAVAGE

offered his arm. "But right now, I believe it's time I take you to the new man in your life."

As Tink slipped her arm around Conall's elbow, the melodic chords of a harp signaled the start of the ceremony. She filled her lungs with a deep breath before stealing a look at Conall's stoic face.

"I love you, you know," she said to him.

"I love you, too, Tink, and I'm glad you have James. I like him."

Together, they left the tent and followed a flower-strewn path between aisles of all the people she loved best in the world. Old friends and new friends smiled at her in passing, shifters, pirates, Joaidane, and even Peter who merrily played the flute to accompany Princess Teagan at the harp.

Something was strange about that boy, different and not quite human.

But they'd figure that out later, especially since she had all the time in the world to unravel Peter's mysteries. He would be her son soon.

Her misfortune had given her two families who were now a big one. Could a fairy be any luckier?

It seemed improbable, until James stepped into view, resplendent in his finest scarlet coat, his black hair down loose around his face. When their gazes met across the distance, her stride sped to meet the rhythm of her racing heart, until she had abandoned Conall completely and dashed down the row to the man she loved. He caught her in his arms and kissed her while everyone applauded.

Captain Vandry cleared her throat. Two weeks ago, when she'd arrived with her ship and crew, she'd offered to officiate the wedding and sworn her loyalty to Cairn Ocland.

"I suppose we should skip to the important bits, yes?" she asked, a twinkle in her uncovered eye. "Do you, Admiral James Hook, accept this woman as your wife, to honor and cherish as long as you both shall live?"

"I do."

"Belle of the fae, do you accept this rapscallion of a man as your husband, to honor and cherish as long as you both shall live?"

"I do."

"Then I see no reason to delay you further, and I happily present you as husband and wife to all who stand in attendance, both beloved family and cherished friends. May the gods—and the stars—smile down on your union as brightly as they did upon your meeting, and may you always sail with their grace and protection." Captain Vandry paused, then grinned. "Go ahead and kiss her again, James. We all know you want to."

Tink beat him to it, throwing her arms around his neck and claiming his lips. James pulled her in tight against him and met her with equal fervor, and the world around them ceased to exist. Her adventure to find a companion of her very own may have ended, but the journey of Tinker Bell into her new life as a fae had just begun.

And, standing beside the master of all pirates, she'd rather have no one else by her side.

About the Author

Vivienne Savage is the pen name of two best friends who write everything together. One works as a nurse in a rural healthcare home in Texas, and the other is a U.S. Navy veteran. Both are mothers to two darling boys and two amazing girls.

All of their work varies in steam level, so pop by the VS website for details on which series is right for you.

Newsletter:
http://viviennesavage.com/newsletter

Facebook:
https://www.facebook.com/Savage.Books/

Website:
http://www.viviennesavage.com/